Taken by The She

"She disappeared down the harbor so quickly, out to sea. She looked me in the eye for about a hundred yards, trying to swim back. She just wasn't making it."

Grey's eyes were wide, staring over my shoulder somewhere. I knew she was seeing it, but I didn't think the guilt was so necessary.

"She got caught in a riptide." I shrugged quietly. "Did you holler for her to swim sideways? Get out of the stream?"

"No."

"Did you swim after her?"

"No." She looked at me long and hard. "Don't even say it. It's not what you think. I surely didn't look to drown anybody. I'm just a bitch; I'm not a murderer."

"So...what was up?"

She swallowed. "I was frozen to the side of the boat. I couldn't move. I was hearing this terrible shriek. It was coming out...from over the ocean. This girl was being sucked, very quickly, toward the sound of the shriek. My friend Lydia was right next to me, and she said she never heard it."

THE
SHE

ALSO BY CAROL PLUM-UCCI

The Body of Christopher Creed

What Happened to Lani Garver

THE
SHE

CAROL PLUM-UCCI

HARCOURT, INC.
Orlando Austin New York San Diego Toronto London

www.HarcourtBooks.com

First Harcourt paperback edition 2005

The Library of Congress has cataloged the hardcover edition as follows:
Plum-Ucci, Carol, 1957–
The She/Carol Plum-Ucci.
p. cm.
Summary: After his parents are lost at sea, Evan Barrett and his older
brother leave their seaside home in West Hook to escape bad memories,
but years later even worse questions emerge when Evan is asked to
help a fellow student deal with another sea-related tragedy.
[1. Brothers—Fiction. 2. Interpersonal relations—Fiction.
3. Sea stories.] I. Title.
PZ7.P7323Sh 2003
[Fic]—dc21 2003047754
ISBN-13: 978-0152-16819-3 ISBN-10: 0-15-216819-2
ISBN-13: 978-0152-05453-3 pb ISBN-10: 0-15-205453-7 pb

Text set in Sabon
Designed by Cathy Riggs

E G H F

Printed in the United States of America

To Frank Schaeffer

ACKNOWLEDGMENTS

Many thanks to Tom O'Rourke, formerly of the Coast Guard in Atlantic City, for his help with all sorts of seafaring issues, from the precise wording of a Mayday to what happens when a ship does a three-sixty in the water. Same thanks to Dwight Webster, captain of the *Suzie Q4* out of Brigantine, New Jersey. Guys, just don't be waylaid by my poetic license, *capisce*?

Thanks to Trey Severs and the other students of Jean Serber's English classes for their help with slang.

My most gracious thanks to Sally Turkavage for teaching this dumb Protestant the Hail Mary and any other Catholic issues I managed to get straight.

Thanks again to my editor, Karen Grove, for always being there, and for beating me up good on those first two drafts. My slothfulness is ever indebted to your perfection, woman. I still want to be you someday.

Thanks to Dr. Rafey Habib, most excellent professor of philosophy, for giving me so much to think about for two years in grad school and for helping me out with

Saussure for this manuscript. If I thought it were remotely possible to be you, I would want that, too.

Thanks to Ed Okonowicz, author of *Terrifying Tales of the Beaches and Bays* and its sequels, past and future. Thanks for allowing me to quote and for blessing us all with the salty tales of the coast that make for great bedtime popcorn chomping.

THE
SHE

The old moon is tarnished
With smoke of the flood,
The dead leaves are varnished
With color like blood,

A treacherous smiler
With teeth white as milk,
A savage beguiler
In sheathings of silk,

The sea creeps to pillage,
She leaps on her prey;
A child of the village
was murdered today.

—ELINOR WYLIE
   "Sea Lullaby"

EIGHT YEARS AGO

THERE'S DEATH WEATHER OUTSIDE MY HOUSE. I
know about death weather, no matter how often Emmett
tells me I've got bats in my attic. The wind is rushing off
the sound since maybe fifteen minutes ago, making the
drapes stand straight out from the farthest window in the
living room. Dad forgot to close it before driving with
Mom down to where they launched their freighter. I'm listening. Sometimes my ears can hear through the dark,
past the ocean and everything that rattles, so as to confuse you.

I've got the red army cornered by the blue navy under
the coffee table. Emmett's on the couch reading some fat
high school book. Usually he'd be bugging me because he
says nine is too old to play navy men, but not tonight, because he's reading with a highlighter pen. At least, he
wants me to think he's reading. But I see his eyes looking

up, though his head's down, and he's watching the curtain, same as me.

It's like the black dots of his eyes get wider and wider, though he doesn't move. Finally, he's looking down again. But something makes me think he's not really reading. He's thinking of our island's *Ella Diablo Agujero,* which means "she-devil of the hole," though that's a hard term to spit out. Since the first time I heard her, I just call her The She.

My dad thinks that's funny, and he says now half the islanders are calling her The She instead of *Ella Diablo Agujero.* I think it's the half that believes in her. The She lives in a hole under the canyon, which is the deepest place where you can fish out there. The She is big, and she doesn't get hungry too often, but when she does, she'll catch hold of a ship over the horizon, and she'll eat it. I heard her shrieking once, right before she bit down on one. Not many islanders can hear The She. Emmett used to say I was baby shit in a diaper, but he had to quit that after The She ate a small yacht and some fishermen we knew. I'd been shrieking on and off all that morning two years ago, when I was seven, because that's the only way to cut the shriek of The She. That night my dad read us the Coast Guard report and mumbled, "The old bitch didn't even spit out half a life jacket."

I'm watching my brother, and I know he's remembering tonight's dinner table fuss between Mom and Dad over The She. Emmett's been in on their fights for a couple of years now, always taking Mom's side. Dad was laughing quietly over his coffee mug—telling once again how when a husband and wife set sail on the same vessel, The She gets jealous, and she swallows the boat into her whirlpool and spins it down into the hole under the canyon floor, eighty miles out.

Emmett's allowed to say "horseshit" now without getting sent upstairs, and Dad was shrugging him off, but I didn't like how Dad's eyes wouldn't go along with his smile.

Dad said, "I'm not saying I believe any husbands-wives superstitions of the deep, Mary Ellen. I'm saying some of the crew's a little touchy about these things, that's all. If you want to replace Lowenberg while his wife's in labor, just don't expect the other crew to be your best buddies."

Mom said, "When did I ever? Goddamn superstitions, they're all just a poor excuse to keep women off the water. Those guys can be satisfied that I've become a flight paramedic—and deal with it once in a while if I want to help out on the freighter I used to own and drive."

I don't like it when they fight. I like it when Mom's peaceful, which has not been this week, so I felt almost glad when Dad caved in, because then she'd be peaceful for a couple of weeks after she had been at sea.

I look from Emmett's pretend-reading eyes back to this curtain, and I can't help it, I'm listening beyond the wind to see if I can hear The She. I can't tell Emmett this. In fact, I can't let him catch me even looking like I'm thinking about it. Seventeen-year-olds are strong, and they don't think nice.

And I know, as sure as I'm sitting on this rug, that The She is real, and she's out there. I can't hear her tonight, and I'm glad of it. It sounds like plain old wind. Big wind. It's whizzing through the bayberry trees out front, making a *shatter shatter shatter,* and the ocean is going *thunder thunder thunder* beyond it. The She makes a different, angry noise. It's the pain of undigested crew down in her guts that makes her moan rise to a shriek. It's a shriek that stays behind the waves, but it's not the waves—it's separate from the waves. I've heard her shrieking about the four freighter ships she's eaten since 1920. She also ate a fishing boat in the 1970s, when my dad was a kid, and when I was in second grade, she ate the yacht with our friends the Gormleys on it.

I glance back at Emmett before moving a few red men closer to my shoe box, where the blue navy is about to ambush them. The navy always wins in my stories. Emmett's eyes are stuck on one spot on the page. He's not reading; he's just pretending.

I look away quick as his gaze darts over to me, as if to say, "Don't you dare start in with your crap, because I am in charge tonight, and I will beat your ass, just like I did when you were seven and scared the piss out of me."

So, I'm playing and playing, not wanting to remember that day, but I can't help it. Mom, Dad, and Emmett were racing around because of sudden storm warnings and the full moon, and high tide was coming, and Dad hadn't cleared his family portraits out of the crawl space yet. Twelve generations of sea captains on the Barrett side, twelve portraits wrapped only in newspaper. He was trying to get them upstairs, and Mom was trying to lock down the shutters with her electric screwdriver. Emmett was hauling sandbags down to the edge of the property, and I was with him, and that's when I heard her.

It was a screaming so plain from out over the sea, different from the waves, more human, more shrieky. I started shrieking to cut the sound.

"The She! *Ella Diablo!* She's doing it! Right now, Emmett!"

He had me by both arms, and he started shaking me because I had scared him once already that day. In the morning I had screamed, hearing The She, and then word came in about the Gormley yacht's Mayday. Mom was telling Dad at noon that the Coast Guard wasn't saying the yacht foundered yet, because there was no wreckage. Dad said, "Holy shit, did you hear Evan screaming about The She this morning?"

When Emmett was sandbagging, I started in screaming again, and he was shaking my head loose. I pushed one hand in his face to get him off me, screeching, "Can't you hear that? Can't you hear that?"

Then I was caught between his huge arm and his side and he was whaling the hell out of my thigh, accusing me of trying to upset Mom, until I bit him. He let go, but I'd caught the worst of it, and Mom came around threatening to send me off to boarding school if I didn't quit with the superstitious crew talk. She asked why I didn't think it was a traditional man-devil instead of a woman she-devil, and she stalked off muttering, "My own baby... You're so lucky that was Emmett whipping on you instead of me..." The She had shut up by that point, so I was quiet.

Dad missed his friends, the Gormleys, but couldn't help getting out one of his books when Mom wasn't looking: *Terrifying Tales of the South Jersey Coast.*

West Hook has all sorts of theories, from faulty hatches to how maybe all the people working those missing ships got rich quick running drugs, and they went to live it up in South America. My dad says he believes in something out there, though he doesn't say it when Mom's around, because she starts in on him. I don't talk about The She, but I'm always listening, waiting.

Emmett's back to reading again. I move a few more of my red guys, and the rain starts in. It changes from whipping wind to clatter wind so quickly that I can't help looking at him again. Sleet's all tapping on the windows, but he doesn't close the one that's open. His head is still down, but his eyes are back on that drape. They move to the floor, searching through the pattern on the Oriental rug for something I can't figure out, maybe nothing.

I strain my ears. No shrieks. Just rain. Still, I don't like the way Emmett gets up too slowly and looks out the window onto the porch, the window that faces the sea. We're a hundred yards back from the beach, and a thick patch of bayberry trees lies in between, so you can't see anything. I don't know what he's looking at. Maybe he doesn't know, either. I just know it's weird he went to that window instead of the one that's wide open and threatening to freeze us...almost like he doesn't want to close it. He wants to listen, too.

He's thinking about The She growing jealous of lovers on a ship, about the canyon that my parents have to pass over. It's only been three hours since they left. I know he's thinking what I am, because I ask him, "Whereabouts are they?" and he doesn't have to look at his watch.

"About eighty miles southeast." He keeps his back to me, staring into the black. Finally, he turns, steps over my army men, and moseys back to Dad's office as I hear the radio warbling. I follow him as far as the kitchen.

I can hear Mom's voice coming out of the ship-to-shore. "*Goliath* to West Hook. Emmett, are you there? Over."

Wind shrieks through the radio, sending my heart into my neck. But I remember how the wind always shrieks when we get caught in a storm on the ship. It's a different shriek than hers, it's separate, though the radio makes every sound seem together.

"West Hook. I'm here. Over."

"Emmett, shut the south-face window in the living room before you turn in. Your dad forgot. Rain coming. Over."

"It's here, Mom. Where are you? Over."

"Coming into the canyon. Got off course a little bit. Somehow. Over."

"What do you mean, 'somehow'? Over." He thinks them getting off course makes no sense, which it doesn't. The *Goliath* is more than three hundred feet long, and the pilothouse has every finder known to man on it. Depth finder, current chaser, wind reader, automatic navigator, weather fax.

"Uh...don't know. Loran receiver says we're well into the canyon, but we're not. We've only got depth of twelve hundred yards. We misplaced a few hundred somewhere. Over."

"You see any swells break when you crossed? Over."

He's asking because sometimes the swells break into waves right at the edge of the shelf. I'm always asking Dad if I can drive through them.

"Uh..." I hear Mom laughing. "There's a lot of white stuff winking at me right now, Emmett. Hard to say. Looks sort of like...black-bean soup, coming to a boil in a pot. Weird water tonight. Why? You worried?" Her laughter rings through, and she says, "Over."

"No. Over."

I know he is. If not worried just...itchy, antsy. I can tell things like that about the people in my family. They can't tell about each other, but I can tell about them, and Emmett is itchy.

"Good. In case you start to worry, think of the ninety steel girders we've got down in the hold. You know how much that weighs? We're not going to wander too far off course, functioning computer or nonfunctioning computer. Over."

"Yeah, I know. I just...I don't know. Where's Dad? Over."

"He just went to spit over the stern. He's coming in... Let me put him on..."

Spit over the stern is something Barrett sea captains always do in a storm, because it mixes their body with the sea so they can "reach an agreement" with her if they have to. I don't like that Dad is deciding to spit.

"Barrett here. Over." My dad's voice rings through.

"It's just me, Dad. Mom says you're off course. Over."

"We're over the pit of the canyon. I'm sure of it. Never underestimate a captain's intuition. It's this fancy-schmancy new depth finder. You know how I hate technology, but, hey, it was Mary Ellen's boat before it was mine, and if she wants to use up her trust fund loading it up with contraptions, well, God bless her. How's Evan? Over."

"Playing with his army men."

It's a real say-nothing answer, but I don't miss the little click in his voice. It tells me I've been making him nervous. He's been thinking about The She and blaming it on me. I can tell he's stalling about getting off the ship-to-shore.

"Dad, what's it look like from the stern? Over."

I don't like my dad's laugh. It's his dinner table laugh, from when he was trying to laugh off the superstition about a husband-wife team bringing bad luck to a voyage.

"Weird, I have to say. Your mother's describing it... Yeah. Black-bean soup being stirred in a boiling pot. Over."

They're all laughing now. I can hear Mom in the background. I rush up to the doorway of the office to stare at Emmett. There's a warning barreling up my throat. But I know it will sound like baby shit in a diaper. Still, the image of a stirring pot fills my head, some giant, invisible she-devil finger spinning the waves slowly, then faster, and faster, and faster.

He has his back to me, and he's leaning on Dad's desk, staring out at the rain and sleet beating against the black window, hearing the sounds of the angry ocean.

"Black-bean soup, huh?" He's stalling, stalling... doesn't want to be alone with me. "Don't let the DEA hear you say that. They'll be going through your hold with a toothpick, and you'll never make it to Jamaica without paying that late penalty. Over."

Some boats run drugs when cargo is short. One boat tried to fake a disappearance and sent a Mayday saying The She was after him. He got caught, but I could have told the Coast Guard he was a liar, because I didn't hear The She when he was supposed to be getting his boat eaten.

Dad's talking again, and I don't like the sound of it. They're talking about the water, and cracking jokes about the Bermuda Triangle, and they're sort of laughing, but still.... "Emmett, here's the weirdest thing. The wind. Can you hear that wind whipping? Over."

"Plainly, yeah. Over."

"Well, when you go out on the stern, you can't feel it.

You can hear it, all right. It's like it's coming from every-where...and nowhere. Over."

Emmett gets silent for a long moment. "You ever see anything like that before? Over."

A long cackling came, like a spitting between the sounds of shrieking winds. Dad doesn't answer the question. His voice gets louder and clearer, like he's got his lips pressed right up to the handset, like he doesn't want Mom to hear.

"Emmett, you know what's in my desk drawer, bottom, left-hand side. I know you don't like to hear about it, but...do it for the old man, okay? Over."

I back up out of the door frame so Emmett can't see me when he turns. But I hear him open the drawer, hear what sounds like a paper being shoved into his jeans pocket. I peek one eye around, and the corner of a paper is sticking out of his back pocket.

He sounds annoyed. "I don't see why you're working on scaring the shit out of me if you're saying it's just a mild rainstorm and you're completely on course. Over."

"Don't scare so easily." Dad's laugh came through. "I'm just talking to you from my intuition. If you want to drive your own vessel someday soon, you've got to learn to listen to it. All the toys in the world will not replace intuition."

"Yes sir."

Neither of them sounds too happy. And they had forgotten to say "over."

"And Emmett."

"Yes sir."

"Don't forget to take good care of your brother. Over."

I figure this is as good a point as any to make my grand entrance. "I want to talk, too."

"Hey, little buddy." Emmett puts his arm around me, which is weird. Sometimes he's pleasant enough, but he usually doesn't touch me except for an affectionate swat. Most of the time he's torturing me.

And I know my intuition, but suddenly my intuition is all gone from me. I feel lost at sea. I'm all turned around inside of myself, clicking the button and hearing them laugh. I feel like I'm dreaming.

I've used the ship-to-shore to talk to Dad many times, and so Emmett leaves after a minute or two, telling me he has to get in the shower.

I don't usually like being on the first floor by myself. The times my parents let Emmett watch me, I'm like a puppy, attached to his side. But you don't follow somebody into the shower. I cut a few more jokes with my parents, promise to brush my teeth, and I go back into the living room.

The rain-sleet is hammering at the window. I look at the clock. Nine-forty. I am usually in bed at nine-thirty, and suddenly I'm way, way tired. I pick up my navy men and start putting them back into the box. But my arms feel so heavy, I have to stop a couple of times, hold up my hand, and look at it.

I say to each sailor, "Go to sleep," which feels weird. I don't talk to my navy men usually. But I keep doing it.

"Go to sleep, go to sleep…" I glance up at the window Emmett had forgotten to close. It's too heavy and high for me to shut, though that curtain's still flapping up to the ceiling, making me cold with this wind. "Go to sleep…"

Half of me wants to go upstairs to bed, but my whole body feels chained down here, like there are weights on my feet and shoulders.

And all of a sudden, I hear her.

I drop the shoe box so I can put my fingers to my ears, but I'm stepping all over navy men and I'm heavy and my heavy arms won't reach my head. I know The She and it takes me a minute to realize this time it sounds different. It's definitely her. But she's shut up in a box or a tomb. The sound is buried, not loud and free from over the ocean. She's…behind me. I spin.

Looking past the dark kitchen, I suddenly don't care that it's darker back there or that I'm rushing toward her voice. The closer I get to Dad's office, the louder her shrieking gets.

I stare at my dad's empty desk chair, then the radio, hearing what my intuition tells me is a dream, but I'm wide awake.

"Coast Guard, this is the vessel *Goliath*. We are approximately eighty-four miles southeast of Atlantic City. We just lost power and a valve below the waterline. We have a list. We are caught in something, a very heavy current pulling us northeast. We are being...sucked—Mayday, Mayday. Coast Guard, this is the vessel *Goliath*—"

I grab for the handset and push down the button, which stops the shrieking, at least while I speak. "Mom? What's wrong? Over!"

The shrieking mixes with her voice while she's talking to me, to Dad, it's all mixed together. "Oh, shit, we got the baby, Wade! Evan! Tell Emmett to...Wade! What the hell is that? Over the port stern! Look with your eyes! Mother of God!"

I want to jump through the radio to get to my mom's screaming Maydays, and I want to bolt upstairs to get Emmett. I end up backing out slowly, hearing The She until she has almost overpowered my mother's voice, which is screaming. The sound is all through me then, coming from the sky, the beach, the radio.

I'm up the stairs, throwing open the bathroom door, but the light is out, the air is dry. I tear down the hall to the big wooden door and the stairway that leads up and around to the widow's walk. I pass my mom's padlock, hanging open, and try the stairs that go up and up and round and round. But I'm still a thousand pounds and I can feel myself being sucked down...into black, deep, dizzy, swirling black. I croak, "Emmett...," but I'm falling backward...forever and ever falling.

I

*"A fool's brain digests philosophy into folly,
science into superstition, and art into pedantry.
Hence University education."*
—GEORGE BERNARD SHAW

ONE

I sat down in physics class two days before Thanksgiving and went through this trail of amazingly satisfying thoughts. First, it was my last physics class before a four-day holiday. Second, the view out the window almost made the class worth having. There's something about old, tall buildings and taller, new buildings, and cabs, and horns, and traffic rushing along JFK Boulevard that is almost as good as television. After Thanksgiving, Christmas lights and store windows would be a decent enough distraction to keep physics boredom from killing me.

Which brought me to my final satisfying thought: I considered it my solemn duty to amuse my friends and fellow humans in the meantime, and some fun with physics was on its way.

People were groaning because Mr. Maddox had come in with his laptop, which meant a Maddox superdeluxe-o PowerPoint presentation (super in his opinion only). I had "borrowed" a copy of his file to make it less sleep worthy, and I now was doing my straight-face relaxation exercises. All my friends say I have some genius for disrupting classes, but that's not really true—there's just one major trick involved. It is majorly important to keep a completely straight face.

Mr. Maddox lowered the lights, and up on the big-screen TV we saw, MR. MADDOX'S SUPERDELUXE-O PHYSICS IN MOTION, FEATURING...

People were yawning. I yawned, looked at Harley Ehrlich, and winked.

She did a double take, having seen the wink. Then she groaned and whispered, "Are we going to have pea soup dripping from the ceiling again? If so, I don't know how you expect him to see it in the dark."

I kept my bored face. She cracked up. She said once that the more bored I look, the better it is.

FEATURING...SISTER AMOEBULAS...THE SCIENTIFIC NUN.

And there beside Mr. Maddox's superdeluxe-o letter-ing was his little animated nun icon, which he had fallen in love with back in September. She zipped across all his slides, pointing at this and that with superdeluxe-o sound effects. We'd quit wondering back in September if the superdeluxe-o sound effects would have Sister Amoebulas quacking like a duck or breaking glass or honking like a car horn.

Mr. Maddox clicked to the first screen, which was sup-posed to explain to us the difference between the guts of a proton and the guts of an electron. Harley sat forward slowly, staring. She had noticed, though I'm not sure anyone else had yet. This nun icon was just slightly different than Sister Amoebulas. A little taller and thinner.

"You touched his nun?" Harley turned to me. "In a Catholic school? I'd have left the nun alone and had my fun with some other graphic."

But she didn't understand the whole story. The night before I had seen up on farts.com this little nun character that looked alarmingly like Sister Amoebulas, only with a whole new and different set of sound effects. I was a victim of circumstance.

"They call her Sister Mary Flatulence," I whispered. "She's...a rip?"

Then this little cartoon nun's habit blew out in the back, and a spark cracked, and she broke this way-nasty-sounding wind. Mr. Maddox froze, and I think everyone else did, too, except Harley, who murmured, "Touching a man's software. That's got to be worth a couple of Saturday detentions."

It took most everybody a couple of more sound effects before they believed they were seeing a nun run all around the energy equations, her habit billowing backward to the sounds of yesterday's Fart of the Day.

Harley turned to me, shaking her head. "What'd you do, steal his laptop?"

"Just copied the file onto a disk. Do I look like a hood?"

Mr. Maddox was not being very smart. He kept fast-forwarding through the screens, hoping this edit job would end, but he was just giving the class more and better effects. On the sixth slide, the nun was twirling, dancing on top of a molecule, bowing to one side. *Pooooh...* She bowed to the other side, and a fatal car accident resounded instead of a fart.

"All right. Mr. Barrett, do you have my real program, please?"

People were laughing more at me, I think, than at Sister Mary Flatulence, because they could never believe I could look so totally clueless. I didn't think he'd point the first finger at me. We had a couple of big-time comedians in the class who were better computer whizzes.

I sat up, coming out of my half sleep. "Wasn't me."

He flipped on the lights, and I blinked sleepily, casting confused glances around at the Cheshire cats having fits up the aisle. He had turned down the volume, but had failed to stop running slides. I watched the nun dancing all over the top of Mr. Maddox's lightning bolt, her dress billowing with what now amounted to SBDs.

"I think it *was* you, Mr. Barrett."

I shook my head, tiredly. "It *wasn't* me. I don't think that's funny." I looked at the nun's billowing outfit with stunned awe. "I don't think that's at all funny. I'm a mature person who was raised better."

I watched people cracking up in that desk-pounding way, and it was going over the top. The two cheerleaders in the class were away at some competition, and the queen of the bitch patrol, Grey Shailey, had gone to Maine because her grandmother was dying. That left no one to groan and cast me disgusted glances. The laughter was ripping with nothing to cut it.

"Mr. Barrett, by virtue of the fact that you are the only person *not* laughing, I would say your guilt is apparent. Between today and yesterday, I've lost about a half hour of teaching, thanks to your comedy shows." And then, he was waving the orange hall pass at me, orange meaning proceed to the gestapo's office, do not pass go.

I had forgotten the pea soup thing was just yesterday. Seemed like a hundred years ago. Clever class pranks are a necessity, in my heart, because most people got tired of doing them after, like, sophomore year. We were seniors, in a barren wasteland of yawns, which my big brother said would change again in college. A couple of his dormies at Penn reprogrammed all the phones in the dean's office so the Three Stooges answered the voice mail. I just couldn't wait to graduate to college, where immaturity reigned supreme.

The class was all moaning, "Come on, let it roll!" Mr. Maddox's ears were red, and I could see hurt in his eyes. I didn't think most people could see hurt in a teacher, but I was like that. I could read eyes like most people could read the title on a book jacket. I was seeing maybe a couple hours' work in this presentation when he could have been watching *Monday Night Football*.

I moved over to his laptop and started pushing buttons. "Mr. Maddox, put yourself in my shoes. Some of your less apt friends send you up to this...this really rude Web site. And you see a nun who looks so much like dear, sweet Sister Amoebulas. I'm sorry, I just lost all of my self-control."

I had restored his program off the hard drive while blathering. Then I kept scrunching my face in a way that said, *I'm sorry. I'm sorry.* I think most people hate to say "I'm sorry." But it is a secret weapon, because teachers don't expect it, and if they look completely mean next to someone who is being totally apologetic, people will think they are jerks.

Sometimes it works, and I needed it to, because of how they stack up things to have a domino effect in Catholic school. My brain started to follow the trail of dominoes, and I wished I would think harder before I pulled stuff. This orange hall pass would mean my third Saturday, which would mean my third missed soccer game, which would bench me for my final season. Three Saturdays also meant Emmett or Aunt Mel would have to show up here and have a charming conversation with the principal about how I don't apply myself. That meant both my car keys and transit pass would end up in Aunt Mel's desk at the university. All because two cheerleaders and the queen bitch weren't here to frost everybody down.

I had apologies barreling out of both eyes, which Mr. Maddox had been staring at, and, finally, something passed through him.

"Please, Evan. Allow me to teach up to the Christmas holidays without any more comedy shows."

I put my hand up, like, *swear,* and as I moved to my

seat, people were murmuring, "Lucky bastard…too lucky, Barrett…"

I did have this reputation for being extremely lucky, and it wasn't just weaseling out of trouble. Last year I totaled my car in an ice storm and walked away without a scratch. I got kicked in the face in a soccer game, and the doctor said the guy missed my eye by a sixteenth of an inch.

And I *felt* lucky. I could gaze out at the buildings during physics and not have to worry. Emmett understood physics completely, and he patiently explained any overly painful homework. I concentrated on girls' thighs for about five minutes, feeling lucky about Catholic schoolgirls' uniforms. Then, Mrs. Ashaad stuck her head in the class.

She apologized, said she was leaving for a holiday flight but first, "I need to speak to Evan Barrett in my office before I go."

A groan whizzed through the air with the word *lucky* echoing through it, and Harley got too jealous. She watched me getting my books and muttered, "Boy, you really are an optimist. What's so important it'll take up the whole period, unless it's something bad?"

"She probably wants me to, uh, 'volunteer' for something else," I whispered. Emmett laughed sometimes about our Orphaned Kid Syndrome, how it makes us warm up to nice adults more easily than others do. It never hurt anything, except that I got asked to do more stuff by the teachers and principal.

"Confident, aren't you?" she muttered, casting me a smug glance. "The only thing I can think that would take all period is that you've been busted for hacking into the administrative file and reading Bear his grades."

I spun to see that Mrs. Ashaad had left the door open, but she was not out in the corridor—which meant she had gone back to her office and wanted to tell me the whole thing in there. *Hacking. That was a biggie.* There was a big legal notice about hacking posted in the administrative corridor, which nobody bothered to read, but we got the idea that this was definitely expulsion material based on the thick black type and the lengths of the paragraphs. I'd done it for a worthy cause, of course. Bear's dad was threatening to sell his Mustang back to the dealer if he got lower than a C in anything. Bear would have slept with that Mustang if he could have wedged it under his pillow. He just wanted to know how much fast-talking he would have to do when the last quarter ended recently. I took pity on him.

I went as calmly as possible down the corridor, trying to decide if Mrs. Ashaad could possibly know about this. Could a hack be detected and traced backward to the source? I didn't know. But I was a very lucky person who was having a very lucky day, I reminded myself. I walked into her office, actually grinning.

"Sit down." Mrs. Ashaad pointed to the armchair in front of her desk.

I sat, and she kept staring, smiling suspiciously. Actually that's not unusual. I think she wore that smirk for the fighters, the loadies, everyone.

"How are you, Evan?"

"Fine. Yourself?"

She only stared more. My insides started turning hot, and to fight it off, I let go of a line or two. "Of course, you can always ask Emmett how I'm doing. He told me you cooked a great meal on Friday night."

"Where were you?"

"Mrs. Ashaad, um…it would be like sitting down with the gods. I wouldn't be able to digest my food. If you don't mind, um…I'd like to enjoy your company around here and…" I trailed off.

"You like to keep your school life and your private life separate." She didn't look hurt. In fact, she looked amused. "I've had plenty of the students at the house for a meal. Some feel the way you do. I'm just surprised. It's usually those not so involved with everything."

"Well, much weirdness comes from having your brother decide he's friends with your principal and her husband." I shifted around. "Especially *my* brother. I mean, he's a very nice guy, but I'm stumped. Really."

She dipped her head from side to side, thinking about this. "He talks quantum physics with my husband, and then I don't have to."

But he was twenty-five, and the Ashaads had to be pushing forty-five. The fact that her husband was a math professor didn't cut it with me either. He taught at Penn, and Emmett was finishing the philosophy program at Drexel.

"And he's an atheist. You're principal of a reputable Catholic high school." *Which I may be expelled from in about ten minutes, so would you get on with it, please?*

"He's a well-behaved atheist. That's all a good Catholic can ask for these days."

She kept staring and smirking. I couldn't help squirming around a little. "Tell me," I asked, "does he find a way to bless himself at the dinner table when you say grace?"

"No. But he's honest, and I appreciate people who are willing to defend things they believe in. Not that I can entirely follow his little vaults over the bar of reason, but he enjoys our company. He says many of his friends are older."

Yeah, Orphaned Kid Syndrome. I didn't want to bring that up. I let the silent standoff go on for about five seconds, then, careful not to take my head out of my hand, I asked, "Why are you looking at me like that?"

"To see if you're guilty."

I didn't move a muscle. Though my body was filling with heat, I could have sworn there was nothing behind her eyes but amusement. She makes herself a hard read sometimes, so I stalled with another joke.

"Um...I know the way I broke up with Callie McCabe last week was not very, um...*discreet*? I shouldn't have done it on school time."

"Ah yes." She kept glaring but a slight grin crept up.

"Another illustrious member of the female student body bites the dust following your charming send-off lines."

"You don't know what she did first."

"Tell me," she said. I didn't think I could tell the principal that Callie McCabe sang the onion-ring underarm song right in the face of a sophomore with some sort of constant body rash.

"Let's just say I ought to listen to Emmett more about why he doesn't get in relationships. He keeps saying that really nice guys often find themselves attracted to really mean girls."

I looked at my watch without seeing the time, and forced myself back into composure, using my "nerves of steel," as my friends loved to call it. I looked Mrs. Ashaad dead in the eye until we'd both blinked about three times.

Her face relaxed finally, the smirk turning to a smile. "You'd be amazed at what your fellow students confess to when the principal calls them to the office for one thing, and they think it's something else. Out it comes. They're defending themselves before I ever have any idea what it is they've done."

I'd heard this about her. Somehow the rumor of her little tricks didn't prevent people from having vacuumhead when they got in here and spilling their guts about God knows what. Expulsion always hangs over your head in a Catholic school. I doubted kids in public school pissed themselves so easily in the principal's office.

"I'd say right now you're not looking *too* guilty of anything." She was opening a folder on her desk, but I didn't want to look down at it because she wasn't looking down yet. I was amazed at how other people could not read eyes like I could. This was the *principal,* for God's sake, and she couldn't see the sparks and seizures of guilt flying through my head. She looked down finally.

The upside-down Kids Helping Kids logo stared at me from a form.

"I want you to do a KHK service project for me, Evan." Mrs. Ashaad was filling out the form now, not looking up.

See, Barrett? You're having a lucky day. My only bad thought was that I wasn't sure I needed my heart to grow another three sizes, which is one of the "joys" of KHK projects. And I didn't see the need to shrink my kick-back-and-relax hours three sizes again.

"God knows you did enough with little Miguel. I wouldn't ask you to do another long-term mentoring project this year. There's certainly not as much time involved in this one. A couple of visits should do it. I'm not saying it will be easy for you…"

She looked up at that point, but I was hung up on the statement before the last one. "A couple of visits? Doesn't foster care tell you that's not the way to approach a little kid?"

"This one isn't from foster care. It's a seventeen-year-old girl. She's in Saint Elizabeth's."

I just stared at her. Then I started shaking my head,

though I wasn't sure which I was wary of: the seventeen part, the girl part, or the Saint Elizabeth's part. *Saint Elizabeth's.*

"She's in..." I almost said, *the nuthouse.* I shoved my fingers up to my lips. "What could I possibly do to help somebody like that?"

"Somebody like what?"

I got her gist pretty quick—people in mental-health facilities are not something to be stereotyped—but I was still completely baffled.

"I know she is not babbling and cracking into walls, if that's what you mean, Evan. I went to see her yesterday."

Mrs. Ashaad went to see her...so this was a student from here. Maybe somebody I knew. "Mrs. A, if I were up in Saint Elizabeth's, I would not want anybody from school knowing where I was. I can't believe that she would want some guy to—"

"She asked for you."

I sat there in stunned silence, all *What the hell?*

"Her family spends the summers in West Hook." She watched me, and I stared just as blankly. So I had lived in West Hook a long time ago. That didn't make me a psychotherapist.

"And?"

"She was out sailing, and there was an accident. She hasn't been able to get past it."

She kept staring, and behind her eyes I could see only black, like a major disturbance in the Force. I kept shaking my head because I didn't get how this related to me, and then suddenly I did. But it still didn't make a whole lot of sense.

I laughed a little, then quit to say, "Okay, so you think...because I lost parents in a boating accident way back, half my lifetime ago...that I could be of some help to a girl who had a boating accident last summer?"

She nodded, watching me. I thought of my parents sometimes. When I did, I usually saw one thing in my head: the color gray. Like a gray door, like a hatch onto a roof that was gray, locked, nailed shut. I mean, I had nice little memories of playing Frisbee with Dad, and Mom making me laugh sometimes. I wasn't some total repressive. I just liked my life with Emmett and Aunt Mel and didn't feel the need to go into that memory bank very often.

I got sort of edgy watching Mrs. Ashaad fill out something that said "Underage Visitor's Pass" at the top. I tried to stay calm but couldn't help remembering last year. I'd had some very bizarre memory surges after some poor excuse for a human being actually slipped me acid at a party. I was too drunk for it to register until I was home in bed. Some totally great memories from my childhood surprised me by showing up...and then they changed.

At that point I figured somebody must have messed with me because I'm not normally so mentally energetic. But I got up out of bed and wrote down every last thing about my parents' deaths like it was happening again before my eyes. I thought it had to be some bizarre truth serum, some memory drug that someone had slipped me.

But Emmett hauled me down to Pennsylvania Hospital the next afternoon because I was remembering some shricking so plainly that I was actually holding my ears. He didn't like to talk about West Hook any more than I did, and he was also scared shitless that I might be dead of some drug poisoning by nightfall.

The hospital lab showed it was just a small dose of LSD-25, which usually wears off in three to four hours. It had worn off. The only problem was that I was left with these awful memories. They didn't wear off so easily.

I spent the school week zombified, then took my first trip to West Hook in a long time. I had such a bizarre experience down there that whenever I thought about it, it still seemed like a dream. The only important thing is, I came back with my sanity again, with a sixteen-year-old head on my shoulders, no longer wondering if my parents could have been eaten by something I had at one time called The She.

Emmett would not have approved of my methods for getting my sanity back. So I never told him about going to West Hook. I never told him about the writing I did under the influence, either.

"I don't see how I could help some sick girl, Mrs. Ashaad. I was just a little kid who, you know, saw it through a little kid's eyes, and eventually forgot a lot of it."

"She's getting professional help. No one expects you to be a shrink. She just seems to want to talk to someone who's been through something similar to what she's been through. That's a normal, human response. I'm assuming it wouldn't hurt you to talk to a person in need."

"No…no," I muttered, but my mental alarm bell was going off madly. Emmett explains away my intuition as just me having a really keen perception for small details. Maybe a lot of the time that's true. Like I noticed Mrs. Ashaad had been careful not to mention the person's name—almost as if it was important for me to commit myself before she said who it was. Like maybe I knew this person and wouldn't want to go.

She tore me off a yellow copy of the form, and I saw "Grey Shailey" written there, and the walls moved three feet inward. Her best friend's voice whizzed through my head with some tale of Grey being in Maine for the past three weeks because her grandmother was dying. I dropped my hand on my knee, thinking, *Your lucky day, huh?*

I do feel like an extremely lucky person, but I'm also aware that there's a catch. When I'm unlucky, it's almost beyond human comprehension—like losing both parents.

"Grey Shailey had a boating accident, and somebody died," I heard myself say, and didn't quite believe it. So I repeated it. "A *boating* accident."

"Yes."

"Jesus. That's almost enough to make you believe in—"

I stopped short of saying "the she-devil of the hole," because I'd just taken the Lord's name in vain, and sometimes Mrs. Ashaad could write you up for that, depending on her mood. I just sat there apologizing, trying to figure out the mysteries of the universe.

I've solved a few mysteries since I sat staring at this form and this visitor's pass. But I'll admit, there are some things that will never be explained to me, maybe because the answers don't exist. I can't explain how the girl who was responsible for my acid-inspired memory surges ended up in a boating accident nine or ten months later. It ranks right up there with your mother accidentally sending her Mayday over the ship-to-shore instead of the ship-to-ship, while you're playing with your toys on the floor.

"I'll go," I told Mrs. Ashaad, and stood up. I had a thought that maybe this wasn't so unlucky. I wasn't concerned with Grey Shailey messing me up. She'd thrown me for a loop by slipping me acid and thinking she was so goddamn funny. But I got past it; I'd been fine about West Hook again for nearly a year. I was more concerned with how gratifying it might be to see her in hospital clothes, not looking so beautiful and stuck-up for once.

TWO

When I got home after soccer practice, the light was on in the study. "Emmett?"

"I'm here."

I wandered in and threw my backpack and coat down beside his reading chair. He was facing his monitor, with his back to me, looking at a page full of small type.

"Aren't you supposed to be teaching tonight?"

"The week before Thanksgiving, the university does a Wednesday, Thursday, Friday schedule on Monday, Tuesday, Wednesday. It's something I don't quite understand. It must have to do with dollars and cents." He beckoned at me without turning around. "But it means I can sit here and start the final chapter of my dissertation. Read that line."

I looked where his finger pointed and read, "'Saussure discovered that the relation between the sign and signifier is arbitrary.'"

"Do you have any idea how significant that has long been to literary theory? To philosophy in general?"

I patted him on the head, watching him stroke his beard contentedly. There was a bowl of pears on top of his bookshelf. Aunt Mel was great for putting bowls of fruit around. I reached for one, felt it was soft, and bit into it, sucking the juice down the back of my throat.

"And if the university thinks it's Thursday, I take it Aunt Mel *is* teaching."

"The university doesn't *think*; the university *knows*. If the university says it's Thursday, then it's Thursday." He turned and looked at me, his eyes glowing with pride over his dissertation.

He pointed to my pear. "The way we think of and speak of this pear, that is known as the sign," he said, then pointed to his mouth. "The word alone, *pear*, is a signifier."

I stuck the juicy thing to my mouth for another bite. "If it *is* Thursday, how come we're not sitting down to Thanksgiving dinner? You hear from Opa yet? We doing dinner at the Hyatt as usual?"

He sighed. "I wish. Opa's having problems with his diabetes again. Circulation. He's having some pain in his legs and doesn't want to drive up here on Thanksgiving."

I flopped into Emmett's reading chair and groaned. Opa had open-heart surgery the year our parents died, which had thrown his diabetes over the top, forcing him to sell his business and take it very easy, though he still enjoyed monthly trips to Philly to see us. I didn't like to think of Opa in pain, but I liked my family traditions un-tampered with. Opa had taken Aunt Mel, me, and Em-mett to the Park Hyatt for Thanksgiving dinner for the past seven years. It was a great spread, with everything from turkey to Maine lobster on the buffet.

"He can get a massage in the spa before we eat," I ar-gued. "Besides, he doesn't drive. He gets driven. What the hell is the difference?"

"I guess that's what happens when one lives in a soci-ety where some have more money than others. Those with the money get to make all of the decisions. The decision is…drumroll…we are going to East Hook. He's having dinner catered at the house."

I shuddered, watching Emmett's back as he turned to face his monitor again. Aunt Mel was a philosophy pro-fessor who had "discipled" Emmett, as they loved to joke, and both were socialists. It sounds crazy to your average American, and I'd found out not to broadcast it. But it seemed there were a lot of people like that at universities, especially in the philosophy departments. What made our situation even funnier to average people was Opa. He had an endless, sprawling house and had owned an endless, sprawling business. We're talking major capitalist here. Emmett told me once that his wealth exceeded that of two recent presidents.

Emmett disliked my grandfather's house even more than I did. The place was right on the bulkhead of the har-bor, and it had huge windows in every room. If you looked out any one of them, you would think you were on a boat.

"I hate being inside that house," I told him, shaking my head in disgust. "Everywhere you look, there's water."

"Yes. It could make you seasick. I'll pack us some Dramamine." He typed a few words and stuck up one finger. "Actually, the water doesn't make me as bilious as the collections. It's inconceivable to me why one man needs fifteen ship models, and all the while his house-keeper has to rely on that ridiculous excuse for a public school down there to educate her offspring." He spun around and grinned sympathetically, watching me glare and chomp. He pointed again. "Sign, signifier. If the rela-tionship between the thing and its word is arbitrary, that makes language *everything*."

"I don't want to go. Maybe I'll go to Harley's. Thank God I never went out with her. That's one friendship I'd hate to ruin."

"*Everything*, Evan. You don't get it." He spun back again, having some sort of subtle, educated glee-fest. "It means that if we didn't have language, we couldn't think, at least not in concepts. We wouldn't know anything."

"So?" I turned the pear around and looked at the chomped part. I didn't know if I agreed with him. "I'm starved. And even if I didn't know this pear was called a *pear*, I would still eat it. Aunt Mel leave anything in the microwave?"

"She said to order in Chinese."

I groaned and reached to pick up the cordless beside him. "I'm going to turn into a Chinese person if I eat any more beef and broccoli."

"Now, now." That was Emmett's shortened version of a lecture on how Americans ought to not complain about all their food choices. "If you're sick of Chinese, try Japanese. That sushi place is delivering now—"

I shook my head at his brilliance. "Why would I want to eat raw fish tonight, when I've just been informed I'm going to the shore on Thursday, and I'll have to smell it wafting off the beach?"

"Then get a pizza! It's food. Food is for the belly. Language is for the mind. And that's what I mean when I say everything is learned through language. If language is the source for every idea you have, then there *is* no other source."

I hit speed dial ten, which was pizza. "Pepperoni?"

"That's fine. I'll have to try this out on Mrs. Ashaad next time she asks why I won't say grace at her table."

I had about ten seconds to figure out he was saying that God is a man-made concept that came with language. By the time I ordered a pizza and hung up, I could barely remember Emmett's argument leading up to it. That's how philosophy was for me. It was like chinning yourself on a bar with one arm. You can't stay up there for too long.

"Why is it so important to you to disprove Mom and Dad's Catholicism and everything else, Emmett?"

"It's not," he said, typing a few more words. "I just

want to understand what's completely true. The religious angle just happens to be a by-product."

I finished my pear, staring at his back, not exactly be-lieving him. "Nah. You're on a soapbox. That's what I think. And I think you ought to leave Mrs. Ashaad alone and let her believe whatever she wants to believe. That's one thing about America. We've all got rights."

"True."

"Mrs. Ashaad gave me a new KHK project today, speaking of her." I tossed the pear core into the waste-basket, choosing my words a little carefully. "Only, it's not mentoring this time. If you can believe this, she wants me to go see a girl up in Saint Elizabeth's. She had some sort of a boating accident in West Hook last summer. Mrs. Ashaad says she's haunted by it, though I don't know what I'm supposed to do about it."

"*Haunted*. That's such a dirty, nasty, little word. In other words, there's a deceased."

"Yeah."

"And Mrs. Ashaad thinks you can help her?" He spun slowly this time and stared at me. No smile.

I nodded. "Actually, it's worse than that. She said the girl herself asked for me. She must have heard about Mom and Dad somewhere along the way."

"I can't tell you what to do, but...I really wish you would pass this one up for something else."

I could think of a dozen reasons why I shouldn't go, but nothing he would know too much about. I had al-ways been careful not to mention Grey as the source of the acid I took last year. After taking me to the hospital screaming about West Hook, Emmett might have found some enjoyment in calling the cops on her. I had wanted to kill Grey, but I wasn't sure I wanted to get her expelled and busted, if that makes any sense.

"Why shouldn't I go?"

He drummed his fingers on his jeans, almost nervously. Finally, he said, "You were very young, Evan. Even with your bad experience last year, there's a lot you still don't remember. Believe me, it was a very, very bad business down in West Hook. Aunt Mel and I have done our best to create a very nice life for you up here. I don't want any girl perchance throwing you into another tailspin. I'm sorry for her, but there are plenty of professionals available for her to talk to."

A very, very bad business. I thought that was a good expression for an atheist to come up with, somebody who could no way, no how, consider the existence of some superstition about the canyons off the Jersey coast. Well, I didn't believe in any she-devil, either—except maybe the one I was going to visit tomorrow.

I remembered Grey telling me at Bear's party, "It's like an oxy." *Oxy, my ass.* I had just been a way-trusting, drunk fool who wasn't looking for the difference between a football and a marble. I didn't even start to realize what this thing could do to me until I was alone in bed. Grey had been long gone by that point.

But she'd heard. She had played a stupid game of slice and dice with my brain. It brought up a clear, vivid picture of what happened the night my parents died, right up to the point where I was climbing the stairs to the widow's walk. The widow's walk is high up. Some of the oldest houses at the shore have them—it's a tower with a porch, where sea captains' wives went a hundred years ago to watch for their husbands coming home from sea. One memory surge reminded me that I hadn't been able to climb the stairs. I'd fainted or something...wasted precious time.

I squirmed, thrust an arm around Emmett, and stared at his gray type. It gave me a safe feeling to know that I was living with very smart people, even if I didn't always understand them. I just figured if very smart people loved me and treated me with the respect and kindness I got, I couldn't be as awful as I felt I was sometimes.

Emmett rubbed his beard, sighing. "I ought to have made you see a shrink last year. I don't know what was wrong with me."

"No, Emmett. I'm fine," I told him, being careful again not to mention my trip to West Hook. "I wouldn't have gone. I wouldn't have gotten anything out of it."

He kept rubbing and smiling in a way I didn't like—it was what most people would take for pleasant, though I knew him better, and knew that smile meant a "pleasantly judgmental" remark was about to fly.

"You didn't think *at the time* you would get anything out of it, probably because a psychotherapist would have no grounds upon which to disprove the fearful existence of a character that picks thirteen-ton shipping vessels out of the water and eats them."

I laid my head onto his shoulder and let him rub my back affectionately as I cracked up. "I'm sorry. It was short-lived. It was gone again...in a week."

"If you want, I'll call Mrs. Ashaad and tell her I don't think it's a good idea," he offered. "She knows how many charities Aunt Mel and I take on, that we're not inordinately selfish. Only when it comes to you."

I lifted my head and almost said, "Do it," just because Grey Shailey could push my buttons like nobody else. I probably would have, if it hadn't been for how much I just wanted to stand there and stare at her up in a mental-health facility and gloat. Bear and Harley and about four other friends knew of my trip to West Hook, so Grey probably knew about it, too. She had known my flipped-out and desperate state of mind that week. She'd had plenty of chances, and yet she had never even said she was sorry.

I told Emmett I would go see her, meet the minimum requirements of this KHK project, and then forget about it again. But I didn't like how I could feel his eyes piercing my back as I went to answer the pizza man's buzz.

THREE

I'm not any expert on being mean, even to Grey Shailey. So I kind of rearranged my strategy before heading off on the subway after school ended on Wednesday. It was about three in the afternoon when I got on the train at Seventeenth and Walnut, with Jupe under my coat. I looked like an amazing fat person from the waist up. Jupe was my twenty-five-pound lop-eared rabbit, a gift from Aunt Mel, whom I had "trained," more or less. Most magicians could pull a little white rabbit out of a top hat. I could pull Jupe out of a garbage can, though I wasn't planning on doing that trick. Most magicians could make their rabbits turn into pigeons and scarves. I could make Jupe shit cupcakes by sleight of hand. I practiced the trick on my friends, though Emmett said I could have a nice job doing little kid birthday parties if I would clean up the agenda.

I would do this thing and I would tell my friends, "Jupe is the only creature in the world who shits cupcakes.

Nobody else shits cupcakes, including us, so…"—meaning don't get too impressed with yourself. I thought maybe Jupe and I could lay a few hints on Grey—to change the subject—if she asked me any up-close-and-personal questions, or if the situation got too tense.

I kept that game plan until I got to the gate and looked up the winding walk of Saint Elizabeth's. It was a gray day and the sun was low, so at three-forty-five it was dark enough that all the lights were on inside. This place looked like a combination of a gothic mansion and a modern country club. I could feel my brother's thoughts running through my head as I went up the long walk, looking over the neatly clipped grass and bushes and back out the wrought-iron fence to what lay on the other side. Brick row houses smacked of low income, with drooping drapes and blankets hung in windows. I could hear babies crying, dogs barking, a woman's shrill voice rising from the sidewalk as if in an argument. There were a lot of souls packed into this neighborhood, one on top of the other. The neighborhood surrounding the haven of Saint Elizabeth's was not Rittenhouse Square, where I lived in the town house Opa used to keep for business. Grey was sent here by rich parents, to be protected from the world's problems by a high iron fence and a football field of grass and trees, and to loll around until she got over the fact that people die.

When I signed my name to her sign-in sheet, I noticed the only other name on it was Kevin Shailey, her attorney-father, day after day, twenty times in and out. *Daddy's girl.* He was paying for the whole thing and visiting her every day, probably ignoring the surrounding neighborhood because his little girl had a little problem. I sighed, promised to keep Jupe off the floor, and followed the lady in an expensive business suit down a couple of long corridors. I was ready to be not so sweet.

Grey was in a TV room with little couches and chairs, but the TV was off. She was standing by the window, looking out. She was alone in the room, and the echo of the woman retreating down the corridor again made me wonder if people on her ward were able to get passes to go home for the holiday, and if so, why Grey had not. She turned, sizing me up, I think, to try to detect my mood. I didn't smile. She was wearing a hospital orange top, but her own jeans. She looked washed out and like maybe she'd been crying. The sight of the orange shirt and some obvious wear and tear on her good looks made me keep my irritation to myself.

She glanced down at Jupe the way bitchy girls do when they're looking you up and down. She met my eyes again.

"Your rabbit looks happy, but your face looks unhappy. I take it you're not happy to see me."

I put Jupe down on a plastic chair while I took off my coat. I took it off slowly and set it down, unwrapped the scarf from my neck, threw that on top, stuck my hands in my pockets, and leaned against the wall.

"What's happening?" I answered. "Food any good here?"

"You're still pissed. All right. Starting from the top. I owe you an apology."

She raised her eyebrows at me, like maybe she was hoping I would say, "That's okay." I raised mine back at her.

"I'm sorry. I should not have slipped you that acid and told you it was an oxy. Even though you should have known, Mr. Blind-and-Dumb. Oh, God." She dropped into a chair in front of the window and held her head in her hands. "This is not very easy for me. I'm terrible at apologizing."

I moved toward her, only because I could hear real sniffs full of real tears. The best I could do was grab a Kleenex out of this box on my way past and hold it under her face with two fingers. She took it and blew her nose.

"Just bear with me..." She stood up again. "Yesterday I made up what they call around here 'The List.' That's a real Catholic phenomenon, 'The List.' I should have gone to Stillwater. At any rate, there's about fifty names on it, and you're the first, so..." She passed me and walked over to the chair beside Jupe, then rubbed his fur. "...so, sit down. And let me work on this."

I pulled a chair up and sat down facing her. After about fifteen seconds, she went on.

"Evan. Evan Barrett, maybe not the nicest kid in school, but the nicest cool kid in school...I am...terribly sorry about what I did to you. It was my own fault. I shouldn't have done it. I'm sorry I thought it was funny afterward. I'm sorry I was mean to you after I heard about your visit to Pennsylvania Hospital. It's just that I thought your damn brother would send someone over to bust me or something, and it's not like I'm any big-time user or I've ever sold the stuff! Wait—"

She sighed, scratched her hair through with her nails. Her normally shiny, short blond hair had turned into an untamed mess, almost ready for dreadlocks. "Back it up. Take out all that stuff I just said—that excuse about why I was mean to you after the party. Start with, I'm sorry I was mean to you afterward…"

I actually started to listen to this, not because I sensed any real regret in Grey but because this apology was getting to be like an engineering project—in avoiding all casting of blame.

"I'm sorry I pretended I never saw you in the halls…" She started watching me hopefully, like maybe that was enough.

I coached her, "I'm sorry I sat two seats away from you all last spring in—"

"Yeah, that, too."

I just let her cry, because it was very obvious she would not be doing this if her own life had not become suddenly very uncomfortable for some reason. She was doing this for herself, not for me. I waited.

"So. Can you forgive and forget?" she finally asked, looking miserably at the tissue clutched in her hand.

"Keep working at it. This…the list you're talking about. Do you have Soundra McLelland on it?"

"Is that any of your business?" she snapped, then shut her eyes and let her breath out like she was sorry once again. "No, Evan. I skipped her. I don't know how I'm supposed to march up to a girl with one leg and say, 'Sorry I gimped around behind you five or six times.' Can we just leave that one alone?"

I didn't say anything.

"So what does your rabbit do? Do you pull him out of a hat or something?"

I couldn't believe I had been good-hearted enough at one point to think I might actually do some tricks for her. "No, he was just bored and needed to get out of his cage."

She wiped her nose and stood up again fast, moving back to the window. "Look. Evan, I've heard all the stories. I know you were dreaming...or having flashbacks about your parents' death. I know Bear sat on the floor of your town house with you the next morning, while you lay there holding your ears and yelling, 'What was that fucking noise?'" She shuddered. "Do you think that doesn't make me feel bad?"

Her apologies were so to the downside of horrible, I really didn't want to respond to them. Memory surges don't only bring back something that happened. You also jump back into your feelings at the time, your age at the time, and I bounced into a nine-year-old head that made me see my parents getting sucked into a whirlpool that was actually the belly of some terrible sea hag. It was like stepping into an alternate universe, where you start to question everything you believe, and sleep is all but impossible.

"So what are you doing here, Grey? What can I do for you?"

"I'm here because..." She paced a little aimlessly, back and forth. "Do you know what panic disorder is?"

"Yes." Aunt Mel had it, said twenty-five percent of all people have some degree of it. Big deal.

"I got it in August. In September, I realized I could get away from it via my parents' wet bar. I switched around a lot, vodka one night, Johnnie Walker the next, so my mom wouldn't miss anything. Then one day I was going to sneak some into school, you know? I've had my fun on weekends, but I'm not a loadie—not a school loadie. I just decided, 'No, I'm not doing this.' I finally broke down, decided to confide in Mrs. Ashaad, and she got me in here. So here I am."

I was a little more impressed with that story than if she'd told me she had been caught. Sounded like she'd come here of her own free will.

She went on. "At first I didn't think the accident last summer put me here. It happened a whole month before I started losing it, and I got good pretty fast at drowning the symptoms. I thought I was coming for panic disorder and the substance abuse that followed, and the accident was just some awful thing. I tried to tell myself I wasn't responsible for it, which I wasn't, exactly. And it worked, until I got up here. Now I can't stop thinking about it."

She wandered over and sat down across from me again. "So go ahead. Abuse me for not caring right away that somebody died."

I resisted the urge to ask, "How does a beautiful girl

get to looking like shit?" It wouldn't have done anything except make me feel better.

It was my turn to get up and pace. "Unfortunately, I don't know if I can help you, Grey. That whole business with my parents was a long time ago. I was a little kid. I don't exactly remember much."

She just stood there watching me, and before I knew it I was doing what I hadn't wanted to: reciting personal details that followed my parents' passing, just to fill the silence.

"There's not a whole lot to remember. They disappeared at sea, went down fast. No boat, no wreckage. I moved in with my mom's dad over in East Hook, and when the school year ended, Emmett managed to talk my grandfather into letting us move up here with Aunt Mel. There's enormous picture windows and views of the water from every room in my grandfather's house. Except one or two of the bathrooms. I think Emmett realized it wasn't the place for me when he kept catching me playing with my toys in one of those bathrooms. We've been here with Aunt Mel ever since. I guess you could say I've grown pretty happy."

"Unless we're counting your bad time last year."

I really didn't want to get into that, either. So I answered her personal questions rather than go there. I thought maybe she was stalling.

"Where was your grandmother?"

"She died when my mom was fifteen."

"Out at sea?"

"No, she had cancer."

"I heard you had all these relatives who died at sea."

"That was on my dad's side."

She kept watching me like she was interested, so I searched my memory for what my father used to tell me. It seemed like a good way to be charitable without getting personal. I could take her mind off her problems by telling her harmless little details. "We're from thirteen generations of sea captains, and every few generations, one of them would go down on a ship. Leave an offspring to carry on the family fun 'n' games."

"Your mom? I heard down in West Hook that she actually owned her own freighter?"

"She was paying it off slow. She bought it from my grandfather, who made them."

"That's your rich grandfather?"

"The one and only. Phillip Starn. She had to sell it to my dad, though. She tried different crews, but...the sea is new ground for females. It didn't work out very well."

"Yeah, I heard about that."

I kept staring out the window. I supposed she was talking about the rape, before Emmett was born, when a few of the crew got drunk and disorderly in port in North Carolina. She pressed charges against one guy, and the crew stiffened up, torn between knowing right and wrong and living by this code of honor where one seaman never turns on another. My mom had then tried a "no drinking on my boat" rule, which went over about as well as putting a "no drinking" sign outside in the bushes at a high school party. It had just been a lot of anguished talk I'd heard between her and Emmett when I was little. And since Emmett and I had made it a habit not to talk much about Mom and Dad, it was all very hazy.

I shrugged, didn't see how this would be interesting to Grey, but she started to laugh a little. "And your mother has a sister, a Starn, who is a...a *communist*?" She blasted out a laugh. "God. Does your grandfather go around with a bag over his head? What an awesome scandal."

"She's a socialist." I turned and stared at her, thinking if she didn't get that smirk off her face I would leave. "That's one reason I don't go to West Hook, Grey. The summer people have too much downtime. They squawk and carry on as if everybody's business is their sole responsibility in life. Aunt Mel teaches philosophy; she's got tenure. And yet she's not so above it all that she won't go down to one of the soup kitchens on Christmas morning to mop the floors, which is more than I'd wager your mother ever did—"

"All right, I'm sorry." She put her hands up, then wiped the smirk off her face. "I'm sorry." She looked serious, like she realized she was apologizing again, and apologizing is a serious business. "My mom gets so drunk on Christmas, she's asleep on the couch by noon."

She came over and leaned against the window, facing me. "Maybe she's why I'm here. Maybe I don't want to be like her. Maybe I don't want to go through life thinking only of myself until I realize there's no self left...or maybe there never was any self to start with." She turned, put her forehead up to the glass, and I felt my eyebrows shoot up. "I know I have spent almost my whole time in high school never really appreciating the things I have. And I was really…"—she sighed—"…*mean*. I didn't consider other people's feelings. And now…I'm sitting up here, while everyone down at school is laughing. 'Ha-ha, serves her right for thinking she was so much hotter than'… whatever. I'll bet Soundra McLelland is having a real field day."

"I don't think anybody is taking time from their lives to talk about you, Grey. I heard about you from Mrs. Ashaad."

I would have thought she might have been surprised that she wasn't the talk of the school, but all she did was mutter, "Guess Chandra's better at keeping her word than I gave her credit for." She started laughing as she started crying again. Chandra Clemmens was her best friend. "So. I hear Soundra McLelland is running track this year! I heard they fashioned her some sort of bionic metal leg over at Presbyterian Hospital! Hell, that's a great way to get your mug in the paper—"

"I'm out of here." I went over and picked Jupe up off my jacket, but Grey followed and grabbed my arm before I could get my coat on.

"Look, Evan, I'm not here because I'm a piece of shit. I'm here because I'm a piece of shit who doesn't want to be one. All right? I know I have a ways to go."

"Grey, you know what I used to think of most when I thought of you? I thought you were a lot of fun. At least, you were fun until you turned my life upside down. It was *temporary*. But I guess I woke up at that point. What in the hell gives you the right to treat people like they're some sort of cartoon characters? As if we were all put here for you to amuse yourself with?"

I thought she might lash back at me, tell me to leave. But she just kept laughing and crying at the same time. She took Jupe out of my arms, fumbling until he was cradled in her arms, and she held him, rubbing his fur. But her eyes met mine, cold and mocking.

"What, you want me to sit here and blame it on my parents or something? You want me to say they were like that first? Okay. I guess they were. But I can still remember knives going through me when my mother used to sit talking on the phone, talking about one girlfriend to another, when she'd just gotten off the phone with the first one. I can remember her laughing about blackballing some lady from one of her charities because the lady was obese. I knew her whole life was wrong. Sometimes I think you can see that most clearly when you're just a little kid. I made my choices. I'm not blaming anyone."

It was the most disarming speech yet, but I think I liked best how she was treating Jupe. She was scratching him behind the ears, which was something he liked but that did nothing for her but make him relax and be heavier on her arm.

"The, um, the accident last summer, um…" She swallowed and wouldn't look at me. "It was more of the same…if you can stand to hear it. Lydia Barnes—a summer friend from New York you wouldn't know—she and I were at the yacht club down in West Hook, fooling around on my Sunfish. The sailing director came down the dock, said there were some Girl Scouts coming over, and he wanted to know if we would take them out sailing. Something about them earning a badge. We thought they would be little girls. They show up. These girls were our age. *Our age,* and still in the Girl Scouts. Lydia started in— No. That's wrong. Actually, *I* started in. 'We've got to flip the boat, scare the shit out of the one we take for a sail.'"

Grey plopped down in the chair with Jupe, and I eased into the one across from her again. I wondered if I should go get her another Kleenex. Her eyes were still hard, but flooding over big time. "I didn't know she wouldn't be able to swim. And I don't see why…why it is that Lydia and I could not have just accepted that. Girl Scout, our age. What's the big fucking deal? What is wrong with us? And not only that. But looking back? She really wasn't a big dork. She was really cute. Vice president of her class at Trinity. Looked like future college sorority material. I think that got under our skins even more. How dare this Girl Scout not fit with the mold we dreamed up in our heads?"

I grabbed her a Kleenex and sat down again, watching her sniff and blow. I had to say my thought, being that I was human myself. "Grey, I think we've all made fun of people. Some people just make you twitch."

"Yeah! Like the idea that you could actually become a dork yourself, if the tides turn just a little!" She pulled at her orange shirt with one hand, like she meant herself.

I just went on, "And you said you didn't know she couldn't swim. I mean, how many people from West Hook, whether they're summer people or not, don't know how to swim?"

"I didn't say she couldn't swim; I said she wasn't *able* to swim. Her parents said she did know how to swim." She stared off into space. My intuition went off big time. Seemed like some weirdness was about to fly, and I shifted around a little, looking down as Grey glanced into the darkening corners of the room.

"So...why are you saying she wasn't able to swim?"

"Just...the fact that she disappeared down the harbor so quickly, out to sea. She looked me in the eye for about a hundred yards, trying to swim back. She just wasn't making it."

Her eyes were wide, staring over my shoulder somewhere. I knew she was seeing it, but I didn't think the guilt was so necessary.

"She got caught in a riptide." I shrugged quietly. "Did you holler for her to swim sideways? Get out of the stream?"

"No."

"Did you swim after her?"

"No." She looked at me long and hard. "Don't even say it. It's not what you think. When I say I didn't consider other people's feelings, I surely never looked to drown anybody. I'm just a bitch; I'm not a murderer."

"So...what was up?"

She swallowed. "I was frozen to the side of the boat. I couldn't move. I was hearing this terrible shriek. It was coming out...from over the ocean. This girl was being sucked, very quickly, toward the sound of the shriek. Lydia was right next to me, and she said she never heard it."

FOUR

The TV room was completely dark by now, save the little light coming in from the spotlights out the window and the hallway behind me. I wanted to reach for the lamp on one of the tables, but I didn't want Grey to see my face. I groaned and rubbed my forehead with my fingers hard, thinking how it seemed like bad luck—bad luck that I would share something with Grey Shailey, even if it was the possibility of weirdly shaped eardrums.

She tried to pull my arm down. "Evan, Chandra was there when you were going through some of that remembering stuff last year. She told me you were talking about some shrieking noise…and about your parents. You said Emmett couldn't hear it. It sounded to me like this shrieking had something to do with your parents when…you know."

I just groaned.

"So you did hear it." She was pulling on my arm still,

and I just let it drop, let her lace her fingers through mine and almost squash them with her clammy hand. "I need to know what that was! Have you ever looked into it? Have you ever tried to figure out how you could hear something that a person standing right beside you couldn't—"

"No!" Actually, I had looked into it a little last year, but I hadn't gotten any answers that were worth repeating to your average, cynical person.

"Well, don't you want to know?"

"No." I was sure there was some scientific explanation having to do with how my ears are shaped slightly differently than other people's. "I don't believe in any *Ella Diablo* that haunts the Baltimore Canyon, Grey."

"Me neither." She blew her nose and whispered, "But I can't stop hearing it. You go through your life, never giving any thought to stuff that you can't hear, see, smell, touch, or explain. You don't give any thought to those stupid beach bonfire stories...except that they help break the ice, help you nuzzle up to some lifeguard you've been hot for. Now? I don't know. This sort of changes everything. There's all these stories about Saint Elizabeth's. There's a catacomb under this place. I asked the nun about it, and she says it's just a former wine cellar, and now they keep files down there. But when I asked her if dead people really were buried under the floor, she avoided the subject. She told me...the dead rise in Christ or something. You ever heard any of those stories, Evan? About the catacombs of Saint Elizabeth's?"

I scratched my head for a second. "I heard the one

about the crazy inmate who knifed all her dormies in the 1920s."

"Yeah, well, I lie awake in the middle of the night... listening, wondering if I just heard a scream from down there—from where the administration buried them to cover up the scandal. Or was it my imagination? Or am I rehearing what I heard at the shore?"

A curse rose right up to the top of my throat, but I didn't let it fly. She would know then that I could relate all too well, and I was still hearing Emmett's wise advice on not getting myself involved.

I shook loose of her hand while she laughed. "I mean, if I've heard *Ella Diablo* screaming, why not a ghost, too? Why not the whole schmear? Why not just believe in the bogeyman? How do you know there's not something lurking in a dark corner around here? Do you believe in being haunted?"

I hadn't given a lot of thought to stuff like that since I left the shore. I mostly listened to Emmett and believed what he said, because he'd spent so much time studying reality. "I think stories about hauntings and spirits and monsters have always been used to...control people. Keep the masses in line. It's a form of oppression. And if you're afraid of being haunted, it's really something about yourself that you're afraid of."

"Sounds educated."

"I live with one PhD and a brother who's about ten pages shy of a complete dissertation," I reminded her.

Her tone was a little sarcastic again when she said, "Well, maybe you can quote them to help me explain this."

She set Jupe down on the chair beside her, walked over to a table, and turned on the lamp. The room changed from mysterious and threatening to warm and glowing, just like that. I shook my head, smiling to myself as she brought over a big book. It looked like a library book.

"Since I'm not a drug case, and since I checked myself in here, I get to go certain places now that I've been here for three weeks. I got an aide to take me to the Philadelphia Free Public Library a couple of times this week. Please don't be passing that around school. If anyone finds out Grey Shailey has been spending hours in the library of her own free will, they'll drop over dead. Like I said, I'm not yet a murderer. Anyway..."

I cracked a grin as she turned over the cover page. "I went there to try to explain that shrieking. I looked for articles on pitches and tones and ears and stuff. All I can find is that dogs and cats and mice can hear tones that humans can't. I guess I'm half cat. I looked for articles about, maybe, tidal waves or earthquakes sucking the ocean out, creating riptides or waves that would explain my Girl Scout *and* the shrieking. I looked for something about whirlpools in the Atlantic with far-reaching suction, creating shrieking wind pockets, whatever. The Pacific? Now, that's where to live if you want stories about tidal waves or earthquakes or typhoons or suction. We, unfortunately, live on the mid-Atlantic. Our water does nothing. Except be black, reasonably predictable, and toss up good waves during a storm, according to science."

I threw up my hands, admitting something I didn't want to. "Emmett has said too often over the years that the day before my parents' last launch, he was down on the *Goliath* with Dad trying to fix a faulty hatch. It was one of the center ones that can bust and crack the hold if you're in a storm. And I think your Girl Scout is a riptide case."

"So you're saying they're not related? Then where'd the noise come from?" She opened to a page marked by a torn piece of paper. "This is why I ask if you believe in hauntings. I started looking for books in general on the South Jersey coast. And I came up with this." She pointed to a pen-and-ink drawing of a horrible sea hag rising out of the black ocean. At her belly was an enormous whirlpool, and a ship was being broken in two and sucked down. She had one sailor in her mouth and one in her hand, which, I suppose, she was going to eat next. I heard myself laugh as I shifted in the chair.

"Here's another." She flipped to another torn piece of scrap paper sticking out of the top. A screaming swimmer was being sucked out of the harbor, and the end of a giant tentacle was wrapped around her ankle. Over the water was The She, with many other tentacles billowing up from her waist. The hag in the first drawing hadn't had any tentacles. Different artists, I guessed. She looked hungry.

I closed the book and looked at the title. *Ella Diablo, She Devil of the Hole, and Other Terrifying Tales of South Jersey.*

I stood up. It was cold in here, all of a sudden. I walked over to the window. They had put the night-lights on out on the grass. There was no cemetery associated with Saint Elizabeth's, except maybe the one said to be under the building itself. But there were two gravestones at the far reaches of the property, over by the wrought-iron fence, which belonged to the man and his wife who had donated the place at the turn of the century. A spotlight had been respectfully cast onto the two stones, so they stood out in the surrounding darkness. The wind was kicking up outside. The grasses blew in front of the stones, and the trees rustled, and it made those stones look so incredibly still and upright.

Grey read, " 'Residents of the Hooks and neighboring barrier islands tell tales of the *Ella Diablo* of the Baltimore Canyon, eighty miles off the coast, who will rise out of the deep when certain rules that she established have been broken. If husbands and wives sail on the same vessel, she will become jealous and seize them. If people swim in odd numbers, she will make it an even number. Dogs chasing sticks at low tide are her favorite delicacy, and numerous dogs, bathers, and even sizable sailing vessels have been disappearing around the canyons for hundreds of years.' "

She turned the page. "Here's one eyewitness account, taken from a crewman's diary at the turn of the century. Want to hear it?"

I forced myself to nod, just because she seemed in need of telling it. Her voice was wound up.

"He says, 'She came in nothing but a small rainstorm. I was looking over the stern, as my job on our ship was to watch a following sea. I could see her rising out of nowhere, so black in the blackness, only because the stars behind her were disappearing. And then she revealed her face. Two white eyebrows cracked the blackness, then a hideous mouth opened and thrust itself out at me. I turned and ran for the captain, but he was on his knees paralyzed by a noise I myself could not hear. Shally was with him, the bowman. Since no one else was on deck, and since he was my captain, Shally and I knelt and prayed over him. I kept my eyes tightly closed, so as not to contaminate myself by the sight of this hideous abomination. But she sent driving spit and hiss all over the deck, all over me and my captain, sending us to a port list where the mast almost touched the water. But she failed to devour me and my captain, possibly because I was reciting my captain's prayer. It was a strong and good one. She took her cursed form back into the deep where she came from, and spared our vessel. Unfortunately, Shally was lost. We lit every torch lamp and searched the surface into the day, but nothing was seen that night except her belches of sea foam, and the following day, the surface was as if she had never come.'"

I had my hands on my lips, pulling on them like it might ease my sudden case of gut ache. I had my back to Grey, staring out the window, so I'm not sure she noticed. She just went on.

"I read somewhere in here that the number of ships that disappeared off the Jersey coast over the past three hundred years is something like nineteen."

"I've heard Aunt Mel talking about that," I told her. "She says you can't count any that disappeared before the days of radios. Anything could have happened in the old days. The captains could have been toting stolen goods or pirate treasure and lived out their lives having fun in Madagascar."

"Whatever. I went to the library to find out about tsunamis, tidal waves, and the shape of the human ear, and I come out with this book. I couldn't find anything else on the South Jersey coast. It's like any book of science in that library was hidden. It's almost like...something intended for me to have this."

"Don't get carried away," I muttered. I'd been pretty calm, though that picture and stern watcher's story had rocked me up for a minute or two.

"And I felt so strange asking Mrs. Ashaad to see if you could come up here and tolerate me for an hour. My thought was that I had brought some terrible memory surge ordeal down on a kid who lost his parents in a boating accident...then I have a boating accident? It's too creepy, too *Ella Diablo*-ish."

This time I laughed, holding back from saying, "If anything, it's more evidence of a just God than a wailing she-devil." I understood her little hell. I didn't know what to say.

She snapped the book shut. "I thought you might be a little more helpful. Or at least supportive. As I understood it, you were no calmness king last year at this time."

"No, I wasn't," I admitted, and thought back on it. "I'd heard my parents' boat going down on their ship-to-shore radio, and I must have made myself forget that whole night somehow. When it's too much for a kid to stand, what's that called?"

"Repression?"

Sounded right. "For years, all I could remember was waking up in Emmett's bed the next day, and him and Opa coming in and telling me the folks had gone missing. Last year, some of the night before came flying back."

She walked over to me, put a hand on my arm, and her forehead hit my shoulder as I stared into the little spotlights outside. I could feel actual sympathy and regret wafting off her. I didn't look at her, but I put a hand on top of hers. I might even feel sorry for Jack the Ripper if he had heard that shrieking.

"What did it sound like to you?" I couldn't help muttering.

"Like a thousand cats in a fight, only higher." She'd whizzed out that answer kind of fast, which let me know she'd given some thought to it.

"Not bad, Grey." I turned and walked back to the chair again, plopping into it. "Look. I was helped. But it was probably not in any sort of way that would help you."

She pulled her chair right up close and grabbed my upper arm again. "I heard you took a trip to West Hook that's been, like, shrouded in secrecy. You won't even tell Bear what happened down there."

I sighed. *Why would I tell what would sound ridiculous, even to my best friends?*

"Look at me, Evan. I'm a waste! Whatever it is, *I believe*, okay? Right now, I would believe *anything*. So don't think I'm going to laugh at you. What did you do, go see Bloody Mary? Did you drink some of that rotgut stuff she serves up to people so they can talk to their dead relatives? I'll talk to a dead Girl Scout. Maybe her body is caught under some shoal, and that's why it never turned up. Maybe there's not any she-devil, not any hole. Maybe that screeching we heard is just...some funny wind pocket that weirdly shaped ears can hear. I do believe in talking to the dead. I mean, I would...probably...if Bloody Mary could tell me—"

"Bloody Mary." I laughed up some scorn. "She's *easy* to believe in. She uses tonics and powders and potions. She throws bones and reads cards and charges real money. And there's people who have heard this or that impossible-to-know detail from her about the dead. I suppose Bloody Mary might have a little real power of some sort. But, also, I don't know anyone who spends summers in the Hooks who has ever been to her sober. She's like a giant giggle. Except that there are some local islanders my grandfather cringes over, who went to her about an actual dead person. Supposedly, she's got no problem telling the gory details if she's asked about somebody who died a horrible death. I haven't stooped that low yet."

Grey watched me like a hungry cat. I got scared she would drool on me. She said, "Some people think you went to see Edwin Church."

I turned my head slowly and looked at her, trying to gauge what she would be thinking. She didn't look too impressed. She shook her head. "The sailing director at the yacht club says he's just an old burnout who was a POW in Vietnam for too long and came home to drop too much acid. In spite of all the education."

I turned my gaze back to the floor. That's about what I would have expected someone to say.

"Why'd you go to him?" She took the leap of assumption, and I figured, *Okay, why not just tell the truth?*

"I don't know."

"What do you mean, you don't know? You must have felt there was something he could do for you."

"Grey, I didn't even have a reason to go to West Hook, okay? I just...felt it, felt like if I didn't go, I'd go crazy." I stood up and wandered a few steps aimlessly. "I'm just that type of person. I feel things, and I do them. I drive my brother crazy sometimes. He's got to have a *reason* for everything. I just have to have a *feeling*."

She said nothing but watched me in a way that made me think she might not laugh.

"I guess I was looking for something, just like you are, only Bloody Mary is out of my league. She runs that tattoo place, and I do remember having one thought that if I went to her, she might get under my skin somehow. I'd walk out with some multicolored snake on my chest that I wanted like a hole in the head."

She cracked up a little, and I ignored it.

"Edwin Church...I don't know. I went to visit my old house, which Opa hasn't had the heart to sell yet. And when I was standing in there, I just knew I was going to take a ride out to Sassafras to visit him. He's not dramatic like Bloody Mary, but there's that whole business with his hands."

"What about his hands?"

There were a few choice pieces of gossip in West Hook that only the natives knew, and I wondered if this could be one of them.

"I'd only heard tell of one person he'd ever done this for, and I was a little kid when I heard it. So I wasn't even sure it was true." I let my breath out, shutting my eyes, because as much as I'd gotten from him, it was still embarrassing to try to share it. "But he claps his hands, rubs them together, and sticks them up to your temples. Like this."

I stuck that fleshy, thumb-knuckle part of my palms up to my temples and pressed, shut my eyes. "He said it's something he learned when he was a POW. It's karate, or mystical, or something. He doesn't explain it very well himself. He just does it, and then...you can see things."

Before she could start in on me, I collapsed in the chair again and blathered. "See, that's why I'm saying it wouldn't be any help to you, Grey. If you're more into going to libraries or something, talk to my brother. He knows better libraries than Philly Free, and he's kept up his seaman's license, if you can believe that. I'll bet there's a lot of information about the sea he would know how to get...if he wanted to."

"Did you tell him about Edwin Church?"

"No way. He lives in a...a 'closed system,' as he calls it. Nothing exists but the physical universe and what we learn from each other. He would think Edwin Church is as ridiculous as Bloody Mary, and he would kill me if he knew I'd gone. He would say all I did was replace one superstition with another. I replaced a sea hag with some other higgly-piggly horseshit Edwin Church stumbled on in Vietnam. But if it's undertows and eardrums you're interested in, Emmett's got a lot of professor friends at Drexel—"

She put a hand up. "I'm more interested in results than information. You're a sane, normal, and functioning person again."

"Yeah."

She looked at me in a way that surprised me. Kind of like she was looking behind my eyes, the way I do to other people. Like she was seeing stuff there.

"You don't believe it was higgly-piggly. You believe whatever he got you to see, and however he got you to see it, it is totally true."

I didn't say anything.

"Why are you holding back on me?"

I shifted around and sighed. "For one thing, Edwin

Church is a very, very weird guy. He's probably had more education than my brother and Aunt Mel put together, and yet...he told me he actually does believe in some dark force out over the water. I don't think he'd call it a giant hag, maybe something less Bloody Mary-ish and *slightly* more socially acceptable. Maybe it's like a force of darkness that has no form but has the power to waylay a ship. He said he was very respectful of the tales seamen tell, and beyond that, he wasn't really clear. You could go to him and not get any relief—not if you're looking for the same type of answers that a library could give you. It just so happened...my feelings about going there were right for me."

"So he stuck his hands up to your head and then what?"

"No, first he kind of talked me into this hypnotic trance, same as a shrink would, probably. And then he did that thing with his hands. I was able to see my parents going down in the sea. I was scared to death I would see something like what's in that book of yours. But I didn't. I didn't see anything unexplainable like that."

"What was it?" She leaned up a little.

"It was about the biggest fucking wave I've ever seen in my life."

"A wave."

I could hear her insides trying not to be skeptical. I shifted around again.

"Look, I know the closest tidal wave ever recorded on the Atlantic was across the ocean in the Netherlands. I know it would have taken a hell of a lot more wind, sleet, and rain to create a storm wave big enough to roll the *Goliath*. I know the oceanographers would laugh. But that's what it was."

"I think that's great you sound so sure," she said, but her voice was forced. Not that I could blame her for thinking maybe I belonged in here with her. If you're going to believe in visions, why not just believe in The She? What the hell's the difference? I really didn't know.

But I hurried on. "I believe it, not just because of how I felt when I was seeing it. He did that trance thing to me twice. The second time, he covered my eyes with this bandanna he had around his neck. He said, 'If you're seeing that your parents' boat was rolled, let's find out if you can see where.' He spun me a bunch of times, told me to walk. I took about six very dizzy steps. Small shack. I was afraid to go farther for fear of ending up on my face, tripping over the furniture. He told me to stick out my finger anywhere and try to touch something. He put his hands back on my head like that and started breathing out really hard. I reached out toward the left, where I kind of thought his lamp was. He said, 'That's where the sea struck and rolled them.' Then he pulled the bandanna off, and I looked. I was nowhere near the lamp. He has this map on his wall that's about six feet long by four feet high. It's one of those huge maps of the world, where Asia looks like a kid's cutout."

"Where were you pointing?"

I didn't mind answering at that point. It was the part

that would be most hard to argue with. "Of all the places in the world, ninety-five miles southeast of Atlantic City. That's right about eleven miles from where my folks were when they talked to me and Emmett on the ship-to-shore."

"Holy shit," she whispered, then put her fingers to her mouth without really thinking about it.

Jupe had hopped down off the chair, and even though I'd promised the receptionist I'd keep him off the floor, I had forgotten. Now he'd made rabbit poop about halfway across the room. I grabbed a Kleenex, used it to toss the rabbit poop into the wastebasket, scooped him up, and sat down to find Grey staring at me. I looked away.

"Are you...um...going to your grandfather's for the holiday?"

I could sense the next question looming as if she'd already asked it. So I skipped the first one and went right to it. "No way am I going to Sassafras. I swore to my brother that I would leave the whole business with my parents alone from here on in. At this point, that would definitely include steering clear of Edwin Church."

She was quiet for a moment, though I could feel some scheme still baking. Finally, she said, "Evan, starting Friday, I'm entitled to a two-day leave. Take me on Friday, and I'll not only put Soundra on my list, but I'll move her up to second. Right after you." A smile lit, and after a moment it left again. "If maybe she could quit bragging about her bionic skiing, as if she didn't get enough attention, hopping around like a kangaroo, waiting for that thinga-mabob to get made."

"Prosthesis." I got up and put on my coat. "How'd you like to spend a day and a night over the side of a cliff with a broken leg? That was a horrible climbing accident."

"I know! I know! Shit. I cannot believe that passed out of my mouth. Do you think maybe I'm possessed?"

I watched her press her palms to her eyeballs and felt ripped up. Totally cutting remarks from girls like her sent me sprawling backward sometimes. Yet her sincere desire to do better drew my hand to her head. I rubbed the back of her hair, but I was thinking, *If she ever improves, it's gonna take ten years.* "All good things take time, Grey. I think you'll be okay."

Which wasn't saying that I would take her to Sassa-fras. I had promised Emmett I wouldn't get involved in her problems.

"I can tell you how to get there in an outboard from the rental place in West Hook."

"An outboard?" She dropped her hands, confused. "Forgive me for keeping my love of boating to the normal months. Isn't it freezing this time of year?"

I felt strangely outside of myself, like at one point in my life I could have seen myself pointing at her and laughing and calling her "one of those stupid summer people."

"No colder than it is standing in the middle of a field. Just don't fall in."

I left, listening to her whisper evil shit, that I was some

sort of heartless bastard. That was fine. The truth was, I had my peace about how my parents died and about what kind of creatures were real in our universe and what kinds were imaginary. But it all felt kind of shaky. The slightest thing could shake my truth away from me, make me start wondering again if dark forces could rip a kid's parents away and leave no evidence of themselves for anyone but the dead. Then I would just have to live with that. My intuition was telling me that this Thanksgiving trip to East Hook could leave me feeling something less than thankful.

And even though he had been the person who had helped me, I figured Edwin Church had something to do with my fears. The man was a walking contradiction, one I'd known about because at one time he had been a good friend of my grandfather's.

Like Opa, he supposedly had a lot of money. Yet he'd been living in this two-room hut on Sassafras, living off the fish, blue crabs, and clams he caught, since before I was born. He called all that education his "Bloody Mary," meaning, I think, the island witch, not the beverage. He spoke like an educated man, yet he said "I don't know" more than any person I'd ever met. He seemed to know as much about oceanography as any of the experts at the Coast Guard station, and yet there was the legend about his hands, which I now knew to be true. I had asked him, right before he did it to me, "What is this, Vietnamese mysticism or something?" and his answer had been, "I don't know."

His mumbled sentences, evasive tone, and words that

came clearly, like "dark forces over the deep," rang through my head. I figured Edwin Church could shake a person up more than he could help him, depending on the circumstances. Because, basically, there was no way to predict what he was going to say or think. He didn't seem to have a particular definition of what was actual about our universe, except "I don't know." I wasn't going back. Evidence feels shaky when it comes without proof.

FIVE

Opa had sent a limo for us Thanksgiving morning, being he was always leery of losing more family to holiday traffic. The limo had not thrilled Aunt Mel and Emmett, who mumbled all the way over the Ben Franklin Bridge about "capitalist excesses." I liked riding with my feet up, watching the Macy's Thanksgiving Day Parade on the little TV, and felt it was some payback for having to spend a long weekend seasick, eating Japanese leftovers.

Actually, Aunt Mel made me feel a little better when I said that, explaining that a catering service run by Japanese people didn't mean that we would be eating Japanese food on Thanksgiving. She said that families in East Hook frequently hired people of eastern descent to serve them on Thanksgiving, Hanukkah, and Christmas because they celebrated different holidays. Opa had said they could cook anything to perfection.

"Knowing Dad, I'm sure they can," she said, rolling

her eyes with merry affection for Opa. "Though service for four would suffice, I'm sure there will be enough to feed an army."

"Maybe you can take a few heaping mounds to the shelter with you tomorrow," Emmett said cheerfully, to make her feel better. His cheeriness probably came from the fact that he had been into the wine cabinet already, and I could see how he planned to deal with East Hook— by applying numbness.

They had planned it so we would get there just before the meal was served at two, because Aunt Mel didn't want to stand around for hours looking at the big-screen TV and hearing about Opa's latest ship models. She helped out in a soup kitchen the Friday after Thanksgiving every year, so she planned to go back that night. But Emmett and I had no excuse to desert Opa before Saturday at the earliest.

We put our bags in the bedrooms when we got there, then came into the dining room, and I watched Emmett and Aunt Mel exchange glances again as they looked over this spread.

Personally, I thought Opa was a sweetheart when it came to family celebrations. If I couldn't have the Hyatt as usual, there was nothing lacking in the buffet being prepared. Four Japanese men and a lady dressed in white jackets were coming in and out of the kitchen, making the place smell incredible. There was a turkey, a whole plate of lobster tails cooked in a yellow sauce, a ham, and a number of side dishes.

As much as Emmett and Aunt Mel disapproved of "Opa's extravagances," rarely did a cross word pass between them. He was a sweet old guy who never told them how to live their lives, and Aunt Mel once said of it, "Love covers a myriad of plausibility structures." He hugged Emmett and me, kissed Aunt Mel, and there isn't too much bad you can say about a guy who is so happy to see you that he rolls out the red carpet.

The meal wasn't quite ready, so I tried to find a seat in the family room that didn't have the big view of the water. The house was built up high on a huge bulkhead, and like most houses on the harbor in East Hook, the majority of the rooms were on the second and third floors, just in case there was a flood. This second floor view from one picture window in the family room went all the way up the harbor about fifteen hundred yards to the sea, and the view from the other was straight across the harbor, featuring the craggy old drawbridge leading into West Hook and the endless dunes leading to the lagoon and the small town. West Hook was older, more rugged. The only rich people over there were summer people.

It was another gray day—gray sky, gray water—and the wind was causing whitecaps and ridges to bob up everywhere you looked. It could easily make you seasick.

I finally pulled a chair in front of the window and sat with my back to it while Opa poured glasses of wine. He poured me a Coke, and I sat there listening to them talk about his diabetes problems while I fought this retarded urge to keep looking over my shoulder.

When the meal was ready, Emmett and I both moved nonchalantly for the one seat at the table that faced the wall instead of the whitecaps, and when we realized we were racing each other, we sped up a little. Emmett tried to pull it away from me, but I gave him a pleading glance and muttered, "You're older, come on." So he asked the server for another glass of wine, and we both tried to keep Opa from hearing us cackle over our neurotic reaction to his house.

It was a buffet and we were supposed to serve ourselves, but ancient family traditions came wafting back to me as Opa went and stood behind his chair. We stood behind ours, though I couldn't believe he would say a grace on this crew. He never did it in the Hyatt, but he always had at celebrations held here, before my parents passed away.

At least he had the good manners to ask, "Is it all right for an old man to say grace around here? Or do I have to give a toast?"

"Whatever makes you happy, Dad," Aunt Mel said in her usual nice way. He thanked God for his beautiful daughter, most excellent grandsons, freedom, a great feast, in the name of the Father, the Son, and the Holy Spirit, amen. Aunt Mel was even decent enough to bless herself, and when they noticed Emmett didn't, Aunt Mel said, "Sorry, Dad. I think I've created a monster."

Emmett held up his glass as we laughed a little. "A toast...to my aunt for her great intellect, to my grandfather for his great fortitude, and to my brother for his most excellent heart and soul. Great Scott! I'm feeling like Dorothy in *The Wizard of Oz*! Here, here!"

Opa had an ornery twinkle in his eye, and I hoped he didn't plan to start some sort of capitalist debate with Emmett and Aunt Mel. He loved doing it, but I could never see the point. They all loved each other a lot, and the only thing that ever came of those conversations was that they'd all end up laughing.

I took more lobster than turkey, and the food was delicious enough that we all ate in silence for a few minutes. Then Opa called the waiter over.

"There's a paper bag in the hall closet. Would you get it for me, please?"

"Dad, you're not bearing gifts, are you?" Aunt Mel cast him a worried look. "Because you know how we feel about Thanksgiving and gifts—"

"Actually, no. I remembered you had asked me not to. It's nothing, really. Just something I don't want to forget to give Evan."

They went back to eating until the server brought a brown bag to Opa. It was a small one. He pulled out a wool glove and set it in front of me, patting it. I had a heart attack, or close to it.

"Looked like an expensive one. I'm hoping you still have the mate. I stopped by to share a brandy with Mr. Church about a month ago, and he gave it to me. He said you had left it."

I remembered my trip back from Sassafras last November, with only one glove and the icy wind biting my knuckles as I steered the little outboard across the bay. I didn't know whether to kill Opa or not. He wasn't trying to hurt me. He and Mr. Church had been fishing buddies back before Mr. Church moved out to Sassafras. Opa never said a bad word against the man, only things like, "He won't come over here, because he can't reciprocate. Unless I feel like sitting on a crate and swatting greenheads over a toast, I don't get to see him. Which I still do occasionally...for Edwin."

He knew something about the intrigue with Mr. Church's hands. As a kid I'd heard him mention it a couple of times with a hefty shrug. Every seaman in the Hooks seemed to come with his own little set of superstitions, and respecting individual beliefs is just part of doing business down here. I think if Opa was miffed, it was because I didn't stop over to see him on that trip. He didn't say that.

He cast his twinkling, innocent smile over to Emmett. That's who he was trying to get even with, because Emmett wouldn't say grace. I guess he wanted Emmett to know that one person in the family still fit his version of somewhat spiritual. I just took the glove and put it under my napkin, which was a stupid thing to do, because it just made the whole thing look even more suspicious. Emmett quit chewing long enough to glance from my lap to my eyes, and I grinned a little. He didn't.

"The widow Riley called just before you got here," Opa changed the subject. "Said she ran into you in the liquor store."

"We saw her when we stopped to get the wine." Aunt Mel looked at him with a combination of affection and disbelief. "Dad, must you call her the widow Riley? It's just so...vernacular, so Mark Twain-ish."

"Oh." His eyes twinkled more. "She'd be 'someone living with widowdom' or something like that up at the university, I suppose."

"How about Kate?" Aunt Mel suggested. "It's a beautiful name, and it's hers."

"Actually, she likes being called the widow Riley," Opa said. "She introduces herself that way."

Emmett wiped his napkin across his beard, swallowed his food, and said, "Maybe that's because she still feels the constant *suggestion* might alleviate suspicion to the contrary." And he smiled in his politely amused way.

Opa and Aunt Mel laughed. I said I didn't get it.

"You don't remember when the Riley vessel went missing?" Opa asked me.

I glanced at Emmett, who was trying to slip him the thumbs-down sign, but Opa laughed him off. "Come on, Emmett. He's a big boy now. Surely he can hear a little island scandal."

"If it has to do with The She, I would prefer we skipped it." Emmett reached a hand out, rubbed my shoulder, and looked at Opa. "He had some problems with memories coming back, and it's only been about a year."

"Oh," Opa said, like this was news to him. "Why didn't you tell me?"

"Because it was nothing," I said, dredging up some casual tone out of nowhere. If you referred to Opa's health as being a *problem,* he got indignant. He could refer to it, but nobody else could. "I can listen to island stories."

"As you should!" he said, and an awkward smile crept across his face. "I'm not saying it was a bad idea for you boys to move away, live in a change of scene. But you can't spend too many more years pretending like the place doesn't exist. I'm not sure I've liked it going on for this long."

Emmett took a long time swallowing his food, and Opa watched him thoughtfully. He washed it down with a hit of wine and managed to come up with a smile. "You're right, Opa. The island was a big part of our lives. If Evan wants to hear island tales, I have no problem, but I would appreciate it if we could steer clear of the Gormley boat and stories of that nature."

"Gormley boat..." I laid my fork down and chewed, while the name and the circumstances came drifting close in some fog. "Come on. Don't mention a name and then leave me hanging."

"You were seven," Emmett rolled his eyes. "I was trying to sandbag because a northeaster had sprung out of nowhere, and it was a full moon, which meant the tides were going to hit the yard. Now do you remember? Because if you don't, we're not going to discuss it."

I let him think I didn't for a minute. Then I said, "I remember you whaled on my butt like some kind of savage."

They all laughed, and Emmett held up his hands. "What can I say? I was fifteen and impetuous. And Mom was standing right on the porch, listening to you go on and on about that screech you used to swear you heard once in a while. Mom was never fond of that she-devil superstition. She thought it was sexist, and she had enough worries. If I hadn't tanned your hide, Mom would have, and then it would have *really* hurt."

"I always believed you about hearing the noise, Evan." Aunt Mel smiled across at me. "I think it's fascinating. I wish science would hurry up with the explanation. I do remember hearing you cry about it once when I was there. I could see in your face that you were really frightened."

Opa shifted himself in the chair like his leg was giving him some hell. Then he forked a lobster tail out of its shell, and changed the subject. I was glad. Emmett had never believed me about hearing the shrieking when I was a kid—which hadn't bothered me at all in Philadelphia, so long as the issue was buried in some dead zone of my mind. Now I didn't know what to say.

Opa went on. "Shortly before the Riley boat went missing, a couple of the coast's less-favored captains— those who ran drugs from Jamaica, that is—had tried to fake their own disappearances using the superstition of *Ella Diablo,* whom you used to call The She. They gave false Maydays, false coordinates, tried to make it appear they were foundering when, in fact, they had realized the feds were on to them and there would probably be arrests soon. The Coast Guard was too smart, both times. The captains were caught and prosecuted before they could, er, founder. As for the widow Riley—Kate—she's been fighting the same accusation about her husband ever since."

I laid down my fork and slumped back, trying to think of this. I could remember Captain Riley and bits and pieces of my parents' conversations when his boat went missing.

"I sort of remember Mom and Dad not wanting to talk about it. Captain Riley was their friend, but I don't remember them feeling sad like you do when somebody dies. It was more like they were ashamed of him. They must have thought the worst of him or something."

"They had reason to believe the disappearance was a hoax," Emmett confirmed.

"He used to play basketball behind the garage with you, and he taught me how to wing a Frisbee down on the beach," I said. "Captain Riley seemed like a very nice guy, didn't he?"

"Dad always said he was lots of fun, and he was always very nice to me." Emmett turned and asked the server for another glass of wine. I watched Opa's eyebrows shoot up, but I didn't want to be finding fault with my brother for tying one on a little bit. He had gotten a seat facing the water, and I could see all this reminiscing wasn't sitting well with him, either. "But sometimes very nice men have women on the side."

"He had a girlfriend? While he was married to Mrs. Riley?"

Opa nodded, and Emmett patted me on the head. "Yes, O innocent one. She was on the vessel when it, er, went down. It was a big secret to no one, except Mrs. Riley, of course. She still insists they were just friends, doesn't she, Opa?"

"Just friends."

"Well, what was she doing on the boat?" I asked.

Opa answered, "You mean, what was she doing on the boat with a captain and four crew members, all of whom were about to be charged with importing illegal substances with intent to distribute? Except the madam, of course. She was just along for the ride." Opa winked at me. "We certainly don't hold anything against the widow Riley around here, but come on. You're a big boy now. Figure it out."

I thought about it for a minute, my jaw kind of hanging. I guess I was at an age where I would be figuring out that grown-ups I'd looked up to as a kid weren't actually so spiffy clean. But this one floored me. "Captain Riley? The one who made me into the best Frisbee winger in West Hook? You're saying he had a lady friend, he faked an encounter with The She, and now they're living in, like, Trinidad?"

Opa laid down his napkin and applauded. Emmett was shaking his head, glancing at the water out the window, and drinking a pretty big gulp of wine.

So I probably shouldn't have said it, but it was irresistible. "Okay, so...he had a woman onboard. It wasn't his wife, but it was his lover. How do you know The She didn't get jealous?"

Then I laughed, but it came out weird. It didn't last long enough. It sounded nervous, though there was nothing to be nervous about. I just found myself wishing I was up on Broad Street, enjoying a meal at the Hyatt, and I suddenly couldn't fathom why I had agreed to stay here until Saturday without putting up a fight. Up in Philly, the conversation somehow always covered *our* stuff. Opa was a sucker for my class pranks. He laughed and laughed at my stories, and Emmett and Aunt Mel filled in with talk of tenure, teaching, departmental issues, etc. But now we were on Opa's turf. And I think conversations just naturally went to what was important around here.

I figured I would park myself on the family room floor after dinner, below the windows, and watch football until it got dark and I wouldn't have to see the water anymore. Or maybe I would start dialing friends from school to see if any were spending the holiday at their summerhouses, which couldn't possibly have as many views as this place.

I shot a sympathy smile at Emmett, figuring he was thinking the same types of things. He was watching me, too intensely. He didn't smile back.

SIX

We had brandy with dessert, which is the drink of natives and summer wanna-bes in the Hooks. Opa always got me a snifter of that at our Hyatt dinners, just to "keep me a Starn," though I rarely drank any. After watching Emmett hit the wine so heavily, I decided there must be some value in numbness when you've got all these windows to deal with. I drank it, and it did me in. I kept to my game plan of crashing out on the floor of the family room and watching Thanksgiving football. But being that I hadn't had a drink since Grey Shailey nailed me at that party a year ago, I was whizzing a little, enough that I thought it would be funny to let Emmett see me crawl into the family room on my hands and knees to avoid any sight of the whitecaps.

Instead of laughing, he asked me, "Want to go for a walk on the beach?"

I collapsed on the soft rug, thinking of some thirty-seven fucking degrees outside and a lecture that was probably coming my way, now that I'd been busted for seeing Edwin Church. "Why in hell would I want to do that?"

"Because I'm going."

I figured he just wanted to sober up. I gave him the thumbs down and collapsed, my head on an overstuffed pillow I pulled off the couch. I was asleep ten minutes later. When I woke up again, it was because a telephone was in front of my face.

Opa was leaning over me and saying, "Evan, your girlfriend is calling you. *Collect.*"

I didn't have a girlfriend at the moment. And I could see Opa's eyebrows shooting up as he handed me the phone. He had this thing about people taking advantage of him because he was wealthy.

"I'm sorry," I told him. "I'll pay you back."

"No, no, not to worry," he said, but he retreated quickly back to the dining room, and I could hear him giving Aunt Mel the lowdown on his latest ship model. I just knew he wasn't tickled.

"Hello?"

"I thought maybe after that vulgar spread I'm sure your grandfather laid out for you, you might be feeling a bit more charitable about how you spend your time tomorrow."

"Grey, could you not call here collect, please? You've got a cell phone, and it's a holiday."

"They took it at the entrance gate. I'm in the nuthouse,

don't forget. Cut me a break. I get one call a day. I'm calling you instead of Happy and Smiley."

"Chandra and Bear?" I asked sleepily.

"Not quite. Happy is passed out on the couch by now, and Smiley's probably talking to his little button on the side and telling her how much he loves her."

"Oh." I woke up more, remembering that she was in a pretty bad way. "You didn't go home for the holiday?"

"Hell no. I'm coming to see you tomorrow instead."

I sighed. "Grey, listen to me. I just can't go. Believe me."

I heard something like a combination of sigh and groan. "I've never driven an outboard before. Is it hard?"

She was only used to driving yachts and Jet Skis. I rolled my eyes. "It's very easy, Grey. I did it last year after seven years away from the water. It's like riding a bike."

"Yeah, try doing it when you think you're fainting," she mumbled, and I got a little more awake, remembering this panic disorder thing she had. But she went on without any more appeals to my emotions. "I'll still need you to make a phone call for me. I only get one call, and I was imagining myself calling that outboard rental place and getting an answering machine on the holiday."

"You want me to call The Docks over in West Hook?"

"Yeah. My dad used to rent boats from them when he had parties at the house. You need a credit card. Do you have one?"

I was a second cardholder on one of Emmett's cards, but I didn't exactly want that charge to show up on his bill. I rolled over and sighed. "I think that's only in the summer when there's a line of tourists out the door," I told her. "I don't exactly think you need to make a reservation this time of year."

"True...and they'll be able to give me directions through the marshes?"

"It's not hard. You can see his little place almost as soon as you cross the bay. There's only one turn you have to make off the main trail through the mudflats—"

"Well, what about the tides? You can't get back there at low tide, right?" She sighed. "Never mind about that part. I'll look on the Internet."

I could have gotten up on my knees and looked to see where the water was hitting the cement blocks that held up the bridge to West Hook, but I decided I'd do her one better. I could hear her trying to figure all this out herself, from Saint Elizabeth's, on Thanksgiving, when her parents were passed out and/or cheating on each other. It did things to my heart like make me want to be normal toward her.

"I think Mr. Shields will probably take you out there himself. He owns The Docks, but he's got nothing to do this time of year, probably, except watch television—"

"That would be so cool." She sounded relieved. "What do you think he'd charge me to take me out and pick me up again?"

I started to say fifty bucks, but I stopped myself. My heart was doing even weirder things inside of me, like going out to her.

"Probably nothing," I lied. "I'll call him for you. I'll set it up."

I pulled my wallet out of my back pocket and eyed up this credit card of Emmett's. I figured I could say I bought a jacket in Mr. Shields's bait and tackle store if Emmett asked me any questions.

"Just show up an hour before high tide, which would be..." I actually got up on my knees, looked out the picture window facing the bridge, and saw where the waterline was. "Show up around nine A.M. Looks like low tide was at four by where it's hitting the pilings under the bridge, which would make high tide ten. Is that too early?"

"I can leave anytime after seven. And you sound like a real sailor."

Suddenly I could see Emmett walking across the bridge with a very red face and a package in his hand, a white bag with red lettering. I figured he'd walked to the West Hook CVS and bought himself something instead of walking the beach. I collapsed back on the floor, laughing at everything.

"Yeah, I'm ready for my longshoreman's test. Look, I've got to go. I'll set the thing up for you, but I've got to do it before my brother gets back in the house, and he's coming across the bridge right now. I told you he's not into Mr. Church."

"Evan, thanks."

"No problem."

"Evan?"

I really just wanted to get off the phone, make her phone call, and forget the whole thing. "Yeah?"

"I got Soundra McLelland second on my list. After you."

I just smiled, shaking my head.

"I just wanted you to know that," she said. "I'll call her tomorrow from my cell phone, when they give it back to me on the way out the door."

"That's good, Grey," I said, and my voice sounded a lot warmer than I really wanted it to.

"Actually, don't get too excited. She might be skiing. It seems to me that sometime last year, I heard her telling a couple of people *loudly* that her family goes up to their chalet in Vermont over Thanksgiving. Hey, does it cost less to buy your skis if you only have to buy one?"

"Grey?"

She shut up kind of fast.

"You want me to make that call or what? Because my brother's coming."

"Yeah, Evan. Thanks. Really. I'm grateful. I'm...really, supremely...grateful." She sighed a long one, then muttered, "Oh, fuck, I'll never get it right," and just hung up.

I dialed information and got the number for The Docks. Mr. Shields answered on the first ring, and the television was blaring in the background. I could hear little kids' voices shrieking, too, which meant he had picked up from his house. I remembered it was Thanksgiving, and in Philly, people wouldn't have picked up at all.

"Mr. Shields, hi. My name is Evan Barrett. You wouldn't remember me, but—"

"How would I not remember Wade and Mary Ellen's kid?" he asked in a friendly way that kind of stunned me. "I ask for you and your brother every time your grandfather comes in the tackle shop. I guess he doesn't tell you, since everyone's always asking."

He asked about school and the city, and I answered all his questions while hazily realizing he hadn't recognized me last year. I'd rented the outboard to go see Edwin Church from Mr. Shields. I'd gone in there wearing a hat, sunglasses, and a wool scarf, and I'd paid cash. Now he was giving me the impression our names were still household words down here. I felt shocked and guilty for not having been a little friendlier.

"So what're you going to do with your life? You going to come back, drive your own freighter someday?"

"No..." I stumbled, wondering if I needed to sound apologetic. "I never had that urge. Sorry."

"*Mmmm*...that's quite a long tradition you're breaking there, kiddo. We don't get either of the Barrett boys back, eh?"

I didn't know what to say. It felt eerily cold in here all of a sudden. I tried to shake the nap out of my arm while I hunted for words. He finally went on himself.

"Well, guess I can't blame you. Freak accident with your parents. Maybe one of these days your grandfather will hire one of my diving crews. I keep telling the old man, a big part of closure for your family in this case would be to find the wreckage."

There was a silence, and I sat up, trying to conceive of how superstitious people could be down here. I remembered Grey reading the day before, reminding me that The She sucks everything down into her hole beneath the canyon floor. In other words, to find the wreck meant, in his mind, that the ship had foundered in some more natural way.

Mr. Shields was blathering in that "native islander" way I remembered. Actually, the natives gossiped a whole lot less than the summer people did. They were more accepting of each other; whereas the summer people from Philly were known to be more snobbish and judgmental. Somehow they also were more reserved.

"I keep telling your grandfather I'm hooked up with this ace, crack team with a bubble drum that'll dive the canyon for thirty thousand. Stop any wayward talk that might still be haunting these parts, if you know what I mean."

I sat there completely stunned. The room got even more cold as I let my arm go limp in amazement. *Thirty thousand dollars? To find my parents' wreck and prove it wasn't in some she-devil Hades beneath the canyon floor?* I laughed, though the whole concept made me some combination of jumpy and disgusted. I thought of Emmett's words—"Superstitions control the masses." I felt glad at least that my grandfather wasn't one of the masses.

"Well, it might have been nice to get any remains

back," I stumbled, but put some intentional emphasis on my next words. "*Just* so we could have had a normal burial!"

If he caught my disgust, he didn't keep it. "So you been out on the water since?"

"Uh, yeah. Once. In fact..." I sat there dizzily, feeling chilled to the bone. I could barely remember why I had called him, or I was too confused to make up a lie. "In fact, I came to you about a year ago. Last November."

This time, he was silent.

"I'm sorry," I went on. "I should have been more talkative. I wasn't feeling really great, and I rented an outboard to go see Edwin Church."

"Oh, my lord," he breathed in awe. "You were that tall, good-looking blond kid. You really have grown up! Well, I'm not sure a trip to see Edwin Church is the perfect cure for what ails a person. Depends on what you've got, I suppose. My belief is, live and let live. Everybody has their own thing. Whatever works for you, you know?"

"Yeah, well, going out there to see Mr. Church helped me a lot," I said. "I'd like to go out there again tomorrow. Er, actually, it's not me. It's a friend of mine from Philadelphia. She asked me to call and find out if you were busy. She thought maybe you could take her out there."

He made a noise that sounded like a verbal shrug. "I'm not exactly setting the world on fire this time of year. Could do with a little extra cash. How much time does she need? Which piece of Edwin Church will she be finding useful?

The oceanographic institute piece? The Sigmund Freud piece? Or that, uh, eastern mystical schmear none of us really understands?"

I had to laugh at that. There was no way to describe Mr. Church, and considering that, Mr. Shields had done a pretty good job. And he hadn't laughed, hadn't sounded judgmental at all. I had spent a couple of hours out there, and I told him that.

"It'll probably work out best if you just want to work around high tide," I finished.

"High tide's at ten. I'll get back and it'll be time to pick her up again. Oh well, I'll catch some striped bass for the missus while I'm back there. What's the young lady's name?"

"Grey Shailey. She's tall, blond, very pretty, but with sort of a hardened criminal look around the eyes." I let the joke fly, just to squelch my sudden feeling of being outside myself again. Like I was in Emmett's body, looking down on me, and this whole visit sounded ludicrous. "She's summer folk and has been a little bit under the weather. Don't let her drown, okay?"

I listened to him laugh, though the sudden coldness in the room was starting to spook me bad. I heard a clanking sound behind me and jumped around. I realized where the cold had come from, and why I'd just felt like Emmett was looking down on me. Emmett was back there. He was pouring himself another glass of wine, studying the label on the bottle so hard that I knew he wasn't really studying it. He had stinging red ears and a red nose. This house was so different than our place in Philly. We didn't get drafts from open doors because the lobby was three floors down. We had creaky wood floors and Oriental rugs. This place had cushy, silent, wall-to-wall carpet, at least in most rooms. I'd been ambushed.

"I have to go now, Mr. Shields." I was in deep shit over payment now, because I could in no way give him this credit card number with Emmett all but on top of me. "I'll bring you the cash tomorrow."

"Fifty dollars, up front," he told me. "No refunds. If the weather's bad we'll set a rain date. Spit on it?"

It sounded a bit tightfisted to me, but somehow so familiar, like I had been hearing business done that way my whole life. "Spat on it."

Emmett was doing more of that studying thing, only this time it was the darkening sea, which I knew for sure he couldn't be studying so intensely.

"Did he just say to you, 'Spit on it'?"

"Yeah." I scratched my head, watching the rug uneasily.

"*Mmmm*... You fall back into old ways easily," he said too cheerfully, "cutting business deals with local fishermen."

"I don't know what made me say that. I never heard it before—"

"You heard it plenty before. The fact that you *spit* on it without any actual recall of that custom? That makes me feel *infinitely* better." His sarcasm was overtaking his cheeriness, which made me stare. I watched the glass of wine going to his mouth.

"I thought you just got sober."

"I did."

"Well, could you stay that way a while, please? I'm not used to talking to my brother when he's smashed."

"I wasn't smashed, Evan. I was...loosening the tight joints. Don't worry. If I start slurring, I'll go lie down. Guess we're both seeing each other in ways we're not accustomed to." He tore his eyes from the sea finally, moseyed over to the couch, and plopped down on it. "I'm not accustomed to thinking of you as being reckless."

"Reckless?" I realized grimly he must have heard me talking to Mr. Shields about visiting Mr. Church. "I wouldn't call a little ride in an outboard across the bay reckless, Emmett. I was doing it in third grade. As for seeing Mr. Church..." I didn't know quite what I wanted to say about that. "Can we just leave it at you have your peace and I'll have mine? I don't mind your beliefs. I think you could extend to me the same—"

"Courtesy?" he broke in. "I always try to be courteous. I don't think courtesy is the issue at all. I don't think it would be discourteous for me to remind you—nicely—that my beliefs are a little more thoroughly investigated than are yours."

There wasn't a whole lot I could say to that, because "You're wrong" would have been somehow wrong, though it felt right. I bit my tongue.

"Besides, I wasn't...at this moment...addressing any belief system of yours that would propel you to the feet of a man like Church. I was talking about this Grey Shailey person. Is this the girl you were telling me about on Tuesday night? She's in Saint Elizabeth's?"

I nodded.

"She's in Saint Elizabeth's, and obviously she's got some kind of weekend pass or a release coming her way, and you are sending her to a man like Edwin Church."

I rolled over onto my elbows, bouncing my fingers off the carpet, thinking about this. The way he put it, yeah, it sounded reckless.

"No, wait..." I stumbled. "I'm just an innocent bystander in all of this. I have never told anybody I went to see him. She put it together, called me up to Saint Elizabeth's, begged me to put her in contact with him. I'm just being...*diplomatic*." It was a word I knew he liked.

"Well maybe we should be *courteous* to all but save *diplomacy* for those who are well. You were not a well person yourself when you, obviously, came down here last year and didn't feel the need to tell me."

I figured we were into it now, and I should just stand my ground. "Yeah? I was perfectly well when I came back."

He looked at me, almost with a flash of interest. Emmett didn't like things he couldn't explain, and usually he would have been a little more smug, I think. But he was drinking, and the look lingered on me long enough for me to feel maybe he was in some weird, vulnerable spot— away from his desk, his books, his dissertation, his cronies in the philosophy department. All he had was picture windows, wine, and me.

"I think...I need to hear this." He lay down and stared up at the ceiling, probably so I couldn't read his eyes. He knows how I can read eyes and it spooks him sometimes. I couldn't see his eyes, but I sensed this was more of a curiosity question than something he planned to argue. It sounded almost resigned more than argumentative. He was searching for something...in strange territory.

"Place makes you feel strange, doesn't it?" I crawled over to him, got up on my knees, and patted his hair sympathetically. He shut his eyes and turned them away from me, twirling the stem of the glass on his chest. I could feel pain crawling off of him, bad memories. Because he wouldn't let me see his eyes, that was all I could read, but I gathered that his pain was like mine had been. He wanted to know what had become of our parents.

"So...what did our illustrious Mr. Church do to you, Evan?"

I decided to skip all of what might have amounted to gory details to him and just get to the punch. Maybe he was just vulnerable enough to listen to me on this one.

"It was a wave, Emmett. A monstrous, fucking wave. The biggest wave I've ever seen."

I could feel him tighten, but his voice still sounded diplomatic. "So, in other words, he did that second sight... *thing* on you. That *thing* with his hands that I used to hear about."

"Yeah."

"And it was a wave."

"Yeah. I know that sounds completely crazy. I only believe it because—" and I went through the whole thing about touching the map. He never moved, never tried to interrupt, never did anything but blink.

After I finished and a bit of silence followed, he said, "I wish you had come walking on the beach with me."

"It's freezing."

"I know, but I wanted to talk to you away from Opa. He's taking a nap now, I think. It's safe. There have been some things I've wanted to share with you—I was ready to last year. I thought you were old enough and enough time had passed. But that incident with the LSD made me put it off longer. Now? I find out you've been throwing yourself at the mercy of subhumans like Church, and you're sending your sick friends to him. You're my brother. I love you. I want to convince you to stop it."

He sat up, and I figured he had fooled me into telling him about the wave and the map. He could do that to me sometimes, lure me into saying something he could take apart, just by not showing me his eyes and keeping his voice even. He's one of the few people in the world who could get away with it.

He went behind the bar, and I could see the white-and-red bag. Only now that it was up close, I could see the bag was worn, like it had been around for a lot of years. He had a loose-leaf notebook full of papers, which he held up to me, not looking at all happy.

"Edwin Church has some weird little power," he said

softly, but I knew just from knowing everything about Emmett that he was being sarcastic. "He can make you remember things more clearly. On a good day, he can even make you see the future. He's touched by God. He sold his soul to the devil. He did both! It's a highly opinionated world out there, Evan. And you have to be careful, because these days, *everybody's right,* and if you don't believe me, *ask them.*"

I didn't know what was in the binder, or what exactly he was rambling on about, but I hated it when he got this condescending tone. "Uh, you're holding that damn thing up like a TV evangelist toting a Bible. Maybe you should come down off your high horse and say whatever it is you have to say."

He lowered it and apologized. "Everybody's right. There's no way to find truth in this world, except for one. And here it is."

He held the thing up again. Couldn't seem to help himself. *"Evidence."*

He sat back down on the couch and opened the black book as I crawled warily up and plopped down beside him. My heart turned hot and started banging, though he was being vague enough that I couldn't have said why at the moment.

"I don't think Opa told you the story about the Riley boat to make pleasant chatter. I think he was laying a big hint on me, telling me it's time I opened the floodgates of debate. He's right."

He turned the first page, and a hefty legal document stared back at me. I looked where his finger pointed and saw the name of my parents' boat, the *Goliath*. Then my eyes bounced up to big bold letters at the top: SEARCH WARRANT.

SEVEN

"Oh, shit," I breathed, over and over, following his finger down this page, seeing these all-too-real names and facts: "Name of Vessel: GOLIATH. Location of Port: THE BASIN, ATLANTIC CITY. Owner/Operator: WADE BARRETT, MARY ELLEN STARN. Date: NOVEMBER 10," and the year, signed by a judge, and by two men who had the word "Agent" after their signatures and "DRUG ENFORCEMENT ADMINISTRATION" beneath. The blue ink where the DEA agents had signed was now fading, but I ran my finger over it, hoping it might just disappear.

I didn't know what exactly this had to do with my parents' death, but some sort of black energy was rushing off Emmett, making me feel electrocuted. This had to do with the man who rocked me in his lap and told great stories about our ancestors. And it involved a woman, a flight paramedic, who came home with tales of saving lives while reciting her version of the captain's prayer: "Lord, give me a stiff upper lip."

"None of this will make any sense to you if I don't start from the beginning. The night they disappeared was not the beginning. It started two years before, I would estimate."

He turned a page and pointed to a cassette tape in an envelope that fit into a three-ring binder. Emmett's way of keeping things organized for research had always gotten on my nerves. This was beyond reckoning—a three-ring-binder plastic job for a cassette. The cassette was dated about six months after Mom and Dad died, and marked "Talk with Mrs. Riley" in Emmett's scratchy handwriting. I guess that meant he'd been to see her and taped the conversation.

His voice went on. "About two years before Mom and Dad's boat disappeared, the Riley boat disappeared. About two weeks before the Riley boat disappeared, Mom and Dad had dinner at the home of Claude Lowenberg. He was Dad's first mate. Remember him?"

I nodded. "I just remember he was a very quiet guy."

"Still waters run deep. He had a lot of friends. A lot of people trusted him. He'd heard some things that he shared with Mom and Dad. In essence, Captain Riley was in a lot of trouble, shall we say."

He turned the page again, and there was a search warrant that looked pretty similar to Mom and Dad's, only it was a Xerox in black and white, and was more grainy looking. And the names were different. This one read,

"Owner/Operator: CONNOR RILEY." And I snapped my eyes up to the darkened picture window, not really wanting to read any further.

Emmett kept on. "Captain Riley had come on tough times. A lot of the container ships had. Federal Express had come onto the scene, driving prices down at UPS. The freighters were losing a lot of business. Sometimes the owners would get tempted to bolster their incomes illegally. They would drop off a small load of furniture in Jamaica that didn't really even cover the cost of the trip. They'd also pick up something to make the trip worthwhile—"

"Oh, my God," I breathed. I let him talk on about Captain Riley running drugs, feeling it was about to hit closer to home, and the gray hatch was slamming in the wind.

"Captain Riley had delivered a huge amount of Colombian gold up to Canada and had gotten paid for it." He pointed to a newspaper clipping that followed the Riley search warrant. It covered the disappearance, mentioning Connor Riley had come under suspicion of drug trafficking.

"The DEA didn't find the shipment or the money, but they took a lot of his files, things lying about on his desk, and among them were some scrap sheets he'd scribbled out, with phone numbers, delivery names, estimates of his profit. He realized they would eventually put it all together and arrest him. They'd get him on circumstantial evidence, unless they came up with a witness, I don't know..."

I looked at him funny when he said "I don't know." It

was the first sign that he didn't know every last detail about this story. It made me want to listen for flaws in his arguments, in spite of how this black book intimidated the hell out of me.

"Captain Riley decided to take Claude Lowenberg into his confidence. Riley said he was going somewhere safe from the law, and was going to fake a disappearance. On top of that, he was looking to pass around his cartel contact in the Caribbean, if any ships wanted to make a few deliveries themselves. And if they got into trouble and wanted to meet up with Riley later, the contact would help them with that."

"Dad told you this?"

"Yes. Almost as soon as they got home from dinner at the Lowenbergs'. Dad appeared to be in shock when he told me. They were friends with the Rileys, and were sorry if they really had been mixed up in the whole illegal business. Mom and Dad wanted no part of it. That's what Dad told me."

"But, you don't believe him?"

"I did. I think at that point, Dad was sincere. I think Mom was, too. Dad encouraged Claude to call the authorities. But Mom was awfully quiet that night. She let Dad do all the talking. She just kind of sat at the edge of the fireplace and looked at her fingers."

"So you're saying Mom and Dad never used Captain Riley's contact in Jamaica, and never did anything wrong."

"Not at that point. The Riley vessel disappeared not even two weeks later. The Coast Guard took a Mayday that sounded very similar to that...that legend you used to call The She. Like Opa said tonight, a couple of drug-running captains had tried to fake disappearances after they realized they were about to be arrested. One gave false coordinates over the radio and added sound effects and hysterical comments like, 'We're being sucked, we're being sucked. What's that off the starboard bow?' Both of them were found and prosecuted. But Captain Riley's boat was not ever found."

"So...you think he faked it really well and got away with it?"

Emmett laughed politely. "If I haven't given you enough evidence yet, get this. By the time the DEA got an arrest warrant, Captain Riley was already lost at sea. They leaned on Mrs. Riley. She had found out about the previous load of Colombian Gold and confessed. Then she swore up and down that her husband had said he was sorry, swore to never do it again, and went to sea to deliver a regular load of goods on schedule. She's kept to that story ever since, even though the Coast Guard found a female name on the crew list. As it turned out, the woman didn't even have a seaman's license but was a waitress over at the Seaview Country Club. The Rileys were members there. Even still, Mrs. Riley rather enjoys calling herself the widow Riley."

"You're saying this waitress was Captain Riley's girl-friend? And it's impossible that Mrs. Riley is a widow?"

"The wife is always the last to know about an affair. Dad used to laugh in disgust and Mom sometimes threatened to tell Mrs. Riley. After the girl's name showed up on the Basin dock log as crew, Mrs. Riley had her chance to reckon with the truth. But Mrs. Riley believes what Mrs. Riley *needs* to believe. A person is entitled to her sanity, especially when she's an innocent party. I'm saying her actual widowhood is so improbable that when I call her by that name, I have to smile into my fingers."

"What does this have to do with Mom and Dad?" I could feel myself taking an educated guess by this point, though I didn't think I could ever believe it.

"Here comes one of the lies I've always told you, which I want to clear up. Two more years pass. I never heard another word about Mr. Riley from Mom and Dad. No matter what he did, they were just not the types to get off on gossiping about it. But remember how I've said now and again that I was on the boat with Mom and Dad the day before they disappeared? That Dad pulled me out of school to help him work on a faulty hatch?"

"Yeah...," I breathed. Emmett had mentioned it a number of times over the years.

"Well, there wasn't any faulty hatch, okay? That's not why I was there. Dad came and got me at school, didn't say anything except that there was trouble on the *Goliath* and they needed me to help. We got to the dock. Nobody was around except Mom by that point. They took me on board. The hold was full of steel girders that needed to be delivered to Jamaica quickly, but the place was a wreck. In the galley, plates and food and cleaning supplies were all over the tables. In the captain's quarters, every last paper was out of the files. Everything left was in these huge, makeshift piles. In the crew bunks, all the mattresses had been slashed and the foam was coming out. A hundred other things were out of order, though all they had in the hold was steel. Thank God the cargo wasn't somebody moving their corporation with all papers in boxes. That would have been a mess.

"At any rate, Mom looked really glum, and all she said was, 'Start cleaning up.' So I did. Dad cleaned up the office, I cleaned the galley, Mom cleaned the barracks. Because they'd never mentioned Captain Riley's stupid proposal after he made it to Lowenberg, I didn't really get what was going on. I thought it was some sort of robbery...until I found the search warrant. One of them had laid it on the counter in the galley."

I interrupted him at that point. "So what did they say? Did they *say* they had been running drugs?"

"Of course not. I was their son. You don't share things like that with your son. But I think what had happened to Captain Riley's income had started happening to them. They were short on funds, and maybe they couldn't make their payment to Opa that month."

For that he had a page of line graphs from a Quick-Books program. They showed Dad's income had dipped sixty thousand dollars a year for two years, leaving the final income at only thirty thousand dollars.

"Mom was so stinking proud, you know. She insisted on buying that boat from Opa at the same price anybody else paid. If she didn't, she said, her crew wouldn't respect her. Not that it really helped all that much. I think they finally caved in, ran an illegal load or two...It probably happened anywhere between once to occasionally. There's no actual way of knowing now."

My head was shaking slowly back and forth, back and forth. I shut my eyes again, to keep from seeing Emmett's neat and orderly little research. But I didn't want to see that wave— *An avalanche of white bearing down on the little cabin in the dark, only it wasn't snow. It was water.* For a year now, that vision had given me so much peace. I wanted it to stay. But it was fading....Even with my eyes shut, this black book was overtaking it, making me feel like an imbecile. Then the book dissolved, too.

I heard voices instead, first far-off, then my room came clear, from back in West Hook. I was kneeling on one side of the bed; Mom was kneeling on the other. We were talking like that. We must have been praying first—doing the Hail Mary before bed—but now we were just talking. Mom was smiling. *Her hair's falling out of her ponytail on one side. Her hands are red and cracked because she hates to wear gloves in winter. They're folded in the middle of the mattress so our knuckles are touching.*

"*Mommy, what's* rape?"

I'm asking her because Dad always says things like, "You're six years old. Go play baseball for about five years." But Mom never glazes on me. And I can see her smile growing bigger, more ornery, before her eyes wander over to mine, way slow. I know I'm saying a bad word, and I know this word has to do with something evil, but she's laughing, like evil has no power over her.

"It's where a man gets his way and a woman doesn't, because his muscles are bigger."

"Emmett told Daddy you got a rape once. Emmett said you told him that."

She's laughing more. I watch her send her body in a circle above her knees when she laughs, and it looks very full of confidence, and I decide I want to laugh like that from now on.

"Daddy knew, or I wouldn't have told Emmett."

"So a bad man was strong over you. It's true?"

"You ever known me to lie?" She drums her fingers on top of my hands.

I'm looking her over. I'm thinking she's the prettiest lady I've ever seen, though she doesn't look like my friends' moms. She's got muscles in her neck that go down under her blouse, come out her fingers, and go everywhere in the room.

"He must have had a lot of muscles."

"Yeah, well. He was a very small person." She laughs again, like she just made some kind of joke that I don't get. She's laughing into the mattress now.

"Mommy, did you put the man in jail?"

"Yeah. For a while."

"Is he out of jail now?"

"He works on the docks, in fact." She watches me for only a second before my thought grabs hold of her, and she wraps her hands around mine. "But don't you worry about him, baby. He would have no interest in you. He'll never do anything to hurt you. You believe me?"

There's no way not to believe my mom. "Do you run away when you see him?"

Her smile dims down for a minute, more like she's confused than like she's afraid. "No...No! In fact, I make sure, every time I'm down there, to say something. I march right up and look him in the eye. Maybe I say, 'Couldn't you move that mop a little faster?' Or, 'Not going out today, Fitz?' He's grounded for life. He'll never see the other side of the horizon again. That's about the lowest thing that can happen to a person of the sea. That's all I do, remind him of that, when I'm looking him in the eye."

She looks peaceful, saying that. I say, "So he didn't hurt you very bad, then?"

Her smile looks different now. Like it's taking some muscle to hold it up.

"Because if he really hurt you bad, you would want to kill him."

She looks past my head at something behind me, with that smile held up like it's working against fifty fishing weights pulling her face down. She'd had folded prayer hands again, but now she turns them over, cracks her knuckles. She stands up, lets her face relax. She's not looking so happy now.

"I'll never lay my hand on Michael Fitz."

"How come? You're strong."

"Yes, I guess I am. In certain ways. I'm strong enough to know that no matter what...two wrongs don't make a right."

Another gray door in my blurred memory had blown open, I realized, only there was no storm above it. It blew open silently, and there was peace up there. Peace and strength. I knew my face was all wet, and I plopped down a foot further from Emmett, because it was bothering me, him seeing me like this.

But I said anyway, "I always thought, even after last year...I didn't like thinking about Mom and Dad because I didn't want to think about how they might have died. It may have had more to do with what I would remember about them when they were living. If I thought about that too much, I would miss them even more."

"They were good people, Evan."

"The thing I remember most about them was how they were so strong."

"They were that."

"So then, what's making you think this? They *said* they didn't want anything to do with Captain Riley's drug running. The search warrant on the *Goliath* turned up nothing, right? Or they wouldn't have been going out to sea the next night. They'd have been under arrest."

I didn't even like saying that last sentence. *Arrest* and *parents* are terms that sound ludicrous when put together. Emmett got up and poured himself more wine.

"Evan, the DEA is a very busy organization. They

wouldn't have done this on a hunch. They had reasons. They had evidence."

"What evidence?"

"I don't know. The grounds for a search warrant are always sealed until charges are brought. In that case, they are unsealed and a copy goes to the defendants' lawyers. If no charges are brought, the grounds remain a secret. The boat disappeared too quickly after the search for any charges to be formulated. And it's expensive to execute a search of a ship that size. They wouldn't have spent the money if—"

"How can you accept it without even knowing what their suspicions were? Some creepy idea that your parents are buying and selling illegal stuff that will go down to lowlifes, like those guys who hung around in their old bomb cars out in front of West Hook Junior High School?"

"Just that the government was so well organized. I think one thing Mom and Dad didn't count on was the DEA coming to haunt Opa and me the way they did. This was after they hadn't been able to prosecute Riley, and they were extremely pissed when Mom and Dad quote-unquote foundered. They questioned me for four hours the next morning. They talked to Opa for days. They even tried to talk to you, do you remember that? Two men and a woman in suits? They came to the house?"

I had no recollection of that whatsoever, and told him as much.

"Well, you had no memory of the disappearance to help them with. You kept saying Opa and I told you in the morning. They gave up on you after about five minutes. They tried to come back to me days later, but that's when Opa started hiring lawyers like crazy to protect us. It spared me further questioning, but the only other thing it seemed to accomplish was to slowly bust a couple of Opa's heart valves. And I'll never forget the looks on the agents' faces when I was so adamant about Mom and Dad describing the sea to me. 'Black-bean soup, coming to a boil,' according to Mom, and Dad describing a wind you couldn't feel. I felt pretty humiliated by those mannerly smiles. Especially since they had brought six bound volumes of notes they had taken on the Riley disappearance, probably to intimidate us. Aunt Mel and I looked through them when they were questioning Opa. They knew every crew member's mother's shoe size."

He dropped his head back and rubbed his eyes with one hand. "Evan, I went through my hell back then. I was the age you are now. Believe me, I felt the same way you do. Only, I didn't go to Edwin Church, my God...I wish you had told me! Now he's stirred you up to think some... fantastic...motion picture...fiction phenomenon—"

I put my head in my hands, thinking of something like a chilly heat shooting through me when the man had touched me, and the vision that came so crystal clear. I could still see it. *White avalanche descending on a cabin in the dark.*

"It seemed so real!"

Emmett rubbed my back as I wiped my eyes on the balls of my hands. "I'm sure it did. Evan, the desire to believe what you need to believe is ever so powerful. I think *desire* is the most powerful force in the universe. There's only one thing I know that's stronger. *Evidence.*"

He turned the page again. My neck creaked when I looked this time, like it was rusty. I stared at an old-fashioned sandwich bag. It looked kind of dingy. He had stapled it to a blank sheet in his anal-retentive research way.

"I emptied it when I found it. Smell. I bet it still smells."

I bent my head down as he opened the baggy and I sniffed hard. Marijuana. Unmistakably.

"When I got home after cleaning up the *Goliath,* I took this out of Dad's desk drawer and emptied it. I figured it would be only hours before the DEA came to the house, so I threw the contents into the ocean."

"Great. Are you saying Mom and Dad were loadies?"

"I'm saying they must have smoked it occasionally. I never saw them do it. I think it was probably just Dad. Mom didn't even drink. After the disappearance, Aunt Mel and Opa and I were cleaning up the house, and I remembered I had never put the trash out on the road. I dug the little bag out and saved it."

"Why?"

"*Why?* Fortunately, Aunt Mel was with me most of the time early on. She made me go and get it, and we talked about it when Opa wasn't around. She was educated—

knew the difference between saying, 'This is the truth because that's where the evidence points,' and saying, 'This is the truth because I happen to love the people involved.' Love and truth have no correlation. Love helps create little theories that make you feel better. Sometimes the truth does not feel good. Does that mean we shouldn't seek it out? Does that mean we should believe a lie?"

"If the truth is something awful, why not just leave it the hell alone?" I breathed.

"Because we can't. Obviously, you couldn't either. You remembered something, that thing you used to call shrieking. And you had to go to Edwin Church. For what? You wanted truth. Human beings are always searching for the truth. Aunt Mel and I have committed our lives to it. If you're going to figure out what's at the core of the universe, if you're going to spend your life telling people truths, then it's a package deal. Even if you're not a philosopher, you're still a human being. Life is all we have, and if we can't look at it honestly, are we really living?"

"Just stop for a minute."

He did, but it didn't really help me grip on to where this might be going. Gray doors. Now there were a hundred of them floating around in my head. I couldn't think.

"Just cut with the Philosophy 101 and tell me what it is you think Mom and Dad did, besides run drugs. We didn't get to the part where they're dead yet."

I could hear him swallowing a huge gulp of wine, and I wanted to shout, "Hey, that's really dealing in reality!" But it wouldn't have done any good.

"Plainly, I'm saying they were trying to fake a disappearance. They were trying, though they ran into some insurmountable problems that got them anyway—"

"Jesus Christ." I said it to shut him up again, feeling my eyes dredge up so much sop that everything was swimming. But his voice rang clear.

"Listen to me, Evan. They would never desert us. Not for long. Here's my one leap of faith, all right? I try never to take those leaps, but I do have common sense, and I'm allowed to apply it. I might not have thought my parents could succumb to greed or pride or Mom's stubbornness or whatever. But I am still certain, beyond any shadow of a doubt, that they loved us. They were planning to get us to them. As soon as they were safe from scandal, a possible prison sentence, everything that would ruin our family, and ruin your life and my life."

I wiped my soppy eyes and turned to look at him. He was tucking one lip under the other, up and down, so his beard was sticking out. I felt that the pain in his eyes was almost entirely for me. He'd gotten used to his over the years. It amazed me that I'd lived with him all this time and he'd managed to keep it from me. He was trying to think of me. I tried to keep from attacking him.

"So then, what happened?"

"Here's where they actually died." He pointed to the new page, a satellite picture showing a huge swirly hurricane floating ominously beneath the dip of Florida and down southwest of Cuba. "This is a hurricane we didn't hear much about on the news because it never hit land.

Hurricane Marco. November eighteenth to November twenty-sixth. On the nineteenth, winds hit approximately a hundred and ten miles an hour, out over this little piece of the Atlantic below Florida." Above where he pointed, I could see he had mapped out a pencil line from New Jersey with a few angles in it, cutting over a little toward Bermuda.

He followed it down with his fingers. "This is the passage Dad used to call 'whistle free.' He would take it when freight wasn't moving fast. Very few boats cut that far west. He used to do it because if certain unscrupulous captains saw you, or caught you on the radio, or caught wind of where you were going, then they could contact your client...if not steal your run with a lower bid, then get a piece of the next one. If Mom and Dad went this way trying to get to the Caribbean, they would have been here on the sixteenth." He pointed to the spot where the hurricane looked most thick. "They would have had to brave it out, take a risk, which Mom was great for. They couldn't send any Maydays because that would blow their cover. I think they foundered right about here. That's where they are."

This spot on the map looked alien enough. He might as well have been pointing at Mars.

"Well, what about the crew? I don't think it's likely that five guys would be in on a scheme like that!"

"There were only four. Lowenberg was off with his wife, saying she was having a baby, though the actual birth record for their child wasn't for another week and a half. In other words, he called out for what happened to be false labor. That's possible. But I think big money was calling everyone's name, and Lowenberg resisted. His wife was his way out. That doesn't mean he'd blow the whistle. Seamen have an honor code of loyalty. Lowenberg probably stretched it to blow the whistle on Riley. He would never, ever do it to Mom and Dad."

"Emmett, this all sounds so incredibly...sleazy," I mumbled, rubbing my eyes hard with my fingers. "I just...I can't picture it in my mind."

"It takes a while. And it wasn't without certain noble intentions. Wade Barrett and Mary Ellen Starn didn't desert their kids. Believe me, bro. If they were alive, they would have contacted us."

I flopped back, staring at the ceiling, trying to decide where to land a thought.

"What does Opa say? Does he really think his own daughter..." I trailed off.

"Right about the time this happened, he was completely unglued about Aunt Mel. She was still in grad school, twenty-six years old, running around shoving *The Communist Manifesto* under everyone's noses. It took a while for her to balance out, grow up, decide she was a socialist and not a radical communist. Opa told me back then he would never have believed it about Mom, but what with Aunt Mel doing that, he said he wasn't exactly sure who his daughters were. I think his exact words were, 'I am through the looking glass, and I don't trust my own judgment.'

"Aunt Mel calmed down quite a bit, but I'm not sure he ever really formed an opinion on Mom. He had open-heart surgery and vein replacements in his legs because of diabetes—all in one year. He can talk about it. But I wouldn't carry it too far, considering his health. His dinner table story about the Riley boat led me to think he was going to tell you this weekend, and I wanted to do it. So I took a nice long walk over to West Hook and got this out of my old room."

He drummed his fingers on the map, and I kept staring at the circled X under the hurricane. Something about this felt wrong, entirely wrong.

I fought back my disgust and took the book into my lap. "So...this is everything. If I read all of this, it'll somehow convince me that my parents were drug runners."

I shut my eyes, felt his hand go on my arm. "It's far from complete. Actually, there's more that I learned after I got so sick of the journal that I didn't even want it around me. It's just important things that kept me from swinging into accepting something for emotional reasons, rather than accepting the truth and learning from it. But if you have any questions, whatever it is you want to know, feel free to ask me."

He was so confident about all of this. And despite all this evidence, it felt inconceivable to me. "You know, I've smoked a few joints in my day. Did a lot of that before last November, in fact. But no one's accusing me of taking it over to the grade school and shoving it under the noses of little kids like Miguel!"

I thought he might jump on me over my little confession, but maybe he'd been more perceptive all along than I'd realized. He just said, "And I would never think that of you. Unless, of course, the DEA started showing up, wanting to search your room, and you suddenly disappeared thirty-six hours later to the wailing sounds of an island superstition."

I shut my eyes again but didn't miss the look of pity on his face first.

"If it helps any, I would miss you very much, and I would always love you," he said.

But it didn't help. All I could see on the backs of my eyelids was that wave, so clear, so picture-perfect...as if it had been done on film. *A white avalanche falling on a cabin in the dark*. I had never known my intuition, which had told me to go see Edwin Church, to fuck me over so badly.

"I could see it so clearly," I said again, so softly I didn't think he could hear me. But somehow he did.

"Evan, there are no huge waves on the Atlantic. There's nothing big enough to founder the *Goliath* without a major massive storm to go along with it. They were riding through a piddling, freezing rain downpour. There weren't even gale warnings."

"So what was that shrieking I heard?" I asked it more for myself than for him, because he had never known what to do with that phenomenon. When he was a kid he would beat my ass over it. Once he grew up, he chose to ignore it.

"I don't know, Evan. But I do know that your choices are clear. Mom and Dad were escaping from the law. Or there's an enormous *She* out there that eats people."

EIGHT

Emmett stared at the television with that book in his lap until he passed out on the couch. I had to take the empty wineglass off his chest and put it back on the bar. I'd spent the time staring out the picture window into the blackness—just staring and wiping my eyes, and staring more. I don't know why I was so suddenly interested in looking at the water. Like I wasn't sick enough. But I could see whitecaps that turned neon in the dark, and at one point, I tried to look away but my eyes found their way back again.

Finally, I heard Opa getting up from his nap. I could hear him padding around in the kitchen; and beyond it, a cell phone rang from far off. I went diving down the stairs two at a time. I got to my phone on the fifth ring.

"Hello?"

"You sound like you just swam the channel. Did you

have to run through that five miles of house to get to your phone?" It was Bear.

"Something like that." I actually grinned in relief, hearing a normal voice. I could also hear a bunch of voices going off around him and a humming sound.

"Guess where we are, my man?"

"In a car," I tried.

"And guess where we're coming? Don't think I didn't hear you bitching loud and clear on Wednesday about being stuck in the Hooks by yourself—just because Harley was bitching louder about not having her Thanksgiving Day party. I solved everything."

Bear's family didn't have a summerhouse, and Harley's was on a different barrier island.

"So who'd you rope into giving you a change of scene?"

"Uh, you won't believe it."

He didn't say the name, which meant he was stalling—which meant I might not love this idea as much as Harley had. Lots of kids from school had summerhouses in the Hooks.

"Here, I'll let her talk to you."

A girl's voice came through the receiver. "Bear mentioned you were lonely, and I was bored." She giggled in an unmistakable way. Chandra Clemmens, Grey's best friend.

"What'd you do, steal the key?" I managed to shrug it off. Chandra was nicer than Grey, and I figured with Grey not around, I would be okay with her.

"I have a key. I told them I was sleeping at Harley's. At any rate, we'll be there in about half an hour. Bear told me you were down there, and I was like, 'Miracles. Evan Barrett at the shore.' What got into you?"

"My grandfather's health. It wasn't exactly my choice."

"Does his house still make you seasick?"

"Very. Emmett's drunk." I wasn't about to give the whole reason.

"Well, you know my house only has one picture window. In the family room. We'll party in the kitchen, okay? Shall we pick you up along the way?"

I started putting on my shoes as soon as she hung up, even though she said it would be half an hour. Then I looked at my watch. Twenty-seven minutes. I forced myself to head for the dining room, where I found Opa padding through from the kitchen with a glass of milk in his hand. I figured I might find him here. He'd drunk a glass of milk at the dining room table every night when I was a little kid. I guess some things never change. He put a lamp on instead of the chandelier, so the room kind of glowed. He sat down at the head of the table, watching me.

"Judging from the sight of you, I'd wager your brother had a word with you."

I could feel that my eyes were swollen and red, and I wondered if I should go wash my face before my friends picked me up. I leaned against the door frame, watching his eyebrows shoot up.

"What do you think, Opa? You really think your own daughter could do that?"

"Who am I to say?" He had that merry twinkle in his eye, which didn't seem to fit the subject matter. But I realized he'd had years to get used to the idea.

"You're her father, who loved her more than anyone."

"Precisely. According to Melanie and Emmett, that nullifies my opinion." He said it quietly. I thought I detected some anger behind that merry twinkle, but I couldn't tell whether it was at Mom, her sister, Emmett, or himself.

I watched him study the glass, turning it in circles on the table. He pushed out the chair next to him, and I went over and sat down. This time I was sitting where Aunt Mel had eaten dinner, and the black hole of the window stared back at me. I studied the whitecaps again. Opa cleared his throat, but I didn't look away.

"Unfortunately, it happened at a time when other family problems had caught me off guard. I was so unprepared for what Melanie had become in college. It annoyed me no end that I could spend a fortune educating my girl, and her education would dictate that Daddy's life was all wrong." He laughed a little but didn't look happy, until he started up again. "But she's settled down to an extent that I could make peace with her...I hope she can live with me. And it's helped me to look back on Mary Ellen a little differently—in spite of your brother's supremely hard line on the thing."

"He agrees with the DEA."

"Don't I know it. Let's not knock it down so easily. Supposedly, unless you believe in the wiles of The She, it's the only theory that works. That's his and Melanie's position, and he certainly can defend it. By the end of his freshman year in college, he was such the logician, he could stump even me. I've been working for forty-five years, manufacturing vessels, employing thousands of people, and here comes an eighteen-year-old to give me something to think about. I had hired a detective right after the disappearance. I thought the detective had done well. Your brother said he had not."

"What did the detective find out?"

"He talked to at least twenty-five of your parents' friends, including the Lowenberg couple, and Claude Lowenberg had been a longtime crewman on the *Goliath*. None had ever heard Mary Ellen or your father discuss becoming tempted in any way to do the drug-running thing."

"Really?" I leaned up to him.

"Yes. That was enough to settle it for me. Your brother said...I forget the exact words he used...something about a logical fallacy." He was chuckling to himself again. "Using a lack of evidence as evidence. I believe the term is *post hoc*, some sort of illogic he said I was using. In other words, my findings didn't eliminate the possibility that they may just have been very secretive."

"He said you talked to the DEA."

"For two days. The agents told me about the search warrant. The kids hadn't told me." He raised his eyebrows, kind of embarrassed. "That didn't look good to the DEA. I tried to describe your mother's pride to them, to which they responded that pride or no, it looks like guilt if you keep it to yourself. Their reasoning for the search was sealed in the courts. The DEA agents said if their grounds and their sources leaked out, it might prevent others from being caught. After a while I quit trying to pry at them."

"Why?"

"Because of my health. And because enough of the locals were supportive that I took my solace in loyal friends. I stopped trying to take it in evidence, which was expensive, time-consuming, and nerve-racking, especially when you're engaged in two major surgeries at once. Nothing would bring Mary Ellen back."

"So..." I rubbed my chin, not knowing quite how to word this. "You never gave much thought to them still being alive somewhere?"

"No." He shook his head hard. "Not after three or four days. I'm a seafaring man myself, and though I can't always say what the sea will do, I am bright enough to know what it *can't* do. If your brother is correct and they went down between Florida and Cuba, or I'm correct and they went down up here, they are dead in either case."

He went into the science of survival, even in a life raft, which I really didn't need to hear. I had to agree with Emmett on that one—if they were alive, they would have contacted us somehow.

He glanced at me, looking sad. "As for your brother, I'm a workingman. I don't have the kind of education that can think its way into every last crevice. The only thing I could poke holes in is your brother. If I wanted to."

"What do you mean?"

Opa leaned to the side to shift his leg, and I could see a combination of love and sadness in his eyes as he went on. "He's the one who's always saying to me that people believe what they *need* to believe. He said it so often that when I would get to thinking of my Mary Ellen as innocent, his words would be the first thing that came to my head." He chuckled, looking a little sidetracked. "I would feel guilty just for having thought it! But Emmett's got some needs himself. He needs to distance himself emotionally from the whole thing. He does that by using his head, which helps him turn off his heart."

"Hmmm." I thought that was an unusual take on Emmett. I'd always thought of my brother's head as holding the secrets to the universe. "But you have to be able to turn off your heart, in order to see the facts clearly."

"That's what *he* would say. But I don't know if that's possible, completely turning off the heart. I think the heart is always working. Whether you want it to or not."

He shifted around, making a pained face over his leg, which he reached down and massaged. I asked if there was anything I could get for him, and he shook his head and went on.

"He's turned out to be an awful lot like your mother, and she was a very, very calculating type."

He turned his glass around some more. "It kills me to say it, but your father was actually the better seaman. At least in my opinion. He had intuition. Mary Ellen's brain ran on six pistons, but my honest opinion is, at least on the sea, that's an inferior quality to what your father had."

"Emmett always told me she was the better captain."

"One thing I'll say of her, she had more working head knowledge, more knowledge of fancy equipment. She knew every last thing about the gadgets I put in the vessels I manufactured. But I would never have found much use for many of them back when I was young, driving my own ship." He shook his head, still smiling. "And she was a bigger risk taker. Your father, he had some sort of built-in warning signal—something Mary Ellen never understood. All the gadgets in the world won't replace that on the sea. I think there's probably a dozen times she might have gotten herself in trouble, maybe even foundered, driving through too big a weather problem, taking short-cuts through the shoals around Florida. He was not as fast as she, nor as ambitious. But the goods were always delivered, and the men always came home safe, so..."

Except for the last time. I almost said it. But my mother had been on board, too. I wondered who was calling the shots on that trip. If Emmett's theory was correct about driving straight into a hurricane, it was probably Mom. After the memory surges last year, I remembered her saying over the radio they weren't over the deepest part of the canyon because the depth finder said they weren't. Then Dad got on, saying the equipment was faulty, and he knew exactly where they were.

According to Emmett, that whole conversation was an act or something. I shook my brains out, trying not to lay a thought on that one. I guess I was afraid of the memory becoming any clearer, and me realizing it actually might have been faked. Maybe I would remember something in their tone, something false, something I wasn't ready to deal with yet. A person could explode if he had to think too much.

"Here's one big difference between your mom and dad," Opa went on again, smiling as he shifted himself in the chair. "Tell me where you remember this from."

He recited what sounded like a familiar poem—creepy, but familiar. "Spin thy safety net thus here; guide me through this deepest drear; guard my crew from early grave, from wailing winds, from witch, from wave. Upon thee I do hence depend, to bring my vessel home again."

He waited, watching me. Emmett had been on the *Goliath* a lot more than I had, and I'm sure Opa wouldn't have had to sit there for so long if he'd asked Emmett. "It was in Dad's quarters on the *Goliath*. Framed on the wall. His captain's prayer."

"Almost every captain has his own version of either a captain's prayer or a good-luck chant hung somewhere in prominence. In many cases, as in the case of your father, it was passed down through generations. Your father's was written by Elijah Barrett, nine generations before him. Your ancestors on that side used to go out on the deck and say that in a dangerous spot, and then they would spit over the stern. I guess the earlier ones felt it brought them luck. Maybe at the end, it was more of a tradition. But your father still confessed to reciting it in a rough patch." He took a sip of milk and set the glass down again. "Now, do you remember your mother's captain's prayer? The one that was posted there when she still drove the *Goliath*?"

That would have been before I was born. But I felt a smile coming over my face. I'd heard this one enough at the house. "Lord, give me a stiff upper lip."

NINE

"I thought we were supposed to be having this party in the kitchen." An arm went around my neck and a joint sprang in my face. I turned my gaze from the blackened picture window in Chandra's family room to this joint, then to her eyes.

"You look seriously weighted down, mister." Her blue eyes, which were starting to look a little glassy, still sparked with fun. "What can I do to get you to stop thinking about whatever it is you're thinking about?"

Instead of answering, I said something obvious. "It's colder than hell in this house."

"So warm up." She took the joint out of my face and a bottle of brandy popped up. She was double-fisting it. "It'll take at least two hours for the place to heat up. Come on in the kitchen. I've got the oven turned on and the door open for you. And you can have yourself a nice little dance with the spirits of warmth and humor in the meantime. Come on. It's just plain ol' brandy, plain ol' Mexican marijuana. Nothing perilous, I promise."

She'd given me the speech about my lack of imbibement at least four times in the past year. She knew what had happened to me a year ago, but I was never sure she knew Grey was behind it. It wouldn't be like Grey to blather something that could ruin her socially, and Chandra had always acted like she had no clue. She weaved both hands in front of my eyes, and I looked from one to the other, thinking, *Screw it.* I took the joint and sent hot smoke down my throat and headed back for the kitchen, where Bear and Harley were playing some board game on the floor in front of the oven, drinking brandy out of water glasses.

"That's not really a board game, it's a b-o-r-e-d game." Chandra followed me in. She put a glass of brandy in my hand. "Take it easy on that stuff. You'll get sick all over your grandpa's superexpensive tiles."

I sat down on the kitchen carpet between Harley and Bear, swallowing brandy, which was as biting hot as the joint. The warmth from the oven felt good. I forced my mind to what was going on.

"What're we playing?" The board looked familiar, though my brain wasn't working very well.

"Clue, you ninny," Harley told me. "The exclusive edition, Bear's favorite game. I would have picked Monopoly. At any rate, you're too late. The envelope's been stuffed. The cards have been dealt. All I know is it was Colonel Mustard."

"In the library with the lead pipe." Bear reached and took the joint from Chandra. I leaned sideways to look at Harley's cards. Colonel Mustard was right there.

Our eyes locked, and she scrunched her mouth around. "We ought to be playing for money, shouldn't we?"

I sat there and watched Harley kick Chandra's and Bear's butts all over the place. Bear hadn't played Clue in years and kept forgetting about the secret passages. He kept rolling the dice to get to rooms. Chandra was talking and drinking and not paying much attention. I didn't smoke anymore, but I sucked on the brandy, just until I was toast, until my gut muscles actually started to relax a little.

"So, we're here in scenic downtown East Hook in the dead of winter. Now what do we do?" Harley asked, dealing the three of them again. I'd said I'd rather watch. "Think the Lagoon Bar would card us in the dead of winter? Seems to me they'd be desperate for some clientele."

"Seems to me we'd stick out like a sore thumb and definitely get carded," Chandra said. "We'll have to watch videos. The stores are closed for the season. Unless you want to go window-shopping at the East Hook CVS."

"That's my idea of fun," Harley said, marking her cards on the clue sheet. "Or we could walk across the bridge to West Hook, go see Bloody Mary. Although she's a lying dog. She told me last summer I'd end up spending a lot of time with a tall, dark, handsome guy in October."

"What am I?" Bear asked.

"You're tall and dark."

Chandra giggled, even though she'd been shaking her head all along. "I don't think I will ever, ever go see Bloody Mary again after what she did to me Labor Day weekend. Grey doesn't know this, so when she gets back from Maine you cannot tell her, okay?"

Back from Maine. Chandra had said it so well. Good friend. I took it she didn't know I had been to see Grey, or she would have at least glanced my way. Bear and Harley looked at her without a clue in their eyes that she was lying about where Grey was.

"You heard about the Girl Scout who drowned when Grey and Lydia flipped Grey's Sunfish, right?"

They nodded. I rolled my eyes, thinking, *Here we go with a dead person and The She.* My friends knew about my parents, but I'd always only mumbled that "their boat sank with them on it." Until last year, that's about all I could remember, so it's not like I ever lied. Even when Bear was with me that horrible weekend, and I was having flashbacks and hearing that shriek, I didn't explain much. He just thought I was having, like, generic flashbacks that had something to do with my parents' accident. I'm not sure he was ever clear on what was going on. It was Emmett I'd asked all my questions of, later.

Chandra blathered right into it. "Labor Day weekend, a bunch of kids wanted to see Bloody Mary because of Grey, whose family had gone back to Philly on Thursday. This story had gotten all over the island: Girl Scout gets sucked out, Grey can't save her, Grey's paralyzed in some sort of shock because of some shrieking she heard, there's no body washing up. You can imagine how spooked people were."

"Yeah, but Bloody Mary?" Harley looked at her like she was trying not to pass judgment, but her eyes widened as she moved Mrs. White into a room. "Isn't she for, like, love interests? And talking to ghosts if you think your summer home is haunted and things like that? You went to her over a real person?"

Chandra looked kind of ashamed but then recovered. "The only reason I went with them is that, supposedly, Bloody Mary hears that shrieking, too. I wanted to hear what she had to say."

My neck snapped up, and I pretended I'd had a crick in it. It seemed to me that I'd known Bloody Mary heard that shrieking when I was a kid. I had no memory of anybody telling me that, but I had caught wind of it somehow. Maybe it had been through Emmett, who thought Bloody Mary was as big a faker as The She was a hoax. He'd probably delivered that news in some snide, big-brother tone that made me want to forget the whole thing.

"She's faking it," Bear couldn't help spewing. "How could she keep her reputation if she didn't have a personal role in every piece of island legend? Didn't the Coast Guard tell Grey to pay a visit to her doctor? Get rid of the earwax or something?"

"Yeah, that's true. Grey went to the doctor. All he found was a mild case of swimmer's ear. I don't think anything to do with swimmer's ear would have paralyzed her on the side of a boat. She's not only a pretty strong swimmer, but she's so not the scary type, you know?"

"So what did Bloody Mary say?" Harley rolled her eyes and stared into the corner of the room warily.

Chandra took a big gulp of brandy, shut her eyes, and swallowed. "Okay, I went with four other people, trying to hang back because I didn't think Grey would appreciate my being there. But she had told me the story personally and nobody else, so I ended up being the one who told Bloody Mary. I couldn't remember a lot of the details. She's got those light green, Nordic eyes from hell that make you freeze up. I think all I said was my two friends had been on this boat with the girl who drowned, and it looked to them like the girl was getting sucked from the harbor and out to sea. I asked what had been sucking her."

"Give me that bottle." Harley reached for it and poured more into her glass. "I don't think I'm going to hear this very well."

She went to hand the bottle back to Chandra, and I intercepted. Chandra went on, "She asked if either Lydia or Grey, or any of us, had heard the she-devil of the hole shriek that day."

I studied my glass, turning it in little circles on the floor in front of me. Harley and Bear just watched her.

"Bloody Mary said she'd heard it. That day. She had this, like, cheesy gas station calendar on the wall in her kitchen. She pointed, and in the August sixteenth square, the day the girl died, there were three X's. She told me she puts *X*'s on her calendar whenever she hears the shriek. She said she usually hears it three times, which explained the three *X*'s."

"She hears that shrieking three times whenever she hears it at all?" Bear asked, but then thought better of it and laughed it off. "She read about the drowning in the newspaper and put the *X*'s on the calendar later."

While they were deciding about that, I felt myself freezing up. The times I'd heard that shrieking, it was some on-again, off-again thing for a day or night. I had ended up complaining about it several times on the same day. I tried to put the whole idea out of my head by getting up and hunting through Chandra's cabinets. She didn't have any chips or real food in there, but I found an old box of soggy oyster crackers and started popping them into my mouth. I figured they would keep this brandy from churning the hell out of my gut.

Harley grabbed the box from me like she also needed a stomach sponge. "So Bloody Mary says she heard that girl being sucked out to sea? By The She?"

My eyes almost popped when Harley called her by that name. It seemed to me I had made it up as a kid, and my dad had told me that the nickname just went everywhere. I didn't know whether to shudder or laugh at my own power.

Chandra nodded. "I swear, I went there ready to believe Bloody Mary was full of shit. But she started, like, telling me *exactly* the same story Grey had." She tried to imitate Bloody Mary's Swedish accent. "'Zhey tipped zee sailboat on purpose.' I hadn't told her that part. 'Zhey all spill out, *your friend* climb on zee hull first.' I never told her that, either. 'Your friend pulls one other girl onto zee hull when it's upside down. Zey look for zee third girl, *whom zey don't like...*' I had never told her about the Girl Scout part, or Lydia and Grey being bothered by this. I just said it was three of them. 'And zhey can't see zee girl right away, until she bobs up thirty feet down zee harbor. Zhen...she gets smaller and smaller, and though her eyes are wide, zhey see she is moving fast, and zhey are helpless. Zhey cannot save her from zee witch, who is screaming.'"

Harley folded her cards into a pile and dropped it in disgust. "I hope you told that raving blond bitch to go back to hell where she came from."

Bear's jaw was dangling, but he turned to me quickly. "Bro, does this have anything to do with that shrieking you were, uh, rehearing the day Emmett took you to the hospital? Tell me it doesn't."

"No," I said quickly. Chandra wouldn't tell her story if she thought it related to my family, and some part of me actually wanted to hear what she had to say. Emmett's words rang through my head. "Your choices are clear. Mom and Dad were escaping from the law. Or there's an enormous *She* out there that eats people." My head was still whirling with information overload. I figured I'd listen now and form opinions later, like when I got safely back to Philly.

Chandra went on, and as she did, I wished I'd told the

truth and shut her up. I did not need to hear her next little speech.

"Bloody Mary gives me this disgusting blow-by-blow. 'Zee girl reaches zee sea. Zee witch quits sucking in air over zee horizon. She extends her longest tentacle, which reaches right to zee edge of zee harbor. She grabs zee girl, sucks her under. By the time she reaches zee witch, she is half drowned, but only half. Because zee witch won't eat a dead body. She picks zee girl up in her bony fingers and chomps down. Swallows. Sends her down, down, down to zee hole, where she remains.'"

"Definitely, she's a lunatic." Harley shook her head, scooping up her cards again. "Don't tell me you believe that bullshit."

"Well, it's hard to not believe the second part after she gave me a blow-by-blow of the first part, which I knew to be true. Then she tells me I can get the girl released. I can get her soul freed, sent on to the great beyond, the light, with this little ritual she does."

My neck snapped up, and I looked at her. I couldn't help it.

"Only she wants fifty bucks?" Bear guessed.

"Sixty-five."

Bear fell backward, yelping like he'd been shot. He laughed his side off. "Please, please, tell me you didn't give that ho any money, Chandra."

"Of course I did! What would you have done? If she'd told you that whole first part?"

Bear gathered himself out of his heap, shaking his head. "She got lucky."

"That's too lucky. How would she know Grey got on the hull first, before Lydia?"

"I don't know, Chandra! Maybe she was watching from the shore."

"It was the height of tattoo season! She wouldn't leave her tattoo shop to come down and see who *might happen to die* in the harbor—"

"She was on her way to the grocery store! Fuck if I know. Some boater saw the whole thing and told her."

"There were no boats around. Grey and Lydia had to right the boat and sail back to say what had happened. *They* reported it."

"Then...she got lucky." He went back to that. "Lydia went to see Bloody Mary first and never told you...Or Grey." He stopped to laugh some more.

"Neither of them went to see her. Lydia's family packed it in and went home right away, and believe it or not, Grey has more class."

I remembered Grey's desperation the day I visited her. "What did you do, go see Bloody Mary?" She was struggling even then about what to do. I knew she hadn't.

"The evidence is right there, Chandra! She's a liar!" Bear tossed Colonel Mustard at her bare feet.

"What evidence?"

"The evidence"—he remembered the secret passage and jumped Professor Plum from the conservatory to the ball-room—"is that you gave her sixty-five bucks, you tart!"

"Look, stop ragging on her." Harley held up her hand. "That was a nasty accident. However Chandra wanted to handle it to make herself feel better is a good thing. I think you should stay off her back."

"I can't help it." Bear was threatening to fall on his side laughing again. I looked at the bottle in Chandra's hand. We had drunk a lot of it. Chandra was still grinning, but walking away, singing merrily to herself as she retreated to the family room. I think she felt frustrated and misunderstood.

I left the room as Bear was accusing Harley of looking on his clue sheet when he fell over, though he'd done the same to her. Harley was making the "invisible third-person pile" out of Chandra's cards, like they were sure she had quit. I followed Chandra into the family room.

Bear said after me, "Don't do anything I wouldn't do, and with Harley, I wouldn't do anything. Ha-ha." Harley and Bear were the type of friends who were always hanging out—and always arguing.

They'd been telling me for some time that Chandra was hot for me, and I could sort of tell it was true. But she was too close to Grey. I had never gotten past the thought that it would bring Grey Shailey into my airspace. I hadn't told anyone but Bear that it had been Grey who'd sent me tripping, and I made him swear not to tell. It was too much of a ball-buster, and I hadn't wanted to give Grey the pleasure of other people hearing it from us. I don't suppose Grey found it useful to tell anybody, either, not after what I went through that weekend. People would have sided with me.

Chandra had sat down on the couch with her eyes shut, and she was rubbing her forehead. Although she was smiling, she didn't look too happy. She opened one eye and watched me plop down on the far end of the couch.

"This is all your fault that I'm babbling on about Bloody Mary! You shouldn't let me drink!"

"I'm sorry."

"I get so...*morose*! Sometimes. Actually, I'm usually a happy drunk. But there's something very *morose* about the shore in the dead of winter. Have you noticed?"

I couldn't help letting some big laughs escape.

She watched me. "What's wrong with you tonight, Evan Barrett? You're looking a bit *morose* yourself."

She was slurring but looking sincerely interested. Not that I would blather about an issue this big.

"You can tell me," she insisted. "I am sitting on a well of secrets, bro."

I watched the seriousness in her eyes and realized that was probably true. "I know about Grey. I went to see her on Wednesday."

She looked surprised. "How did you know?"

"Mrs. Ashaad called me in. Grey had asked Mrs. Ashaad to send me over there. Mrs. Ashaad wrote it up as a KHK, thinking I would like getting some service points. Or maybe she was thinking there's no other way I would go, unless she, like, ordered me."

"Grey keeps telling me that you don't like her anymore, but she also knows that most people don't like her." She shrugged like she was used to that opinion. "For all the things she probably did to you, I'm sorry. That's my job, you know. She gets ugly on someone and then I apologize. We're Jekyll and Hyde. In two bodies."

Chandra was pretty nice. Ditzy, but nice. I could never figure out how the two of them could be friends. I asked her.

"Do you mean, how do we *stay* friends, or how did we *become* friends?"

"Starting at the top, I guess."

"Well…" She twirled a piece of hair and tied it in a knot with three fingers. "Sophomore year, she got the secret flash on me. I did something totally embarrassing, and she swore not to tell. Then, I got the flash on her. I swore not to tell."

"So your friendship started with blackmail?" I grinned down at my thumbs, which were picking at each other.

"Well, that's how we *became* friends. That's not how we *stayed* friends. I mean, you can get to be friends because the person knows you went down on four guys at the same party. I mean, I don't mind telling you. I just don't want the world to know, okay? They were from a different school."

She was ripping drunk, I realized, and would be sorry tomorrow that I'd heard that. I reached over, took the bottle away from her, and put it on the coffee table. Someone had popped a Pepsi, which was still cold, and I put that in her hands. *Too much information, thank you.*

"So why'd you stay friends?"

"We stayed friends because...I understand her." She sipped from the can, looking over the top of it at me with laughing eyes.

"I'm glad somebody does. Everybody needs somebody like that. That's nice she has you." I laid my head back and shut my eyes. The room was spinning just a little.

"That's very generous, considering what she did to you last year. I know about that, too."

I opened one eye, looked at her, and closed it again.

"I think you've been...*great*," she said. "Considering you were remembering the night your parents died and... whatever else. She completely low-balled you. But in case you don't know, she was really, really sorry afterward."

I gazed at the ceiling, feeling my eyebrows turn in. "She had interesting ways of showing it."

"Well, that's one thing about Grey. She doesn't apologize. For anything."

I laughed pretty hard. "Well, guess what? She's going to learn."

I could feel Chandra watching me, and I thought about telling her that Grey was coming down here tomorrow. But I decided against it pretty fast. If Emmett was right and it was stupid to let her see Edwin Church, it would be beyond stupid to let Chandra talk her into going to see Bloody Mary or something.

"She won't let me in to see her. She won't let anybody in. Only you, so far."

I could feel her watching, like maybe I would tell her what Grey was up to. I settled on, "I don't think she would mind me saying, if she's done anything awful to you in the past couple of years, she *is* going to apologize."

That made her crack up totally, and she leaned back, howling at the ceiling. "I'm sure to hear four or five in that case!"

"That's it?"

"Hey." She piped down to just the grin. "Like I said, I understand her. Put some of that brandy in here."

She weaved the Pepsi can over in my general vicinity, and I did it, just so not to be difficult, but I pretended to put more in than I did. I remembered two things about Chandra's drunkenness: She got overly talkative and she got overly flirty. I didn't mind her talking, but I didn't want to dive into some great temptation that would put Grey in my face every day at school, even if rehab improved her enormously. Rehab can't perform miracles. Chandra put her toes on my leg and started flexing them. I bit my knuckles, wishing I could think of something to talk about.

"Okay, so...I told you about my four guys. Now you have to tell me what's bothering you. It's only fair."

I just sat there in silence.

"Must be pretty serious," she slurred. "Your grandfather okay?"

"Yeah. I just..." I was trying to think how to put it so that I wasn't lying and would have to remember how to cover my tracks later. "I just heard some family dirt tonight that I didn't know, and it's pretty awful, and I really can't talk about it, okay?"

She sat up, pulled her feet up cross-legged, watching me. "Okay. Don't tell. I know about awful family problems. It really sucks no matter how you look at it. Because most of the time? You did nothing to cause it. I mean, it's bad enough when you do something and you have to be embarrassed by it. But get this. My dad filed a false insurance claim last year. Fifteen thousand big ones. Well, guess what? In October he got caught."

I turned to stare, and she was nodding at me, swaying just a little, but very sympathetic looking. I almost kissed her. It's like she read my mind.

"Sure makes you feel closer to someone when you tell them some of your dirt, doesn't it?"

"Yeah."

"Good, so can I jump on you now? I've always wanted to."

I put my hands up before I could even think about it, which made her look ready to die, which I didn't really want, either. I stammered, "Let's wait until you're sober. We're on two different planets right now. It just wouldn't mean anything."

She groaned and threw her head down toward her lap. "You think I'm an idiot! That's one of your famous send-off lines that I'm always hearing about in school. The corridors are littered with injured females who've heard all kinds of garbage from you, like, 'You're too important to me! I want to go out with you in a couple of years, when I'm more serious about things!'"

At least she was laughing and not crying. I started to deny it, but first I wanted to think on whether I was serious about what I'd said to her. It had just come flying out. Maybe that meant I wasn't serious. But it didn't matter, because there was an issue here that was serious.

"Chandra, this is not a very good night for me, okay? Besides, you never flirt with me when you're sober. That is true."

She shook her head, picking at her feet and sighing. "Can we just roll the tape back? Forget I said any of that stuff? Especially if you're feeling bad about your family."

I kept quiet, but her face came right up to mine, all sympathetic. "Because you shouldn't, you know. You didn't have anything to do with it, am I right?"

I heard my own laugh hit the air, which surprised me, being that I wasn't even smiling.

"I just told my dad, 'Listen, why ever you did it, I don't care. However you pay it back, I don't care. Just don't think you can put me in public school and use my tuition money to pay your stupid fines and reimbursements. I had nothing to do with it!'"

I nodded pretty hard, feeling resentment build up in my gut—toward Emmett for telling me, toward my parents for whatever the hell they actually did. I tried to tell myself Emmett was right, and I would just have to get used to all this. It was where all the evidence pointed. Bloody Mary had been doing good, proving the existence of some dark force, until she asked for sixty-five bucks. My stomach bottomed out, and I tossed an arm over it.

"And whatever it was, just be glad you don't have Grey's family. They are in a class all their own, believe me."

"She says her mother's a drunk and her father cheats on her."

"He cheats? That would be nice, if he was just a cheat. He's a total cokehead."

I swung my neck to stare. I'd been upset by my dad's little sandwich bag of Colombian gold.

She must have gotten some steam power from my concerned gaze, because she went on a real tear. "A cokehead, and he's a decent lawyer, but I'm telling you, half their money was not made the legal way, okay? Are you with me? And at least when our parents do wrong, they don't try to mix us up in it. That's the goods I had on her back when we started being friends—what her dad did to her freshman year. Not that I would ever, ever tell anyone but..."

She stopped long enough to take a huge sip of soda, but I could see it all coming like a train, and I felt like asking, "What am I? No one?" I didn't really want to hear any stories about Grey being used as a cocaine delivery girl. It would make me feel sorry for her, and I didn't want to.

It wasn't exactly drugs.

"When she was a freshman, her dad *lent* her to a prospective client. At least once, maybe more times. He sent her out to dinner with some fat, aging bald guy in a limo.

Is that the most disgusting thing you've ever heard in your entire life?"

I watched her face to see if her meaning of the word *lent* was the same as mine. She kept nodding, and my stomach flipped almost completely upside down. I hadn't drunk that much, but I hadn't drunk for a year before that. And it was on top of Thanksgiving turkey and lobster butter and whatever else. Maybe it was just that I'd never heard so many puke-inspiring tales all in one day.

"Excuse me." I got up, started walking to the bathroom slowly, but by the time I got halfway there, I was running.

TEN

My dreams that night were all twisted, the kind that keep waking you up because people turn into snakes or eels and then say, "What's up?" like nothing's wrong. This bitch of a stomachache I'd brought home from Chandra's shortly after I tossed didn't help things. I was lying on my side in bed, because lying on your side kills stomach pains, according to Aunt Mel. Maybe that's why my brain tossed up an image of my dad from the side. I was seeing his profile, though I was very close up to him, about nine inches from his ear. His jaw was moving a little, sending his reddish beard a little up and down.

"Spin thy safety net thus here; guide me through this deepest drear; guard my crew from early grave..." His voice is clear; even his breathy pauses ring clear. *"...from wailing winds, from witch, from wave. Upon thee I do hence depend, to bring my vessel home again."*

His eyeball turns until his eye catches mine. Then his

whole head turns. He's looking at me dead-on. I can see
every freckle on his nose, and his eyes, so...deep.

"*When do you say that poem at sea, Daddy?*"

I shot up in the bed, staring through the darkness and
gulping air like I was going to get sick all over again. I remembered I was at Opa's, in the twin bed in the smallest
of the guest rooms, where soft sheets are supposed to
make up for a hard mattress and a hard pillow. I couldn't
move to find my watch and look at it. This one wasn't a
dream; it was a memory.

The more I breathed, the less it felt like I was catching
my breath. I could feel gray doors blowing open, and it
was petrifying, worth trying to fight off. One of those
doors might bring me an image of my parents shooting
heroin or cheating on each other or lying to the cops
or...

Or, or, or...

"*I'm saying it now because I'm going up to Nova Sco-*
tia tonight. There's weather. We Barretts, we always say
that in weather, and I'm not ashamed to tell my own son
so, to tell him we spit over the stern when we say it."

"*Why would you be ashamed to say that, Daddy?*"

"*I'm not. I'm not ashamed of being respectful of the*
weather. I'm not ashamed of thinking that certain sayings
bring you luck, hope, deliverance. That little chant has
been with our family a long, long time. I want you to say
it someday, when the weather tosses your ship mightily."

I grabbed for the crank to open a window, feeling heat
barreling up from the radiator vent below the bed. I liked

the cold air hitting my face, but with the window open I could hear the roar of the sea. It rumbled and thundered from miles out, and the closer part smacked against the pilings under the drawbridge. But, somehow, it sounded better than the artificial heat felt.

"I'll say it, Dad. I want to be you someday."

He's chuckling, rolling his eyes. "Be careful what you wish for. You might just get it—"

I stumbled to the bathroom and splashed water on my face. The room was small, but every bedroom in this monster house had its own bathroom, and I stood by the sink, splashing, swallowing, spitting. It wasn't such a bad memory. It shocked me a little to realize how much my ambitions had changed, but it wasn't like I'd seen an armed robbery. I calmed myself enough to turn on the light and look at myself in the mirror. I had dark circles under my eyes. If you're blond with light skin, those circles look like bruises. I looked like shit.

I climbed back into the bed, wondering which I needed more—the air or the silence. You can't have both on the Hooks. I chose air.

I lay there breathing it in, and suddenly I was seeing the inside of the Burger King at the rest stop on the expressway down to the shore. I had been in there with my dad many times when I was little, when we were driving back from Opa's shipyard in Philly. With slightly less paranoia, I let the memory roll. It showed my dad standing at an ATM machine, some familiar guy behind him, and I don't like this Connor Riley man as much today as I sometimes do because Dad lets me sit in the front of the truck usually, but a man in the truck means I have to squish into the backseat. I come up beside Dad at the ATM, and I can see his eyes growing...his mouth spreading out...his neck doing this little snapping thing to the time of the ATM machine spitting out bills.

Connor is looking over Dad's shoulder now. "Jesus, Barrett, how much does lunch cost? How much did you ask for?"

"I asked for twenty bucks."

They're both laughing. My dad is counting bills in disbelief.

"You hit too many zeros. You're going to be in trouble with the old lady if you don't put it back—"

My dad's shaking his head, pointing to the screen, smiling at Connor, who says, "Holy shit. What're you going to do with it?"

Dad's eyes close, and he's still laughing. He says, "Evan, uh, which is the bigger sin? Cursing or stealing?"

"Stealing," I decide.

"Yeah." He nudges Connor. "Do I raise my boys right or what?" Then he goes, "Shit. Goddamn. Fuckin'-A."

He walks over to the rest stop manager's office and he's cursing more of the same, until he sticks his head in. He says to the lady in there, "Uh, there's a problem."

Then Connor starts in, to the back of his neck. "Fuckin'-A yourself, Barrett. There haven't been any saints named in *about five hundred years. You're past your time. She's just going to keep it! And spend it getting her toenails painted for Mr. Gas-Pump-Trailer-Park. Why do you have to be so noble? Send it my way. I ain't proud—"*

Connor turns, realizes I'm still down there, and gives me a dirty look. My dad gets done with the manager. Then they're going through the Burger King line ahead of me, laughing at each other. But I hear Connor say, "You would never have done that if your kid hadn't been here. Christ, couldn't you just have pretended he wasn't here for about five seconds, faggot head?"

My dad gets jollier over that. "Ask Mary Ellen if I'm a faggot head. And why would I do that for my kid? He's not even old enough to count!"

I stuck my face into the pillow, trying to bring the black back. I thought of Emmett looking at me so concerned before he drank himself into a stupor last night, and now my memory was sending me all the wrong thoughts. I was supposed to be remembering the times my parents weren't trying for sainthood. Like the time my mom hit me with a two-by-four for lighting matches, laid a huge splinter into my ass, and begged me not to tell the teacher the whole time she was picking it out. I knew it had happened, but it was something I *knew,* not something I could picture. The picture was behind some gray door. I tried to imagine my dad smoking a joint. I could get the image for a second, and then it would leave me again. I lost it to the memory of myself smoking a few now and again. *Yeah, I guess that makes me next in line to smuggle a load, compliments of the Colombian mafia, and pass some off to Miguel.*

Stop it! You're using your thoughts to defend them!

I lay there feeling completely pissed at myself, and my anger blew up into this nasty ball behind my eyes, which broke and ran out my eyeballs. But when I took in my first big gulp of air, my stomach quit biting so much. I looked over at the darkened door, just to make sure it was shut, to make sure Emmett couldn't hear me from the other guest room. He was so used to all this information. He was so cool and so together, so, ah yes, the suave professor, minus only the final part of a dissertation. *Fucking Marxist fuckhead.*

I didn't know who to kill. I tried to force my mind through the pages of that black book—search warrants, tapes, maps—just so I could be mad at my parents, who were dead, instead of at my brother, who was alive and my closest remaining family member. But I got distracted too easily. I kept hearing little phrases of Emmett's that irritated me to no end. Like "leap of faith." His one leap of faith had been to assume that our parents had to be dead or they would have contacted us. *Assume our parents are dead.* Calling that his leap of faith sounded somehow kind of cold.

I flopped over, fuming about how Emmett always had this way of making me feel stupid...mentally ill-equipped. I couldn't fume for too long, because my brother was also a nice person, with a conscience ten miles wide. And yet he always tried to understand those who did wrong. He rarely got mad, always tried to understand my side before he got in my face about something. It was hard to find fault with much that he said.

Go out to Sassafras. See Edwin Church again.

I blinked at the thought and almost got sick. I got mad at my intuition for even showing its ugly face around me, especially to bring up Mr. Church. Then I sat straight up in the bed again.

Grey is going out there. Today.

Seconds later I was shoving my legs into my jeans and reaching for my watch: 6:35. She wouldn't get there for a few hours. I kept getting dressed at a slower pace, because sleep was impossible. I couldn't help thinking of some fourteen-year-old wondering what the hell she was supposed to do in the backseat of a limo with some fat, ancient sweat bag. And then I could hear her telling me, as plain as if she were here and talking to my face. "What, you want me to sit here and blame it on my parents or something? You want me to say they were like that first? Okay. I guess they were. But...I made my choices. I'm not blaming anyone."

I couldn't even focus too much on my guilt, because it was huge. I'd had to pick this molested, courageous girl to try to force apologies out of. I let a groan fall out of my mouth, because punching my stupid self in the face wouldn't have helped anything. I needed to meet her at the docks, before she got to Edwin Church, and before he set her up to think "some...fantastic...motion picture...fiction phenomenon—"

Emmett had such a way with words—that much I had to hand to him. Even when he was drunk.

II

"The opposite of a correct statement is a false
statement. But the opposite of a profound truth
may well be another profound truth."
—NIELS BOHR

ELEVEN

The sun was rising to a clear blue sky, the first one in days. I walked across the drawbridge to West Hook, feeling in my pocket for my gloves and pulling them on. My breath blew in streams into the icy air. I had to stop and look down the harbor at that sun coming up, making the surface of the water look like a million diamonds dancing. This diamond dance went out to meet the light of the sun, a giant diamond just above the sea.

I stood there and looked straight down over the rail of the drawbridge. The water wasn't splotched with diamonds straight underneath me. It was dark and bobbed around between the pilings, dancing and carrying on, giving me the feeling it was alive, had a personality of its own.

I heard myself speaking to it. "I don't know if you've got any she-devil hole under you, but I'd say you are a well of secrets."

Of course, I didn't get any reply.

"You really don't want anybody to know you, do you? You're like some bitchy girl. The kind I'm always drawn to and then can't tolerate." It mocked me, lapping and laughing, and I should have felt all sorts of vile hatred wafting off me for this water. But before I knew it, I was sending my spit downward, remembering my dad always spitting off the stern before he hit a storm, "to mix my body with hers, in case we have to reach an agreement."

I didn't know why I did it. I sure as hell didn't plan on having to reach any agreement with the sea. I watched as the spit hit the water, and it gelled immediately, like any other foam cap, and for whatever reason my eyes were filling up again. Things got blurry. I banged on the railing once, and walked on.

The Island Diner was still there, just past the West Hook lighthouse, but I didn't think the waitress, Mrs. Chowder, would be. Honest: Mrs. Chowder. I suddenly remembered Dad busting on Mrs. Chowder when he'd take us in there for the special on the nights Mom worked.

"I met a dentist offshore named Dr. Molar! And there's a minister in English Creek named Reverend Goode!"

"Poor guys, they were doomed. I'd have never thought to work on this godforsaken island if it weren't for my name, Wade, I swear to God. What'll it be?"

She's running through the specials, but he's looking at her and not listening. He's not done teasing yet. He loves to tease. That's why people love him.

"So long as your middle name isn't seafood. Or clam."

"It's worse. It's Flossie. Flossie Chowder? As in, you have to floss the clams out of your teeth afterward?" She blows a puff of smoke over Dad's head as he says no chowder for him, thank you.

Emmett doesn't care that Dad is distracted from us by Flossie Chowder. Ever since he turned twelve, he likes when Dad looks the other way at a table, because he thinks it's funny to be sitting right beside Dad at the table while flipping me the bird.

The memory surprised me a little. There was a lot about Emmett's behavior that had changed so much. Memories of his teasing, fun side came floating back with the inside of this authentic chrome diner. It hadn't changed, except I didn't see Flossie Chowder or any of the other leathery-faced old waitresses, and I didn't see any of these young waitresses smoking. It was one change I could appreciate. I flopped down in a booth and studied some of the guys at the counter who looked like seamen and were packing away huge breakfasts. I guess some things never change.

I ordered a doughnut and a hot chocolate, remembering the hot chocolate in the Island Diner kicking butt. Then I sat there looking at Emmett's black notebook, which I'd brought with me. I had some time to kill, and there was stuff in there he hadn't showed me. I took a deep breath, swallowed, and opened the book, passing the search warrant before I had a chance to get sick again.

There were a bunch of typed pages with dates on them. They looked like Emmett had been keeping a journal or something. I read over his first entry a number of times, because I had written about the same exact period of time when I had Grey's acid running through me. The facts were almost identical. His interpretation was very different.

> *While drinking his coffee after dinner, Dad went through his usual rigmarole about the crew being a little superstitious over husbands and wives traveling on the same vessel. As usual, I had sided with Mom, who went on about it being a sexist excuse to keep women off the sea.*
>
> *Retrospectively, I would have to say this particular conversation must have been rehearsed.*

Emmett mentioned that Mom and Dad had been alone most of the day because he was in school, and they would have had time to plot out how to keep their kids completely innocent of an attempt to escape drug-trafficking charges. He said he had trouble believing that they would talk so normally about delivering steel girders when their hull had just been searched. They should have still been stunned about the DEA and been talking of nothing else, if they were so innocent.

I had remembered the conversation, too. *Rehearsed?* My parents had no training as actors. I did remember my mom seeming uptight over the superstitions and my dad seeming nervous about how the crew would respond to Mom. Had they other reasons to be uptight and nervous?

Would I have been able to tell at that age? I just didn't know.

I tried to do homework after they left, which wasn't hard, considering I was clueless at the time. Evan was playing on the floor. He was giving me the creeps because he thinks he hears The She sometimes. He thinks about her a lot, and when we're alone together on a stormy night, he gets me so creeped out I want to smack him.

When they called, Mom described the sea as looking like soup being stirred. Dad mentioned that he could not feel any wind off the stern, and considering how it was blowing....

When the DEA questioned me later, I mentioned my parents' comments about the wind and water. I thought at the time the agents were very callous to have smiled the way they did. But Aunt Mel and I have to agree: Their comments sounded very much like the local paperbacks from cheesy publishers that Dad used to read and enjoy.

I just wanted to punch Emmett—not because I disagreed with him completely, but because I didn't know what to think. It would have been hard to detect an act, with all that wind and radio static, I had to admit that. Yet nothing at the time left me feeling like it was an act. But I felt stupid, very stupid, now.

*I went up to the widow's walk, and the next
thing I knew, Evan was up there, telling me Mom
and Dad were sending a Mayday. He was pretty
hysterical.*

I couldn't help staring at that part each time I read it.
It was the first detail we would have disagreed on. I had
passed out or fallen backward or something. I had never
made it up to the widow's walk. Emmett was remembering this wrong.

It gave me some bizarre feeling of victory that Emmett
would have messed up the facts. I read the entry over a
couple of times, realizing he must have found me at the
foot of the stairs when he came back down, and maybe I
blathered in my blackout phase, and that's what sent him
to the radio again. My feeling of victory had to do with
his closing words. I could only think that if he had been
wrong about where he found me, he might be wrong
about this next thing.

*When I came back down, Evan had left the
handset dangling on the radio that he'd last been
talking on. It was the ship-to-shore. Mom and Dad
had sent the Mayday over the ship-to-shore. The
Coast Guard couldn't hear the ship-to-shore, only
the ship-to-ship. It's as if Mom and Dad wanted me
alone to hear it. That way, I could describe our
conversation to the Coast Guard, and, of course, I
would say they had been panicking and confused*

and had picked up the wrong handset by accident. And I would sound so convincing, and the Coast Guard would have no record of the actual Mayday to analyze for faked sound effects of screeching and metal snapping.

The problem was, they weren't smart enough. They didn't stop to think the DEA would laugh as they did. Nor did they realize the DEA would keep me for four hours, take meticulous notes, record everything I said, and show me six volumes on the disappearance of the Riley vessel.

I have never, ever seen so much paperwork in all my life.

I have been more hurt by their deception than words can describe. I can only think that they had a plan that was to keep me completely innocent to protect me, and, of course, I would forgive them once we all got together somewhere safe, down below the equator. I would have eventually forgiven all, though it would have been hard.

I pulled on my hair to try to dredge up more memories of my parents being decent and noble, to replace Emmett's thoughts. But I must have used up my predawn energy already, and my mind was an exhausted blank. All I could think of was falling back into bed sometime later this afternoon.

I yawned, reached for my cocoa cup, and realized the stuff was ice-cold. I'd sat there reading this stuff over and over, trying to get used to the ideas. I looked at my watch. It was five to nine.

It's a half hour walk deeper into the island to get to The Docks, and I ran most of it. When I got there, I could see Grey's white Subaru parked outside, and I ran into the bait shop. Mrs. Shields was in there, carrying a baby on her hip, but she said Mr. Shields had already left to take some girl to Sassafras. I laid my credit card down to rent an outboard and didn't give a shit if Emmett saw the charge. He would understand this use.

It was a bitter cold trip to Sassafras Island, and all I could see was meadow grass at first. That's mostly what Sassafras is—a body of meadow grass and swamp that lay in the middle of Great Bay, which separates West Hook from the mainland. The bay pours into the Sassafras swamps at high tide, and leaves them soggy salt bottom at low tide. There was one spot on Sassafras high enough to live on, but nobody had for centuries because of the biting greenhead flies—until Edwin Church came along. Someone told me once that when he bought the whole island from some private owner for, like, thirteen thousand dollars, just after he signed the papers, the former owner said, "Sucker." That was before I was born.

When I hit the inner mudflats, I had to drive standing up to see his cabin over the meadow grass. I took one skinny trail after another, keeping his cabin always in sight. I tried putting one knee on the seat for balance, and looked down, thinking how odd it felt. It was like I had taken this little boat out on the bay for a thousand days in a row—

only on this day, I'd grown a foot and a half. I used to be able to stand straight up with my knee on the seat. Now, I had to stoop funny.

I shook off the memory and felt my anger returning as I reached the little beachhead beside Edwin Church's cabin. I pulled right up onto the beach like I'd just done that yesterday, too. I even remembered to turn off the outboard motor once I started to cruise. I had to stare backward—to try to remember how I'd done it so perfectly. I didn't have time to dwell on magic.

I grabbed the black book, opened Church's door without knocking, and saw Grey sitting at the table in the corner. It looked like she and Church were relaxing over hot cocoa or tea or something.

Mr. Church was standing in the middle of the room, but the two cups on the table left me thinking he had just stood up. He was a tall man, and although he had to be in his sixties, he still had the swaggering muscles of a seaman. His big arms dangled down under a blue work shirt, looking too young and built up to match his head full of thick white hair. He said nothing but raised his eyebrows at me.

I dropped the book on his coffee table, turned a finger toward Grey, and said, "Don't you touch her."

I was trying to be protective of her, so it irritated the hell out of me when she started laughing. And she laughed so hard that she fell off the chair and landed on her butt on the floor.

I circled around Church to get to her. If he knew what

was so funny, he didn't let me in on it. He did glance down at the black book, then kept staring blankly as I got to Grey.

Grey had no manners, the usual. It was typical of her to sit there and laugh at a joke and not think she ought to let you in on it. I reached my hand down for her and kept from snapping her up, remembering she was supposed to be fragile right now.

Church's eyes were a complete blank as I watched him while telling her, "Whatever it is that's funny, either share it or stifle it."

She grabbed for a tissue from a box that sat on the windowsill and wiped her eyes. "Well, he was sitting there with his back to the beach. He never looked. All he did was hear the rental boat, and he says, '*Hmmm*. That has to be Mr. Evan Barrett, and I would perceive that he is angry.'"

TWELVE

Mr. Church raised his eyebrows with this mock innocence that I totally hated. He looked too calm and amused. I glanced around for mirrors that would have shown me arriving but didn't see a single one. That didn't keep me from telling Grey what was up.

"However he did it, it was nothing supernatural, Grey. Don't let him trick you like he tricked me."

"No tricks," he said, very quietly, like maybe he thought his quietness would calm me down. "I just heard somebody beach an outboard without the least bit of clatter. Very few people can do that in these parts…even fewer who could do it at the age of seven or eight."

I felt myself wanting to soften up over the compliment, but then I remembered that how well I drove a boat wasn't important to me or to anybody or anything.

"I guess there's no question about why I'm here," I snapped, figuring he would know I was onto his bullshit.

But he said, "I don't know why you're here. I'm not even sure yet why the young lady is here. But since you're here, would you like something hot?"

The room was a combo tiny kitchen and living room, and he moved over to the stove. Grey was staring at her fingers like they were of interest to her, and I knocked her in the shoulder a little. "If he doesn't know why you're here, then don't tell him anything. He's a big faker!"

With that, Mr. Church turned slowly and stared at me with his eyebrows digging toward his nose.

"Faker? How? What did I fake?"

"You told me my parents' ship got hit by a giant wave!" I shouted. "And that is the most enormous bullshit story!"

He looked confused for a moment, then said, "No, actually, that is what *you* told me."

"After you did that...that stupid thing with your hands! That, that power-of-suggestion...pseudo-eastern mystical shit! How many other people have you impressed with that over the years? What did you do, like, push my hand up against that map on the wall?"

"Is that how you remember it?"

I didn't think he had touched me, but I couldn't be certain of anything right now. He was still staring at me, more alarmed than ashamed, it seemed to me. Maybe he had no shame.

His voice was too quiet and smug when he said, "I don't use that too often. People have to ask me. If I remember correctly, you *begged* me."

"Oh, shut up!" I flopped down in the chair beside Grey. She now had her hands folded between her knees, and her eyes stared blankly at the floor. I thought of asking her to go outside for a minute, so I could keep my family dirt between me and Mr. Church. But I remembered her dad and some fat old guy in the limo, and I almost laughed out loud at myself.

"You shouldn't be doling out false hopes like people's lives are something for you to play with," I snapped, and turned to her again. "Grey, I shouldn't have told you to come here. Don't let him—"

"What happened?" he asked.

I blinked, watching him search through my eyes, as if I wasn't completely taking him apart, or as if it didn't matter.

I pointed at the black book on the coffee table. I could feel myself getting ready to bawl again, and I was trying to stop it, but it was coming up fast, like a freight train. I blathered Emmett's whole story, only stopping to swipe the wet off my face. I told him about the search warrant the day before the disappearance, the stuff on Captain Riley, the map of Hurricane Marco, how Emmett and Aunt Mel had pieced it all together.

He stood there frozen, and as I was finishing, I gestured at the book again, like he could pick it up and look for himself. He glanced at it and back at me, like it was nothing.

"But you don't really believe that's what happened, do you?" he asked.

I landed both elbows on the table, thinking I wanted to smash it to the floor, but I screeched, instead: *"No!"*

Grey was still taking in the floor, like my bawling wasn't upsetting her in the least. Finally, she reached over to the tissue box, and with the same sarcasm as I'd laid on her two days earlier, she passed me off a tissue with two fingers and raised an amused eyebrow.

I snatched it and sat there gazing out at the marshlands, wiping off my face, and feeling like a pot half-full after it had boiled over. I actually felt calmer. I was calm enough that I let the sound of Mr. Church's work boots clomp closer on the wood floor without spinning around on him distrustfully.

He was right over the top of my head when he repeated himself. "You don't feel that your brother is correct?"

I could feel sympathy rolling off him, and I wasn't sure I wanted it. "What the hell difference does it matter what I *feel*?"

"I would say it matters a great deal. Your intuition is very important. It'll even tell you where the line is— whether your feelings are out of love, or whether they're because you honestly don't believe something that's been told to you. If you keep your intuition strong, that is."

Well, I didn't want to feel squat. I shoved out of the chair and wandered around, casting a glance at that map, and then looking at all the things I'd stopped to look at last time I was in here. A year ago the papers taped to the mantel over his fireplace had intrigued me. This time they made me suspicious. The first was a diploma from the

University of South Florida, for a degree in marine science. That one was only faded, but there was another, a master's in social work from the University of Delaware, which was full of tiny holes, like in his younger days he might have had it on a dartboard. Same with the third one, a master's in philosophy, University of Mi—something; it had a big hole in it, as if it had been the bull's-eye of a dart game.

"You really couldn't make up your mind, could you?" I yelled, liking the sound of my loudness. The last time I'd seen all this, I'd reckoned it differently. I'd thought he was a very educated man.

"It's a person's prerogative to change his life's course," he muttered, and I detected more amusement in his voice than I would have liked to have heard.

I could feel Grey coming up beside me. Actually, I smelled her. She smelled scrubbed, like some combo of body wash and shampoo and fabric softener that whizzed through the snot in my head, and when I glanced at her, I decided she must have taken the hour-long shower from hell earlier this morning. She looked a little pale, but other than that, close to her great athletic self.

She pointed to a letter he'd taped up there, too.

It read, "Dear Mr. Church: We would kindly ask that you direct your questions to the pastor in his private study and not attend Bible study any longer. The attendees are finding it difficult to understand the matters in question when you feel the need to..."

I was about to mutter something about not being able

to get along with anybody, but the note cracked Grey up, and I cast her a glance. I thought it was odd she wasn't mad that I'd sent her all the way out here for nothing. It made me wonder if her whole life at home wasn't such a psychodrama that she no longer felt surprised when one barged in on her.

I turned on my heel and crossed back to look out the far window to the meadows. Mr. Church had picked up Emmett's black notebook, and when I passed he was just leafing through it, too quickly to read anything.

"Miss Shailey told me she came here based on your recommendation, and that you were down here for the holiday. I had a feeling the family theories would start to pop at this year's feast—being that they hadn't when you came to see me last year. The day was coming. You're a young man. They couldn't hold out on you for much longer."

I spun on him. "You *knew* about all of this? When I came here last year?"

He was looking down at the weather map of the hurricane and nodded. "In fact, I've seen this volume before. Your brother kept it in your old house in West Hook. Your grandfather took it for a while after you boys moved to Philly. He left it with me once." He snapped it shut, tossed it onto his little couch.

"Why didn't you tell me?" I demanded.

"You didn't ask."

"I didn't ask?" I shouted, five times louder. "I came here looking for the goddamn truth! How could you know

a thing like that and play dumb to it? And decide instead to do some stupid thing with dreams and visions—"

"Maybe I was never so sure this is the truth," he said.

"How would you know?"

He looked sideways for a minute, shaking his head. "I don't know."

I blew my nose again, watching him cautiously. He had started that "I don't know" shit with me last time I was in here, when he was squeezing my head....

"What is this, some Vietnamese mystic thing?"

"I don't know."

"Well, why do you do it if you're not even sure what it is?"

"I don't know. It seems to work, or I wouldn't."

"Is it religious?"

"I don't know."

"Is it psychological?"

"I don't know."

"Well, don't you even want to know what you're doing with your own body? Don't you even feel the need for an explanation?"

"Not really."

"Oh, God!" I fell into my chair and slammed my elbows onto the table again. I would stick to the facts. "How can you argue with my brother's charts and plastic fucking slipcovers?"

"Easily."

I didn't believe him. "The way Emmett put it was, 'I would never suspect you of selling drugs, Evan. Unless the

DEA showed up asking to go through your room, and you disappeared the next night, to the shrill sounds of an island superstition.'" I remembered his smug little grin and shuddered.

"So your parents had an accident the night after a DEA search was executed. Stranger things have happened," he said. "Perhaps the DEA was suspicious only because your father made too many trips to Jamaica. Maybe he accidentally brushed elbows with the wrong guys in port. You know what a friendly guy he was."

I spun in my chair to look at him. "Do you know this for a fact?"

"No. I don't know anything for a fact."

I groaned, flinging my arms at the book. "Look at all this paper!"

"Yes. The academics are very endeared to the stuff. The more paper, the more respectable the project. That doesn't fly with me—"

I exhaled, and what sounded like half laugh, half yelp barreled out with it. I was thinking of Emmett's words in his journal when he'd become so impressed with the DEA. *I have never, ever seen so much paperwork in all my life.* I shook off the thought.

"He said he took only one leap of faith in all of that... which is that they're dead!"

"He's taken a hundred leaps of faith!" Mr. Church countered. "He's taken no fewer than you did last year."

I started to deny it, but he looked so sure that finally my mouth stopped running. I just huffed, out of breath.

"For one thing, don't you think it is a major, *major* leap of faith to accuse decent, normal people like your parents with actions of that nature?"

"*Yes!*" I banged on the table again, surprising myself, though I couldn't say which surprised me more, the quickness of my answer or how stupid I felt for not having asked Emmett that. I tried to remember why I hadn't.

"He was making it sound like everybody was doing it, or being tempted to do it—" I turned to see how Mr. Church would respond to that, and he was shaking his head, focusing out the window.

"Five vessels were either caught or suspected in the years surrounding your folks' disappearance, including Riley's. Let's say there were twice that many involved, just for the sake of argument. There are dozens of freighter ships pulling in and out of the Basin every week. The ratio would be about the same as the number of kids in your school who decide to become drug dealers to those who don't."

I wiped my eyes again, liking his answer, maybe. I said more quietly, "He found drugs in my dad's desk."

I could hear him riffling pages in the book.

"What, this? Big, bad marijuana? I've smoked a few pipes with your father," he said, which snapped my head up. "And your mother, too. Yes, Mommy, too! They were in college. Going to parties thrown by the oceanographers. I was forty-two, having a hard time growing up, I guess. Vietnam can do that to you." He chuckled, then tossed the book back on the couch. "Who knows, maybe it had been there for eight years. I'm surprised your brother didn't have it analyzed."

There was a ring of disgust in his cackle. "However I'm shocking you about the venial sins of your parents' youth, the truth is, it was a major leap of faith for your brother to go from a sandwich bag to 'importing with the intent to distribute.' The only place he's *not* taking a major leap is in noting the close proximity of a DEA search to their actual disappearance."

Well, that was a hard thing to call a coincidence. I tried to think of myself as somebody else—somebody not related to my mom and dad. It would have looked like a hell of a coincidence—enough to make me scoff quietly, the way Emmett did at the widow Riley's story.

"It's a leap of faith for him to dismiss your old friend The She," he said. "How about that?"

I dropped my forehead into my hand, taking one final big breath and letting it out. "Don't even go there. Don't freak me out like that."

"I believe I told you last time I absolutely believe in The She."

"No." I only smacked the table this time. "You said it's possible there's some 'dark force' over the water."

"Let's not get into a semantic argument. Whatever you want to call it. Perhaps the artists' renditions are a bit on the dramatic side."

"Well, I don't believe in The She!" I hopped in the chair. "At least I'm trying not to! There's only so far that

I can go and feel like a sane person! You can't live your life like you're in some sort of psycho altered state!"

Mr. Church scrunched his eyebrows like maybe he couldn't figure out my point. "Do you believe in God?"

"I suppose," I said.

"Do you believe in angels?"

I shrugged. "Probably not."

"Why not?"

I watched him for a minute, trying to decide why not. "Because they're too much like leprechauns or elves or fairy godmothers."

"And what does 'God' sound like? What's the difference? Why accept one bigger force of goodness without the smaller ones? On what grounds are you dismissing one and preserving the other?"

I dropped my head onto the table. "You sound like Emmett."

"Do I? At times there's a razor-thin line between truth and insanity. You have to hit it just right. Your brother would have to believe this: *Opposites need each other.* If you choose to believe in a force of good, you would also have to choose to believe in a force of evil. Because without the concept of *evil* to help define it, the concept of *good* would be all but valueless. Do you understand?"

I watched him retreat to the stove, shaking my head in awe and exhaustion. "What do you do, sit out here your whole life and ponder all sorts of weirdness?"

"*Mmm*...I fish and crab, too." He shook around a

pot filled with water that was steaming. "Sorry, I don't have any marshmallows."

He was trying to be funny, I guess, but my head was too busy trying to pull some sense out of his twisting train of thought. "You can't be saying that...if I believe in God, I have to believe in The She?"

"No, I'm saying if you believe in a force of good, you can't be dismissive of a force of evil. I'm not saying it has to bear fangs and rise out of the deep and shriek. But I've heard enough about that shrieking, lord knows. If I'm going to believe in a dark force over the water, why not believe it has a will, and a character, and can choose to expel an audible sound? On what grounds would I dismiss that?"

I looked at Grey, who looked blankly from me to Mr. Church, but her eyes rolled a little anxiously as they fell again.

"I think there's a scientific explanation for that noise, and someday they'll find it," I said, for her sake as much as anything.

"Scientific explanations. Philosophic explanations. Did you know we're not even sure the universe actually runs on a mathematical system of tens? Our own numbers, which are the basis of proof for most everything these days, are just a theory. The application of them is a leap of faith. Your brother's not so different from Bloody Mary."

I didn't feel like standing up for Emmett right now, though I didn't laugh at him, either. I watched Mr. Church dump boiling water into a cup, put powdered chocolate on top, and look around at the counter. I guess he was looking for a spoon he couldn't find, because he finally stirred the cocoa with a pen. His hands looked so incredibly normal. Just weathered hands that had pulled on a lot of rods and traps and nets. I watched one wrap around the cup as he brought it over to me.

"What's up with your hands, Mr. Church?" I was still thinking hazily of them as having some extreme power of suggestion on the human mind. He had been beating up on Emmett's arguments enough that I could almost be curious about them again, though I was very skeptical. I still had the memory of how they had turned my body kind of cold all the way through. It was interesting, if nothing else. "When did you first start using them that way?"

He put the cup down in front of me, and I wrapped my hand around it to get my fingers warmer. They weren't icy, just clammy. The place was a lot warmer than you would think. There was a woodstove inside the fireplace, and it was huffing and charging full force.

"When I was a prisoner of war, three or four South Vietnamese prisoners were being held there along with the Americans, and I noticed them doing this thing—clapping their hands, rubbing them together, and pressing them to one another's heads. I finally asked what it was all about, and they said it helped them see their families and what they were doing."

"And you just believed them?"

He raised his eyebrows and let them fall again. "Not at first. But there was a Mrs. Church back then. I missed her, and I wanted to know what she was up to."

"So...all the Americans started doing it?"

"They tried. After a time. It's amazing what you'll believe when your discharge date is three months behind you and yet you're still in Vietnam. I don't think it worked for too many of them. In fact, I may have been the only one."

I looked him up and down as he shrugged, like the explanation for that was beyond him.

"How do you know it worked?"

"I wouldn't say it worked in the sense that I got any gratification out of it. I discovered through those experiences that my wife had left me for a man I used to work with. If nothing else, it helped prepare me for coming home to no one."

"You saw your wife with somebody else? While you were a POW?" *That kind of sucks,* I figured, watching him nod, then I remembered what I was supposed to be arguing for. I found myself leaning to the side and saying, "Oh, bullshit."

I kind of flinched at the sound of it, but it had felt like such a natural thing to say.

He raised his eyebrows again, like he was used to responses like that. "You see, to *know* and to *prove* are two different things. You can see that, can't you?"

I shook my head after a minute, more focused on the

idea that I was more insane *this* year than when I had come here last year. Then, I'd come across the bay to Sassafras, imagining that the water was going to suddenly part and some hag was going to thrust herself out of a whirlpool and shriek, "I've long been waiting for you!"

I hadn't heard Emmett's little theories on that trip. On this trip I'd spent a couple of moments hoping that The She *would* rise out of the back bays and start showering me with salt and garlic. Believing in The She was better than believing in the DEA, I figured. I was twice as psycho this year.

"Maybe your brother needs to remember things a certain way, too."

"My brother"—I flopped my head onto my hand, figuring I could crawl onto the floor and fall asleep in front of his fireplace—"is the most honest person I have ever known."

"He's a great kid," Mr. Church agreed softly, almost inaudibly, but I flipped my eyes up, out onto the meadows at the use of the word *kid*. Emmett was twenty-five. I hadn't heard anyone call him a kid in a long time. I wondered if Church had said it that way on purpose. It made me remember Emmett's face when he was a kid in a laughing, carefree house, where the people seemed so not entirely upright...but just kind of—

"Emmett, if you do that again at my table, you're gonna wear my food instead of eat it."

"It was the dog, Mom!" He's laughing down at Otis, who's crashed out on the floor, banging his seventeen-year-old tail against the tile. Otis doesn't care what he gets blamed for.

Mom scoots her chair back and marches over to the counter, while we crack up. Dad calls it the joys of living with three men, but she just doesn't think we're funny. She gets mad. We wait till her back is turned, and thumbs fly to foreheads.

"You ate it," Dad says.

"No, you ate it."

"You ate it."

"Well, since you all ate it, I guess you're too stuffed for dessert. Otis, you want blueberry pie, my man?" She lets him eat some off her fork. That's one of their tricks.

"But, Mommy! I didn't eat it this time!"

Emmett and Dad look at me, and they both crack up. Dad's turning to look in stunned awe at Mom, who's down on her knees. She's holding a long piece of piecrust between her lips, and Otis sticks his graying snout over the whole thing. Their lips meet.

"Your mother is having a supreme moment of hypocrisy, men. I think this means we all get pie...regardless of who ate what."

Mom pulls this ritual with Otis about every other night, but Dad is always stunned by it. He's looking at them, not us, so Emmett takes advantage. He leans across the table so his smile's right in my face.

"You always eat it, you rancid little wet fart."

"Emmett. He wasn't always like he is. He used to be fun. What...made him like this?"

"I don't know."

I don't bother to look at Mr. Church reciting his famous last words. "I mean, it's not that he's not fun sometimes now..." I thought of him laughing at one of Mrs. Ashaad's jokes. He smiled a lot. He laughed once in a while. "Maybe *fun* isn't the right word. Maybe he never really is fun anymore. He's just...pleasant. So he fools you."

"What does he do for fun?" Mr. Church asked.

It took me a minute to think of anything. "He watches *SpongeBob SquarePants*." I could feel my eyes locking in the sockets from the exhaustion of seeing memories. I just stared into the table. "He's obsessed with the fact that when SpongeBob gets full of water and blows up ten times his size, his teeth get bigger, too."

I started to laugh a little but my smile only crawled up halfway when—

—I drop the shoe box so I can put my fingers to my ears, but I'm stepping all over navy men and I'm heavy and my heavy arms won't reach my head. I know The She—

The closer I get to Dad's office, the louder her shrieking gets.

"...we have a list...We are being...sucked— Mayday, Mayday!"

I jumped out of the chair, heard the mug spill over, but I was pressing the palms of my hands to my eyes, to keep everything black. "What is *wrong* with me, with my brain?"

"What are you thinking?" His voice came quietly right in my face.

"I keep having these memories, today and yesterday! They come out of nowhere! I don't want to go there, I—"

"I'd say that's normal, after you hear news that shocks you."

"I don't want to see my parents like Emmett sees them! I don't want to remember them that way! What if I remember them that way?"

"What if you don't?"

The shrieking mixes with her voice while she's talking to me, to Dad, it's all mixed together. "Oh, shit, we got the baby, Wade! Evan! Tell Emmett to... Wade! What the hell is that? Over the port stern! Look with your eyes! Mother of God!"

"She said, 'Mother of God.'"

I could feel his hands on my arms—normal hands, nothing cold or magical. But I wouldn't stop digging at my eyeballs with my palms.

"So?" Church said.

"So, that is one hell of a damn thing for someone to say who's trying to lie their way out of trouble! She's got to bring the Mother of God into it?" I yelled.

It proved nothing, which left me more frustrated, more harshly pushing on my eyeballs, but this time, it was for wanting to see something, not wanting to black it out. I was just too curious.

"Emmeeeeeeeettt!" I'm a whale, trying to climb stairs on a tail fin. I'm stuck in slow motion. Screaming in whale. *"Emmeeeeeeeettt!*

"Come down here!" I'm falling backward, blacking out, stumbling backward one-two-four stairs...gripping the railing. I'm all but lying on it, hearing my dad's words... "He's not a big baby, Mary Ellen! He's just got a big imagination! He'll be better than Emmett in a crisis, I'm telling you—"

And I'm crying like a two-year-old baby, but I'm gripping that railing. The shrieking has stopped. The wind still whips up there, but I'm back to myself, out of the whale's body, or whatever makes me so heavy when the shrieking comes. I'm going up and up till I see the door....

"Aw, shit...I don't think I actually did black out!" It's still gray, though I see traces of Mr. Church's head in deep gray with a light gray halo around it. "I don't think I did!"

He asked, "Why is that so upsetting?"

"Because! It's in Emmett's journal that way! He said I came to the widow's walk and got him! I was thinking he remembered it wrong. Why is he always right? Why am I always wrong?"

"I don't think that's always true."

I let the damn thing roll as—*the wind is dying a little, but it's turning me to ice so I can't scream, can't distract Emmett, who is watching the sea and speaking in a low voice, and I think he's got Opa on the cordless.*

"Emmett!" *He won't listen to me, won't look. I shake*

him. "She's shrieking. She's taking the Goliath! Listen to me!"

He's turning. I can see the whites of his eyes. His mouth is still moving a little.

There's no cordless. There's only a piece of paper in his hand, the one that he'd taken out of Dad's desk. It blows from his hand, flies through the sleet, and disappears over the bayberry trees toward the roaring surf. He darts past me and takes the stairs down two at a time.

My laughter peeled out, sounding strangely out of place and irreverent alongside this terrible memory. I didn't know why I was laughing, except that I could jump into my brother's skin sometimes, and I could feel his future embarrassment over this moment, and somehow it struck me funny. "Dad taught him to recite the captain's prayer three times, then spit off the widow's walk...try to hit the sea. That's what he was doing. He wasn't in the shower."

I was all but squawking like a chicken, and Mr. Church ignored it.

"And then what?"

I shut up, got serious, because he was *punching the phone buttons. I'm hearing water crashing, a deluge, and loud bangs and growling and snarling and crunching, and my mom screaming a Mayday. Coordinates. I'm grabbing a pencil, writing them while Mom screams for my dad to shut up and do something. Emmett backs into me, pressing buttons on the cordless.*

He screams, "Shit!" at the top of his lungs. His fingers are shaking too hard. He keeps dialing the number wrong.

My dad's voice wails from far off as Emmett dials again. "Yea...walk...shadow of death..."

"Goddamn it!" Emmett hurls the phone into the corner and runs from the room. I pick up the corded phone on the wall in the kitchen. I call the operator. Get the Coast Guard. They hear a little kid's trembling voice talking about The She. They hang up. I run to Dad's office, get the cordless Emmett just threw. I get the operator back as I'm climbing the stairs, get the Coast Guard again.

Emmett's screaming on the widow's walk again. I'm trying to shut him up so he'll speak to the Coast Guard, but he won't stop yelling.

"Give them back, you fucking bitch! You fucking whore, I'll kill you myself! I'm going to kill you, you cocksucking whore!"

The story was banging all over the cabin, and after seeing the stunned looks on Grey's and Mr. Church's faces, I flopped in the chair and shoved my own stunned face into my hands.

THIRTEEN

Nobody said anything for the longest time. Then Grey muttered something about, "You're going to drown yourself in bodily fluids," and she had gotten a tissue and was actually wiping up my chin—spit, or maybe it was snot even. I guess they were waiting for me to say something, but I didn't want to cut up on Emmett. I could feel my brother's terror pulsing through my veins, and I remembered as a kid that he had had moments when he could believe in The She—even more than I had.

"Emmett, next time you hit your brother, your father's going to hold you down and I'm going to hit you. You understand?"

"I didn't hurt him, Mom! He just skeeves me out, always looking out that window at night, listening for spooks. He gets me so jumpy! It's disgusting!"

I wouldn't have gotten him jumpy over something he didn't believe in himself—at least at very tense moments.

"He did say not everything was in that book," I finally said, though it was hard to defend him for leaving out parts that would be personally embarrassing.

"I wouldn't call that omission a terrible thing, necessarily," Mr. Church said, quietly. "Maybe he felt guilty and…stupid afterward. Those are hard emotions to write about, especially in light of his probable thought that he had lost valuable time, which might have saved them, when he panicked."

"Stupid…" My cackle sounded way crazed. *Guess he never made that mistake again!*

Church said nothing, but I could read some sort of victory sparkle in his eyes.

"He couldn't have saved them," I added quickly. "The Coast Guard can't beam up like on *Star Trek*."

"Is *he* convinced he couldn't save them?"

"Well, *he's* convinced they died off the Florida shoals after—" I stopped. Then I laughed more, taking the Lord's name in vain a few times. *That kind of lets him off the hook, doesn't it?*

But I was already shaking my head, already trying to disagree with myself. I couldn't get myself to believe my brother would ever fall victim to bad thinking. Especially not with Aunt Mel there looking after him.

"You know, you get me so turned around," I said to Mr. Church. "And I don't understand how you can sound so confident. You admitted a while ago that you sit out here and dream up these savvy little speeches you give."

He shrugged, and I wondered if it was even possible to make him feel insulted.

"But you've got nothing. *Nothing*. No mountain of facts, no evidence," I said.

"I'm sorry if I sound so sure, because I really don't know." Church faced out the window. "Except that I knew your mother and father. I knew Connor Riley, too. They were apples and an orange. You put two sea captains together on the beach in a downtime game of Frisbee; sometimes they look so much alike. They're both laughing, playing jock, cursing like the seamen they are. But you know what I'm talking about. Some people, you see into them, you know they have a soul. Others... you're not so sure. Do you have to be able to *prove* those insights before they become valuable to you?"

I didn't plan on answering, but out of my mouth came, "No."

Enough thinking. I was not a thinker. Church was standing there waiting, too nice, too, too nice. I figured he should have stayed a shrink. The world was missing out on a decent shrink. And he was reminding me of Santa Claus somehow, or of someone actually better. You couldn't insult Santa Claus and expect him to be all, "Oh, well." I felt I could sit by him and give him a wish list, like a kid in need. He was old, and long past Emmett's and Aunt Mel's age of hungriness to become something other than who he was. He had nothing better to do, it seemed, than just be, and get absorbed in whatever problems fell through his door.

"I would like to take a boat ride out to the canyon," I told him. "I want to see the place where they died."

Two-thirty in the afternoon—we were heading out of the harbor between East Hook and West Hook toward the open sea in Mr. Church's thirty-one-foot Tiara, the *Hope Wainwright*. It was named after his mother, he said, one of the two women he'd ever loved. He was better than Santa Claus. He had just waved me off when I promised reimbursement for his fuel, which would probably cost around two hundred dollars, and he had more gadgets and computerized screens on his dash than I had ever remembered seeing on the *Goliath,* which had been more than three hundred feet long. The gadgets gave me a mild feeling of safety. Though I did have my moments of paranoia passing through the harbor, they had nothing to do with the things I felt sure I would have feared most—going four hours past the horizon, getting seasick, or memorializing the dead.

My paranoia had to do, first, with passing my grandfather's house, with so many windows, and I was sure Emmett was looking out of one. Mr. Church had called Opa and told him he was taking me to the canyon, at which point he put me on the phone. I was surprised that Opa didn't object, considering what month this was. He said there was a "warm-water eddy over the shelf" that day, a term I had forgotten, but supposedly it meant we would have smooth sailing. I thought I detected some sort of gladness in his voice as he said, "Wish I had the health, I might join you." I told him not to tell Emmett, and he had said he wasn't that inconsiderate.

My other paranoia had to do with Grey, who had insisted on coming, and I didn't have the heart to stop her, considering I had taken up her whole time with Mr. Church. I had nudged him when she'd gone into the hoagie store to pick up lunch and told him she'd been at Saint Elizabeth's with some kind of panic disorder, and I wasn't sure this trip was a great idea. I had totally forgotten that he had an MSW. He had just shrugged it off, saying something like, "Well, if she's on an antidepressant, she probably shouldn't take Dramamine. Make sure she has a cast-iron stomach." I had seen Grey drink us all under the table, and I thought her stomach could probably hold its own.

Mr. Church paused at the drawbridge, and it opened up for us, sending the roadway straight into the air. We got a little wave from the drawbridge operator, whose name came floating back out of nowhere—Mr. Tommy Downs. I also remembered that my dad used to honk his thanks when we came through the passage in his own fishing boat, so I moved up beside Mr. Church to push the horn button. He must have thought I wanted to take the helm, because he stepped back, gestured at the dash, and before I knew it I had the wheel, and he was honking.

It felt weird gripping the wheel, and something made me turn and look back. Mr. Downs was out of the gate-house with his hands on the railing, just staring. Then I watched him do this thing that sent my heart into my sneakers. I knew why I had looked back. He put two fingers to his forehead and made a wide circle with his right hand.

"You see that salute, Evan? That's for Barretts only. That's for you, little man. Me and you and twelve generations. Give 'im a high one."

I kind of raised four fingers, and dropped them, taking in a glance of Grey with her feet on the stern, hands in her pockets, ski hat on her head, staring into the afternoon sun. She had a bouquet of flowers beside her that she'd picked up at the flower store beside Mac's, the hoagie place. She hadn't said why she bought them. I turned and stared out over the wheel, hoping she wasn't planning on giving them to me for some reason. This drawbridge thing with all the pomp from Mr. Downs was freaky enough.

What amazed me most was how much I remembered, just from my dad letting me drive the *Goliath* and the *MaryEl,* his smaller boat used for fishing. We had a following sea getting out of the harbor, with good-size swells, maybe eight-foot, charging up on us, and I somehow remembered to speed up and ride one's back so the next wouldn't catch us. When we hit the sea, the swells came at us, and I remembered to tack them. Basically the water was calm when we hit open water, and my eyes fell to a compass. The canyon was to the southeast, eighty-five miles, and I watched Mr. Church set the path on the loran receiver. He pointed out a few things I didn't remember, and then I just tried to feel under the boat for currents that would need a little fight and watch for swell patterns. I guess you could say it was like getting back on a bike.

I drove like that for two hours, hitting little more than four-foot swells. Pretty soon after we reached open sea, Mr. Church left me and sat at the stern, eating hoagies with Grey. They had started an ear-to-mouth conversation, which I hoped was about her and her Girl Scout. I felt like a pig, stealing all her time back on Sassafras, but she looked strangely not-angry, almost as if my own problems were some sort of sponge that sopped the problems out of her. I saw them laugh a couple of times.

I didn't eat my hoagie, and I felt glad after two hours on the water. I got this problem I figured I should have thought about before I left shore. I had seen the Dramamine Mr. Church had swiped at in the cabin when I mentioned Grey's problem. It was the old-fashioned kind that makes you want to crash out, and I thought about the little packet Emmett had thrown into his overnight bag with a chuckle. Emmett's was the newer stuff, the kind that lets you stay completely awake. It was there, and I was here, and every swell I had to face was suddenly turning my stomach to sludge.

About four-thirty in the afternoon, I shouted for Mr. Church and made a motion toward the cabin, because I also had to pee. He took the helm. I stared into the cabin head after I went, wondering how soon I would have to drop to my knees.

When I came out, Grey was inside, sitting in the

kitchen booth with her ski hat on the table beside her mittens. She was blowing on her fingertips.

I sat down across from her, taking off my own ski hat and pinching my earlobes.

"You seasick or anything?" I asked, hoping I might not be alone in my idiocy. She had shut the door to the outside, and you could barely hear the engines.

"*Moi?*" She gazed at me. "You've got to be kidding. The only way my parents could ever get me off a boat in the summer was with a set of fins and a scuba tank."

"Really? You dive?"

"Dived my first wreck when I was eleven. Yup." She nodded. "I've done two or three a season every year since."

I nodded, remembering you had to be ten before you could take the scuba course at the Ocean Life Center in West Hook. I'd left after school ended in June of fourth grade, the first year I would have been able to take it.

"Maybe you can teach me sometime," I said, swallowing green.

She watched me for a minute and cracked up. "You know, I'm famous around school for three things: my partying, my downhill skiing, and my scuba diving. You wouldn't know about that last thing, because at the very first party we both went to, people were whispering to me not to talk about the Hooks around you. They said your parents' ship sank with them on it, and you had been a Hook native. They said if you heard any terms associated with salt water, such as *diving,* it would not be a good thing. I was respectful of that."

"You're kidding." I watched her crack up, awkwardly pulling at her mouth over the way she worded it, maybe. I tried to ignore that part. "I had no clue people even thought about it. Not even the most out-of-hand drunk at the most out-of-hand party has ever mentioned my folks."

It freaked me out.

"You've got a lot of friends, Evan Barrett." She grinned. "I won't send this day into the gossip channels when I get back to school, I swear it. But I would love to see people's faces if they could have seen you driving this boat, like you'd just done it yesterday. Didn't you used to go around telling everyone that your grandfather's house made you seasick because of the windows?"

I looked out the little porthole at nothing but blue.

"Dad! I'm really driving this whole boat!"

"You're really driving, little man."

"All by myself!"

"All by yourself."

"You swear? Mr. Lowenberg isn't up on the bridge helping me?"

"I swear on our ancestors."

I jerked my mind to the present and decided to take the high road with some humility instead of the low road about my driving prowess. "Yeah, it's true about Opa's house making me seasick. In fact, I'm very seasick right now. If I don't hurl, it's going to be a miracle."

That totally cracked her up, to where she was slumped over sideways, laughing into her sleeve. She sat up.

"You want some Dramamine?"

I suddenly had a clear recollection of my dad's opinion of Dramamine. A guy taking Dramamine to go to the canyon was like a guy wearing black socks with sneakers. We used to laugh quietly among the family on some fishing trips when he was off for a few days and taking some buyer out to catch marlin. Buyers were notoriously bad seamen, and Dad used to lecture me, "Now, don't laugh in Mr. So-and-So's face, but you can go tell him about the seaweed pie we eat in graphic detail, hee ha..."

"I think I'd rather ralph," I told her frankly.

She just shrugged. "Nothing I haven't seen you do before."

I flinched a little, thinking of a couple of parties I'd gone to as an underclassman where I'd paid a loud visit to the bushes, and I wondered which one she'd been at. I hadn't been thinking about the night she slipped me acid, because I hadn't hit the bush—at least not to my recollection.

I was wondering if maybe I should rethink those memories when she asked, "So, you still mad at me?"

I didn't answer her directly. "Well, you seem to be handling very diplomatically the fact that I stole your whole therapy session this morning. After you drove down from Philly for it, and I just walked across a bridge, having come down in a limo to eat turkey and lobster tails."

She waved her hand like it didn't matter, but she didn't look entirely happy when she said, "I get to talk about my problems all day up at Saint Elizabeth's. That's all I do. Dwell on my problems. So today I get to dwell on your problems. I call that a nice break in the action."

I grinned in relief.

"I would like to have seen one of those hands-on thingamabobs that Mr. Church did to you last year. It would have put the icing on the cake." She ran her fingers through her hair and looked a little more serious. "Truthfully, I wouldn't mind him rapping on my head a little bit. If I could see the bottom of the deep right now…if I could see a dead body down there…it might at least keep me from seeing some huge sea hag chomping down on somebody I actually knew. What happens after she bites you in half? Are you dead or alive in that neat little hole under the canyon floor?"

"Grey."

"Sorry." She glanced toward my knees and then frontward again. "But I don't think I'm repeating any thoughts that you haven't already enjoyed for yourself. Especially right about now. You go over to see Mr. Church. He takes your brain apart, and then it's time to go look for the dead. What do you have now? First you thought it was a wave. Then you thought it was the Colombian mafia. Now? Based on what you see and hear from around the Hooks, you actually have more evidence that it's a witch than a wave that ate your mom and dad."

"Grey." I rubbed my eyes.

She pinched her face with her fingers to break her smile and rolled her eyes like she was sorry. "I'm actually overdue for a dose of Xanax. I can take it every four hours, and it's been"—she glanced at her Ripcurl watch—"six hours, and the sky hasn't fallen." She glanced across the ceiling. "I may actually be licking this panic disorder thing. If you can put up with my mouth."

"Uh, maybe it's not time yet to be such a hero," I said, trying not to roll my eyes.

"In other words, I'm driving you crazy."

I tried to find words that didn't totally bite. "You're about a twelve on the bluntness scale right now. I think I could handle you at your usual six or seven."

With that she grabbed for this little handbag she'd strung across herself under her jacket, tore open the zipper, and brought out a prescription bottle. She stared at it for a minute, then gripped it tightly in her dropped fist. "I've been talking with my therapist about how I've had terrible symptoms for years, actually. I would feel myself starting to... croak, or spin out, or lose oxygen, whatever. And I could put off the inevitable by making some cutting remark. By, like, hurting somebody."

I watched her tap her knuckles on the table while gripping the bottle, kind of lost in thought. "Seriously. When I was around ten, I only used to do it when my feelings got hurt. I was really sensitive, I guess, and would level back at somebody who made me feel cut to shreds. I don't know how it got to be such a compulsion. The doctor says it doesn't matter, but—"

She shoved the bottle back in her bag. "I really don't want to. You don't know how much this means to me. Not being on anything. *Nothing*. Not alcohol, not sleeping pills, not nothing. I'll try harder. If I say anything wicked, just kick me, okay?"

She looked deadly serious, and I had to smile. I admired her guts.

"And let's talk about your life, not mine. It's so much more interesting. Your intuition is very, very cool. I wasn't even scared coming out here today. Did I tell you my book calls this She-Devil Month? I don't know, I just thought if anything was going to happen, your gut wouldn't have brought you this far."

My parents and the Riley boat had disappeared in November, I remembered. But I felt pretty safe today. "My brother says my intuition is mostly just picking up on fine details that others miss, and putting them together in a flash. I feel safe because...she's a rare visitor to the surface, whoever or whatever she is. I didn't hear the noise a lot as a kid. Maybe four or five times at the most. I'd hear her and have this strange heaviness in my limbs." I shook my fingers out, trying not to remember how heavy I'd felt while running up the stairs for Emmett the night my parents disappeared. "But I haven't felt or heard a thing, and this time of year, there're freighters whizzing through the canyon at all hours. Nothing happens to them. It's kind of like...a very safe game of Russian roulette."

She watched me for a few moments. "So, then...what are you expecting to find out there, Evan Barrett?"

"I don't know. I know it's just water...very, very deep water. With probably a hundred wrecks at the bottom."

I don't know exactly what pushed my stomach buttons, either the thought of so much water or some of the things she'd just said in that Grey Shailey frank way. I excused myself to the little bathroom, slammed the door, and got sick in the toilet. I splashed my face off afterward, but there were no paper towels in there so I came out with water dripping down my face.

"Feel better?" She cracked up, pounding her fist on the tabletop. Then she reached behind my head for something, and came around with a tissue between two fingers.

"Fine. Enjoy yourself." I snatched it, wiped my face, feeling better—empty is better than green. I watched her laugh. "Actually, Grey, you look good today. It must be that cold air working in your lungs. I would not at this moment peg you for the sick person I saw...lord. Was it only two days ago?"

"*Salt* air working on my lungs. Being back on the water really helps me, I think. And I think there's something to this whole KHK concept Mrs. Ashaad dreamed up. It's like, you weren't only supposed to help me. I was supposed to help you somehow." She laughed. "I think Mrs. Ashaad meant that I was supposed to help your heart grow two sizes or something, which is not what I have in mind in the way of helping you."

"Putting up with me is great of you. I don't think there's much else you can do." It hadn't occurred to me that she was either getting something out of this or thinking of doing something to help me.

"Well, if nothing else, I brought flowers. When we get over the spot where you think your parents died, you'll get a rush out of throwing them. Two years ago I threw a stick out on a frozen lake for my dog to chase. He fell through the ice. I almost drowned trying to save him, but he never resurfaced." She got a far-off look, the first I'd seen on this boat that she might be spiraling into depression.

"That's horrible."

"Yeah, try watching your dog die when he's the only friend you have in your own house." She swallowed and went on almost too quickly. "At any rate, Mr. Maddox is the ultimate snooze teacher, but he's nice outside of class. He dragged the story out of me, took me down there. We threw flowers out onto the ice, made a little memorial on the bank there. Just a stupid ritual that wouldn't bring Gonzo back. But it really helped, somehow...I don't know how. It just did."

That explained the flowers. I figured it would be very hard to throw flowers out there, but my gut told me she was right. I just couldn't think about it too much, because she raised her eyes to mine with some determined look that resembled the hardness I was used to seeing.

"And there's a better thing I might be able to do. I wanted to see if maybe I couldn't get a bunch of my summer friends together to dive for the wreck. They're mostly older, mostly pros."

I picked up her fingers and squeezed them, deeply moved, actually. "Grey, that is really sweet, but—"

"But what? Tell me the challenges. I am a very stubborn person, and you need to prove something to your brother. And telling me the challenges just makes me more determined sometimes. And less bitchy. I can fight with the problems instead of with people." She pulled her hand away, and I cracked up. It wasn't hard to think of the problems with a dive. I'd actually been thinking about it while I was driving the boat.

"First off, I don't know the exact loran TDs of where they went down. They did give a Mayday, but they gave it over the ship-to-shore, so the Coast Guard wouldn't even have it."

"Why the ship-to-shore?"

"I heard it, and I'd say my mom was freaking, just wasn't thinking. Emmett says they did it intentionally—"

"So, the coordinates are stored in your memory only," she said quickly, like she didn't want to get sidetracked on Emmett.

"I actually have some vague memory now of writing them on something. The wall, maybe. But Opa sends a housekeeper over there every other week. I would imagine they've long been washed off."

"Could Mr. Church help your memory along a little bit?"

I shifted around and flopped my hands on the table. I thought of Mr. Church as some sort of saint right now, but I was going back and forth on whether or not I should believe in his mystical powers. I guess I was trying to be cautious.

"So, what else?" she asked.

"Even if we had the loran TDs, the canyon is a mile deep. The *Goliath* could have landed on the bottom as much as half a mile away from their last coordinates. Finally, the canyon's too deep for divers, Grey. A dive into the canyon would have to be done by a bubble drum. It's a little submarine on a long cable attached to a sizable boat—"

"I know what a bubble drum is. It's expensive."

"Yeah."

"How much are we talking about?"

I flinched, remembering Mr. Shields's comments when he'd quoted his price on a dive and how it would "stop any wayward talk." I realized now he'd been talking about the DEA, not The She. I wondered how many other islanders knew about the scandal and what their opinion was on my parents. Not that it really mattered. I wouldn't have to face them.

"Mr. Shields has some guys he networks with. He quoted me a price of thirty thousand dollars. And if they don't find the wreck, you still have to pay."

"*Thirty thousand?*" She laughed a little, which is what I expected, and so it shocked the hell out of me when she said, "Thirty thousand dollars is actually quite doable."

I thought maybe I'd heard her wrong. "How do you mean? It's not like I can just bust into my trust fund."

"I mean, sometimes we've got more than that just lying around the house."

I watched her look turn from enthusiastic to clouded, though she was managing to keep her grin.

"You're not serious."

"I'm more than serious. I could just...take it. I know all the hiding places. What's my father going to do? Call the police and say his extortion and bribe money was just lifted?" She continued laughing toward the porthole like she really didn't want to look at me.

Extortion and bribe money. I tried telling myself I was dreaming, yet I remembered Chandra's description of Grey's dad, and it seemed like every time I heard something about him, it was something worse than the last thing. I didn't want to stare at her, so I just kept staring out the window, at the blue meeting blue. The sun was starting to sink, but the water was a deep blue, like the sky, so it was hard to tell where the water ended and the horizon started.

I cleared my throat. "I, um, had no idea."

"Most people don't. In fact, I'm not even sure how all he makes his money. Just call him a multifaceted wonder. If it's illegal, he'll do it. Is there a support group for people addicted to breaking rules?" She laughed more at herself, but it sounded forced. She leaned her head on her hand and grabbed a fistful of hair. "He's done money laundering, illegal gambling, extortion, drugs, though I think the drugs are just a hobby to support his own little fun 'n' games. Not that you have to repeat any of that. You know why criminals always end up addicts or alcoholics, Evan?"

I couldn't imagine repeating this to anyone and expecting them to believe it. "No, I don't."

"It's because they have no way to clean up without getting themselves killed. They're afraid to go to shrinks and counselors. They can't tell the truth about themselves to anyone...sometimes not even themselves. I think that's their biggest clog. They're stuck behind their shut mouths, so they have to deaden the pain instead of getting rid of it. That's what my shrink says. I believe it."

"You told your shrink about your dad?"

She bounced a little, taking what looked to be her first shaky breath all afternoon. I watched her glance at her prescription, lying on top of her purse, but she looked away again. "Some. It's one perk of being in a Catholic hospital. The shrinks, they're not only bound to a professional code of silence, they're bound to the Church's. Like priests. It's a good deal. In spite of 'The List.'" She turned her weary eyes and glanced somewhere around my chest. "At any rate, it's a lot harder to bank certain types of money made illegally than you would think. It takes time, if it can go to a bank at all. In the meantime, it sits around for the spending. He thinks I'm blind and stupid like my mother."

"Uh...what if he thought somebody else took it? And somebody else gets their head blown off?"

She shrugged. "Whoever he would blame, believe me, that guy is not on my version of 'The List.' I'd say that's one less subhuman to clutter up our illustrious downtown scenery. Good riddance." She scratched her forehead, looking down at her lap like she'd been caught saying another mean thing and life was too confusing to be anything but comical.

I felt very naive sitting there beside her, but also like maybe I wanted to stay that way. She was living in some sort of cesspool. If I wasn't seeing her fight it in so many ways, I might have gotten the urge to go up and keep Mr. Church company. The situation being what it was, I reached for her hair and ran my fingers through it as she slumped forward with her head on her hand again.

I talked from my gut. "Grey, that's a nice offer. But it just feels all wrong. I'm trying to prove something about my family being *not that way*." They were the best words I could think of, though I watched her more carefully. "It just doesn't feel right using money made illegally, if you know what I'm saying."

Her eyes got heavy, like she was enjoying the head rub but wasn't really hearing me.

"Lord knows, there's enough money in my family. I could talk to my grandfather if I decided I wanted to actually look for a wreck, threaten to empty my trust fund over it, something." Choosing your words carefully is not easy when the person you're talking to is spilling their guts, so I just let fly. "I just don't understand one thing. You've got parents deeply involved in the types of things I want to prove my family had no part of. Why would you want to help me?"

She flopped back in her seat, thumping her head against the wall like she was thinking. "It's not like I want to turn on my family, or wish that my family weren't my family, or wish that my family were *your* family, even if they were dead, or something noble like that." She shut her eyes. "One night when I was about eleven, I got up in the middle of the night for a drink or something. I looked down over the banister, and my dad was down there talking to some guy, and he gave the guy a gun. I saw it. I'd known about his guns since I was little, but I thought, *My dad not only owns guns, but he tells big men how and when to use them. That is cool. That's so powerful.* I always saw him as very cool and powerful. And maybe I still would. The problem is, a couple of times he's pushed me too far. I don't care how old you are, or how powerful. You get a decent coke high, you get stupid. And that's all I want to say about that."

She shut her eyes and thumped her head a couple of more times. She hadn't exactly answered my question, but I thought of Chandra's little tale about her father lending her out. *What in hell kind of a life am I sitting across from?* When Grey had her eyes shut like that, you couldn't see so much of her hardness. It was still there, in her leg pulled up on the seat, in her arm draped over her knee, in her suede jacket, ski sweater, or clunky snow boots. There was nothing overly feminine there, no high heels, long nails, boufed-out hair, or other stereotypes of a mafia don's daughter. Without her eyes to sharpen her face, she looked like a pixie or an angel.

I tried what I thought was a better way to get her mood back.

"Maybe the *Goliath* foundered on the shelf. That's only a hundred and twenty-five feet down. I'll do some more checking around this weekend and see what I can find out. If that's what we decide, then you can teach me how to dive, and we'll dive it together, next summer."

"You're not diving it, no matter what, Barrett." She never opened her eyes, and her words sounded a little slurry, like she might be dozing off all of a sudden. "There's dead people down there. Do you want to be right on top of us when we start bagging femurs?"

Definitely, her mood was spiraling again. I figured maybe I should leave her, let her take a nap or something.

"You want to go lie on the bunk? Up in the bow? It's kind of cozy."

She didn't answer but started knocking her head into the paneling again in a way that looked like it could actually hurt. "Grey, you're not looking so good all of a sudden. Go on, lie down for a while."

"Least *I'm* not puking." A little smile spread out on her face, which I took as a good sign, until she went on. "And I'm just sitting here thinking about it. And even if it is possible, I'm not sure I'm a person who should be diving the wreck of the *Goliath*. Even if it is on the shelf."

"You were doing okay a few minutes ago, if we're right and what helps me helps you."

"Yeah, but I thought I could help because I love to dive wrecks. I never told you *why* I love to dive wrecks." She looked at me with those dangerous eyes and half grin, and never broke her stare as she eased herself to the edge of the booth. "It just gives me some insanely great pleasure to see what happens to people whose lives are more thoroughly down the toilet than my own."

She got to her feet and went into the bow, laughing to herself. I stood up slowly, staring at my sneakers.

FOURTEEN

I got sick again off the stern before we came into the canyon, but not even that completely distracted me from this feeling of having left the planet Earth altogether. I had climbed up on the bridge a couple of times as the sun set behind me. I wanted to get a better grip on what it felt like to look as far as you could in any direction and see only water. It was a wide-open feeling—and yet a closed-in feeling, like you're inside some giant, strangely lit shell that's sewn together all around by the horizon.

At dusk it was a multicolored shell, with purples and blacks at one end, and reds, turquoises, yellows, and oranges at the other. Then complete darkness finally fell. It was like being in a black bubble, except the top part of the shell was covered in enormous white dots. I had totally forgotten how the stars were like flashlights out here on a clear night. The wind was kind of a bitch. It came and went in freezing-cold gusts, working against the closed-in feeling and reminding me that we were a microscopic dot on one of the largest bodies of water on earth. It was humbling.

Finally, Mr. Church cut the engine down to idle and came back and stood next to me.

"Here we are."

I did not feel anything, really. I couldn't sense my parents underneath me, couldn't sense any sunken ship calling out to me from the depths. All I felt was icy wind.

"Now what do we do?" I asked him.

"I don't know."

He was looking at me like I should know. I walked to the side of the *Hope Wainwright* and looked down into the black.

"That stuff, that black that's lapping onto the side of the boat? It's hard to conceive that it's more than a mile deep."

"Actually, we're right on the edge of the shelf. If we go another quarter mile out, the depth will drop that drastically. It's a little rough here. We can cross over if you want, and the sea will get a little calmer, perhaps."

I could see white neon-like stripes out in front of the *Hope,* which sometimes mean you're at the edge of the shelf. I shook my head, then nodded, then shook it again. I didn't know what to do, what I was supposed to be feeling. I was amazed at how this could feel like a normal fishing trip. I really thought that once I got out here, I'd sense the *Goliath* calling me from this direction or that, or some feeling like The She was watching.

Grey came out of the cabin, holding her flowers, and I kind of wished she had stayed asleep. The cutting of the engines must have woken her. I didn't feel like trying to talk to her right now, knowing she might get some sort of gratification out of lives having been ruined worse than hers. Her mouth could curl your hair.

"Did you have a nice rest?" Mr. Church asked her.

"I love sleeping on boats. Thanks." She looked a little better in the lights on deck—less likely to bite.

Did you take your meds? I fought the urge to ask her that, and tried, from the inner depths of my bones, to be someone Mrs. Ashaad would think highly of. I tried reminding myself that this girl had been mauled by old men at her father's request, that she was trying to be better than the cesspool she was living in. It didn't take much more. I was reaching out, pulling her hat down further over her ears, and taking the flowers so she could put on her mittens.

I only said, "Please, try not to say anything awful."

"Okay, I will." She pulled on her mittens.

"Where do you want to go, Evan?" Mr. Church asked, moving back to the helm. "You want to drive?"

"Why not?" I took the helm, gripped the steering wheel, pushed the throttle forward slightly, and we moved slowly across the whitecaps into the canyon. The water ahead was pitch-black, and with pitch-black below and flashlights above in any direction you looked, I got a very free feeling, probably ten times greater than driving on a giant blacktop with no lines and no end in sight. I kept my eyes off the dash intentionally, just to see where my gut might land us. But I could not lose my sense of direction, no matter how I tried to ignore it. I felt myself pulling southeast, though the wind whipped up behind us, sending its icy breath down my neck and onto my back.

It's like I could feel that shelf finally drop, drop, drop, like I was driving a tiny speck over the top of an entire black world, one full of black mountains and black valleys and black hills and black life-forms.

"My folks, they're definitely down there. I just know it." I looked almost straight up as I let the *Hope* pitch forward and take on the swells without using my eyes, and I felt Church come up close behind me. The back of my head was in his chest, and I could feel energy barreling off him. It was so free out here, so free of lights and brick and concrete and horns and cars and floor and ceiling and books and opinions.

I felt free to shed all the shit off my skin, the invisible chains, the things I realized I'd been so subtly taught never to forget—like how to be skeptical. I could even shed my love of Emmett out here, or at least shed those parts that had always made me feel a little bit ashamed of myself, like I didn't measure up intellectually.

"Where are we going?" I said above the engines, but since Church was right behind me, I knew he could hear it.

"You tell me."

"No, you tell me. Come on. Do it, please."

He backed up so I almost fell backward when the *Hope* hit a swell I couldn't see or didn't care about. But then I heard a crack and his hot palms swallowed my temples, seemed to meet in the center of my head. It was keeping me standing. I didn't get that chill through me this time. Maybe I was chilled through to the max anyway. It felt like nothing—like normal, like my whole brain relaxed just a little bit more, like nature taking its course out here in the ultimate core of nature, and the right memories could just drop down off the dusty part of my brain with maybe a little extra clarity. I didn't even care whether it was mystical or right out of some standard psychology textbook.

I only cared that—*I'm writing shit on the wall of Dad's office and my pencil breaks but there's a purple crayon. My hand is shaking, and I can hardly hear Mom because she's screaming, because Emmett is throwing phones and cursing. Then I'm cursing and crying because the whole thing is impossible. I copy the stupid numbers again on a piece of paper, because I'm thinking he broke the cell phone, and the kitchen phone has a cord.*

"East of two-six-six-eight-zero, north of four-two-two-eight-zero. Why did I try to talk to the Coast Guard about the fucking She? Why didn't I keep my mouth shut? They hung up on me! God! Both of us wasted time!"

I had screamed it straight up, and Mr. Church grabbed the wheel on either side of me so I was steadied between his arms.

He said right in my ear, "If two grown adults could pick up the wrong handset, you were certainly entitled! Stop whipping yourself. You were a child!"

He drove like that for another mile, me between his huge arms. I watched the loran TDs on the dash match up with what had just come out of my mouth and still rang in my ears. He pulled the throttle into neutral, cut one of the two engines entirely, and I could hear the waves lapping on the side of the boat.

They drew me over, and I stared into the black, feeling for the *Goliath,* for something spiritual, the voice of my father. I didn't know what I expected to feel, but the old saying of my dad's flashed through my head—"The line between complete joy and complete terror is often thin." I felt absolutely terrified, overwhelmed by something firing at my heart like a blowtorch.

I fell to my knees, heard myself more than felt the words rip loose, "Daddy, tell me you're down there. Tell me you're down there."

Grey was beside me, and her voice was amazingly calm as she thrust a flower into my hand. "Just throw it. Say anything you want. You can talk to them if you want..."

"Scary!" My voice went off again. I might sense they were not down there if I let myself feel anything, and so I pushed at the tears and snot freezing on my face, watching my whole arm shake.

Grey shook my arm and a flower dropped out of my hand and hit the water. She handed me another and said, "Do you have a favorite memorial saying? Memorial prayer? Family saying? You could say that."

"Yeah." I hadn't said a prayer in years, except with a whole group of kids in Mass. So it surprised me when I started in. It was easier to spit out than the captain's prayer, because even as a semi-lapsed Catholic, I had a better idea of where the Mother of God was than where my parents were at the moment. I could hear us all, together, separately, in twos, threes, different bedrooms, different cathedrals in different ports—

"Hail Mary, full of grace, the Lord is with Thee... blessed art thou...Mommy?" She had one of those bloody car accident flights today, and then she paid bills, and now she's tired. I'm shaking her awake. "...Blessed art thou among women, blessed is the fruit of thy womb, Jesus..." It's my voice, and I don't care that she's falling asleep because the real great thing about saying the Hail Mary across the bed with Mommy is that I get to hold hands with her. She's not a kissy, huggy mom like my friends have, so I lure her to me with...

"Holy Mary, Mother of God...getting a whipping from me when we get home, Emmett," Dad mutters, and I'm laughing into my sleeve because Emmett got caught torturing me in Mass again. He can't be still, the usual. He smiles up at the rafters, fifteen, too old to get a whipping from Dad, but he's caught and I'm thrilled out of my tree.

"Pray for us, sinners, now and at the hour of our death," he says pretty loudly, just in case Dad won't find him so old.

"Amen."

I crossed myself with the flower, then tossed it. I was calm again, tossing flower after flower that Grey stuck in my hand, watching my breath come out in steady, icy streams.

"I *know* where my parents are." I knelt there, tossing flowers, kind of amazed at myself, that I thought I would hear my parents' voices coming out of the deep, as if they were stuck down there. If you're brought up religious, I bet you can go for a time and barely think about it, but when you really need it, it punches a hole in the blackness and seems to find you. I didn't understand how my brother came to lose something like that, because it seemed almost to come *at* me, rather than come *from* me. He would say it was my imagination. Well, he was back there, and I was here.

"I don't have to believe Emmett. It's a free country." I could sense the height of illogic in my argument, but I loved it anyway.

Grey was up close to me, wiping my face with a tissue again, thinking I was talking about the *Goliath,* I guess. "Do you think this is where they went down?"

I didn't know what I expected to feel, some sort of knowing that came in some extraordinary way. All I felt was a supreme peace, as unmovable as the iceberg that ruptured the *Titanic.*

"Yeah, this is it. They went down near here."

She stood up, and I heard her exchanging a few words with Mr. Church, but I wasn't listening too well. I reached over the side, put my hands in the icy water, splashed it up on my face, then sunk my hands in up to my wrists, not fighting strongly enough against some urge to stick my whole face into it.

"Jesus Christ, Evan!"

"*Damn* it, boy!"

They were screaming. I was upside down, being pulled at the back of my coat, my legs, until I splattered onto the deck. My face was soaked. I didn't know whether to apologize or not. I wasn't trying to commit suicide, just meet up either with my ancestors or with the water itself, which felt strangely like my possession, my girlfriend, my reflection in the looking glass.

"You crazy Barretts! You've all got a thing about the water!" Mr. Church did not sound contented for once. "If you're going to pull any strange Barrett rituals, don't you do it off my boat! Come here!"

He was pulling me toward the stern, which I crawled to on my knees, then looked over.

"Spit," he told me, and I spit over the stern. "That's what you do when you get an urge like that."

Urge like what? I didn't exactly know what I had done or what I had wanted, but it seemed like something familiar to him. I stared over the stern for the longest time, and finally asked him to cut the engines entirely, just for a couple of minutes, so I could hear nothing but the sea. It was pretty calm, with only gusts of wind rising, so he obliged and I was better able to feel around in my gut.

I stared and stared down there. I can't explain what intuition really is, but at that moment I was certain beyond a shadow of a doubt that we were sitting square on top of a grave.

"I'm going to talk Opa into hiring a diving team," I told Grey. She stood behind me, and I heard her let go of something, an excited laugh, maybe.

"Tell him *I* want to go in the bubble drum. I've always wanted to do that. Tell him they *have* to take me."

She got down on her knees beside me, free again of the poisonous tongue that seemed to grab hold of her. And I put an arm around her, then both arms. I shook her a little. "I know I can get him to do it, if I just handle it right. He's in the right mind-set. I can feel it in my bones."

She smiled up at me, her pretty pink cheeks puffing out and her eyes lighting like soft candles, so free of any thoughts except those that filled my own core. It was like she passed through me, came out the other side, then whizzed back through again. I could sense she had crossed some threshold—moved out of her own set of problems and into somebody else's. For the moment, there was no Saint Elizabeth's, no need for it. There was only the sea, the wreck, and a chance to get in a bubble drum, to set people's lives back in order.

I think I would have kissed her if Church hadn't been standing there behind us. Given that she looked happier and sweeter than I'd ever seen, I think she probably would have let me.

That was my thought when suddenly everything went out of my head except an excruciating pain that cut through my eardrums like a knife. The worst of it lasted about three seconds, and I came out of it seeing Grey holding her ears and cursing, but not looking as nearly mortally wounded as I had felt. I thought my brain would bleed out my ears, but somehow I could still hear.

Grey's voice wailing out in pain. "Oh, *shit*!"

With my head still throbbing, I looked up at Church, who was staring down at us too calmly, with a completely baffled look on his face.

FIFTEEN

The pain moved out of my teeth enough for me to mutter, "Start the engines."

I could hardly hear myself, so I screamed, staring into the blackness off the port stern, where I was sure the noise had come from. "Start the goddamn engines! Get us out of here!"

Mr. Church was fooling with the choke, but before the engines went on, he said, "Evan, it's a perfectly calm night."

"I heard her. We both did!" I could feel my neck pulling forward—trying to see into the blackness—as I wrapped my arms around Grey's head protectively. "She's out there, I can feel it—"

Grey finally quit cursing and pushed herself from under my arms like she had no interest in being protected. She said, "Don't go anywhere yet. I want to hear it again. Maybe we can tell what it is—"

"It's alive." I stared into black upon black. "It's alive."

It had a personality. I just felt sure. Maybe it had something that would love to remind me that certain wrecks could not be found—because they'd been sucked down the hole, below the canyon floor. My nerves of steel felt weak out here, and getting my friends out of trouble at school seemed so paltry. But I saw Grey crawling slowly on her knees to stare into the black abyss off the stern. Grey, who wasn't even taking her panic pills.

I crawled up beside her, saw she was shaking from head to toe, and her jaw shook as she stumbled, "I don't...think so. Not a thousand cats. It sounds more like a thousand teakettles."

I forced my head to go there, to try to rehear it, to match her nerve. "An air pocket...scraping against a head of wind."

"It sounded almost metallic. A jet scraping against an air pocket? At six hundred miles an hour?"

"I wish we had a tape deck," I forced myself to say, but my voice cracked halfway through.

She and I looked at each other, feeding off each other's nerve, maybe feeding off a common thought. If a creature lived out here who could screech at you, take people you knew, eat them off the face of the earth, hide from you, torment you, then life wasn't really worth living. Let her come and eat you, too, and fuck the whole thing.

"I don't think what we need is a tape deck." Grey pushed her voice forward, her attempt to sound casual coming out heroic. "There's got to be some sort of a pitch detector that records sounds that even human ears can't register. Did you hear that, Mr. Church?"

He was standing almost over top of us. "I'm afraid I did not."

I shut my eyes for a moment, letting my breath out. "What do you think it is?"

He didn't answer.

"Do you...think it's alive?" I asked, turning slowly to him.

He was drinking a soda, clutching it in his hand, and it went up to his mouth and he swallowed. "I'd say you're in a bit of a quagmire if it is. According to the tales told, there would be no wreck of the *Goliath* down below, because The She removes all traces of them and sucks them into a hole underneath the canyon floor. Five minutes ago you felt very strongly we were floating over the top of a wreck. So, which is it?"

"I don't know. Well, how would anybody know for sure what happens to whatever The She eats, after she's eaten it?" I asked warily.

"I don't know."

I looked out over the stern, trying to decide if something was watching us, aware of us. I went to wrap my hand around Grey's and she shook me off again, this time more aware of what she was doing.

"I really don't feel like it was alive, but, um, maybe we shouldn't tempt fate until we're sure."

She meant we shouldn't act like lovers on a vessel, which could make The She jealous.

"I think maybe we should just be respectful and be on our way," Mr. Church said. He started the engines. Grey and I stayed on our knees, staring into the abyss, even after he'd put the boat in full throttle. Little lights revealed a following sea out of the canyon, which could make you totally paranoid. I watched the humps chasing us, wondering if they were getting bigger, or if it was my imagination. Finally, I felt the boat bumping over the little whitecaps, which meant we were on the shelf and out of the deep.

I felt slightly better, but not too safe, remembering the picture in Grey's book of a tentacle reaching all the way to the edge of the harbor and Chandra's tale about Bloody Mary saying a similar thing. But eventually my hands were numb from gripping the metal rail on the stern. I stood up, pulled Grey up, and we went into the cabin and shut the door.

She was out of breath and flopped down in the bow, leaning forward, taking off her mittens. I wondered if my nose and cheeks were as red as hers, and I figured they were probably worse, since I'd had my face in the water. I sat down in the booth, squirmed back in the corner, and put my legs up so I couldn't look out that porthole.

I couldn't tell what she was thinking, but I decided she reminded me of my mom, strong and beautiful, making it a matter of principle not to look rattled.

"Mr. Church wrote down those loran TDs," she said finally, and her eyes came up to mine. They weren't hard, just kind of determined looking. "You realize, if you can get your grandfather to fund a dive of that wreck, you can eliminate two awful rumors, not just one."

I huffed, looking down at my reddened knuckles. "Don't laugh at me for saying so, but one of us could die out there. Or both. We could get eaten, trying to prove something."

She smiled a little at the ceiling, reached into her bag, took her prescription bottle in her hand, and stared at it. She squeezed it and dropped her hands. "I don't care."

She sounded deadly serious, and I eyed her fist around the bottle. "Grey, take your meds. Come on, don't be a hero. It's medicine, not a weekend party frolic with the Xanax heads."

"I don't really think I'm depressed, Evan. I'm just being realistic. You tend to look at risks differently when your life is already in danger."

I glanced up at the porthole but didn't look out. I figured if Grey were talking about The She, *all* our lives were in danger. I wasn't feeling inspired to go down in a bubble drum, to be served up like an hors d'oeuvre at The She's cocktail hour. I told her as much, and while she looked out the porthole with respect, I got it that she was talking about something else.

"I didn't realize it for the first week I was at Saint Elizabeth's, but the truth is, my life was probably in danger the moment I walked in there. My dad showed up every day. Did you know that?"

"I saw his name on your visitors page," I said, though

I still couldn't decide how Chandra's tale of him prostituting her gelled with those visits.

"You know why? It's not that he loves me so much. Or if he does, it's in some twisted way. He comes in there all lovey-dovey, and after a week it occurs to me why. He's afraid I'm going to spew some stuff. He's actually petrified."

She kept glancing up at the porthole, and it made me pay closer attention to her. I realized talking about something on shore was taking away her tension over The She. I kept my mouth shut.

"My dad is the type who, um"—she smiled behind her fist and glanced at the porthole again. "He's very stupid in some ways. He's always treated women like they were nothing, you know? A doll to buy jewels for. A lay. A thing to dangle off his arm when he walked into a fancy restaurant. I mean, he was completely blind to the fact that I wasn't turning out that way. He took a lot of chances, talked a lot of business in front of me or let me hear his end of it over the phone, just assuming that I was his sweet little girl and that, like my mother, I would never, ever turn on him because...women don't turn on their men, okay? I have a feeling real mafia dads are smarter." With that, she laughed totally, but it left her quickly and left an ornery look on her face covering a layer of something like terror.

"I guess his wheels started to crank about a week after I went to Saint E's. He got scared and would be really nice.

I wasn't so nice back. Then he started to try to talk me out of being there, saying I didn't need it, the program was stupid. I could see right through him. Then he started to threaten to sign me out himself, and then I threatened him back. I told him if he didn't leave me alone I *would* tell, lots of things. So he'd better get off my case."

I could not get over her nerve. "Are you scared now?"

"Not of him, exactly. He's done some shit to me in his life, but I don't think fathers go around killing their off-spring. He's not that ill."

I thought of Chandra's lending story and didn't know if I agreed.

"The way he put it to me was that he trusted me to get myself fixed up without 'betraying the family.' But he said that if other people knew I was in there, *they* might get a little bit nervous. Maybe some guys who'd watched him spew business in front of me, like I was some trinket, some Barbie doll."

"Sounds like the type of guy my mother used to love to hate," I couldn't help saying. Grey was reminding me so totally of Mom.

Grey smiled, too easily. It amazed me. I thought she should be a hell of a lot more wound up than she was sud-denly looking.

"Grey, what are you going to do in two weeks when you get out?" I asked.

I didn't think she should go home. I figured she ought to rip off thirty thousand to run away with or something, but the thought of her running away felt completely awful. I started to say she could stay with us, then I thought of one of her father's crooked partners breaking in to stick a pillow over her face and silence her…and getting Aunt Mel or Emmett by accident. I didn't know where reality was, didn't know what to say.

"I don't know." Her smile looked weighted down now. "I know I want to clean up my own life, so fuck him. At the same time, I'm not going to turn on him. He's family. You don't bust your family, I'm sorry."

"So what are you going to do?" I repeated, feeling some urgency rise in my throat.

She looked from her hands to me. "For one thing, I'm going to dive a wreck. And if some she-devil comes along to take me down, I'll just look at her and say, 'Whassup, witchie? I sure hope you brought your salt and pepper, because I am fresh out.'"

She flopped down, and I watched her, thinking of how a few short words like that can be jammed with so many unspoken truths. She didn't really care if she lived or died, and that truth showed up even more in her casual shrug, in her ability to flop onto her back and take her eyes off that porthole. It wasn't the same as wanting to commit suicide, but it was gruesome enough, especially when her family didn't seem to care if she lived or died, either. I wondered if my dead parents weren't a better deal than what she had.

I could also see that maybe this dive was keeping her from feeling suicidal. There really was something to KHK projects that I'd experienced myself. I might never have had suicidal thoughts, but I could get depressed as easily as the next person. I'd be going to pick up Miguel—to take him to a ball game or just to the park to kick a soccer ball around—and I'd see him run from the window and throw open the door when he saw me coming up the street. My mood would jump. It gives you a reason to be here, this whole thing about helping somebody else out when their life is too hard. It was more than remarkable, and at the same time a bit humiliating, that Grey might end up helping me more than I could ever help her.

I spent the next hour going over in my head how to get my grandfather to agree to fund that dive. I knew he liked Mr. Church. I didn't know if he would agree to spend that much money just because Mr. Church clapped his hands and put them on my head, and what I thought was a reliable memory came fluttering back. But I knew I could talk a very good game, and I got my lines together while watching Grey rest.

It helped me pass the time without looking out that porthole.

SIXTEEN

When we got within fifty yards of the docks, I could see my brother standing on one, watching us, his cell phone in his hand. Grey was standing beside me looking over the starboard bow, and I nudged her and said, "Uh-oh, trouble."

Mr. Church floated in sideways, and Emmett caught the starboard bow with his foot.

Before he could start in on me, I blurted out, "Opa told me I could go, and he also told me he wasn't telling you."

"I don't need Opa to find you if I want to find you. I went to see Mr. Shields, who said you had been to see Church this morning. I came over here, and the *Hope Wainwright* was gone, and you were nowhere. Do you have any idea how dangerous it is to be out on a boat in November, Evan? Do you know how fast a storm can rise up?"

"Opa said there was a warm-water eddy on the canyon wall and it was perfectly safe," I told him.

"I don't care. If something happens to you, what becomes of me?" He turned to Church. "I'm paying you back for that fuel. I don't want my brother feeling indebted to you in any way."

"Emmett, don't be tacky," I mumbled, climbing onto the dock and giving Grey a hand over. He looked at her, with winter air blowing out both nostrils like a bull.

"And how are you feeling? Do your parents know where you are?"

"Um, believe me when I tell you, they wouldn't care," she mumbled around a laugh, and anyone but Emmett might have thought nothing more than, "This is not the type of girl you bring home to Mother." But I could feel his usual sympathy going out, and he took her mittened hand in his. He turned to Mr. Church.

"You and I are going to have a little talk, Edwin. Away from Opa. I'm taking you over to the diner for coffee, do you mind?" But instead of waiting for him to answer, he turned to Grey. "You're not planning to drive back to Philadelphia at this ungodly hour, are you? There's plenty of room at my grandfather's house, bless his sweet, industrious heart."

His sarcasm was ripping, despite his concern for Grey. I looked at my watch. It was eleven-fifteen, and I wondered if Mr. Church wasn't normally long in bed by this hour. He had another hour's ride back to Sassafras.

He said, "I think I can fit you into my busy schedule," and rolled his eyes at me, like another kid in trouble.

The diner was right across the street from the docks, so we walked over after Mr. Shields's teenage son showed up to scrub down the *Hope*. Nobody said anything, not even Emmett, even after we'd ordered hot chocolate and I cupped the hot mug in my hands, bringing it under my nose so the steam could thaw my face. Grey did the same.

Mr. Church mumbled, "By the way, Emmett, you're looking quite the man these days. I don't think I would have recognized you, full university beard and all."

I guess Emmett caught the dig. "Thank you, I am a full-blooded adult, Edwin. No question. First, I'd like to know what you all were doing out on the water."

It was a hard question to answer, not because we were out to hide everything but because none of us had really been sure. Emmett took the silence the wrong way.

"You were gone nine hours. I don't think there's any question you went to the canyons, but what were you hoping to accomplish?"

Mr. Church found his voice first. "Your brother asked me. I've done it for other people who've lost relatives at sea. It gives them a chance to hold a sort of at-sea memorial that brings more closure. I think that's all your brother wanted."

His kind tone didn't work.

"Edwin, the problem with that is my parents are *not* in the canyon."

"Of course not. They're in heaven," Mr. Church replied, and I hopped in my seat feeling the heat roll off Emmett. This is one of those sticky moments where an atheist can be rendered speechless. There's not a whole lot he could say that wouldn't sound in utter poor taste. He was sharp and found his way.

"That's funny. Based on island superstitions, I would have sworn you'd have thought they were under the canyon floor, stewing in one of the various Protestant hells, or a hole, or in Hades, or purgatory, depending upon which artistic rendering you're paying homage to. See any she-devils out there, folks?"

"Emmett." I found my voice first. "Whatever your problem is, or whatever you want to say, just say it. Stop attacking people."

He waved his hand in the air like he was sorry. "I just feel, and my aunt Mel feels, that Evan needs to accept the truth, and the faster he can do that, the faster he can resume the happy life we have tried so hard to build for him. He can get past this—and with the truth. Not with lies, superstitions, make-believe. I have an army of DEA agents who would tell him the same story I'm trying to tell him. So what are you doing, Edwin?"

Mr. Church blinked at the tabletop. He glanced at his watch, and I thought he looked tired for the first time tonight. "The DEA had to ignore critical information, simply because it didn't fit their plausibility structure. They're not trained to investigate the paranormal, or even the weather, let alone the complex infrastructure of the two of them—"

"I could tell you there is no supernatural, but let me be more diplomatic and say there is nothing supernatural about what happened to my parents."

"Yes, I think that would be far less *arrogant* of you," Mr. Church agreed.

I put up my hands. "Emmett, listen to me. He did that thing with his hands to me again. He pulled loran TDs out of my head, long numbers that I scribbled down eight years ago in a very stressful moment. Explain that."

Emmett wouldn't look at me. His head dropped and he stared at the table so I couldn't see his eyes. I felt an entrapment coming on, but I couldn't hear it in his voice. "So that's what you were doing out there. You were following those loran TDs to...what? To see if you could sense the *Goliath* below you or something?"

I could feel it rolling off him, despite that he wouldn't let me see his eyes, this little tone of his that he used to use whenever he kicked my ass at chess. "Are you *sure* you want to move there, Evan?" I'd be looking all over the board until my eyeballs were bugging out. "Yeah, I'm sure." Boom, a little slide from some innocent-looking bishop on the other end of the board, four moves into the game. "Checkmate. But you'll get me next time." I hadn't yet.

"Yeah," I said cautiously.

"You think you found the *Goliath*?"

"Yeah." I watched him looking at his lap, and since he kept so quiet, I felt my confidence building. "Yeah. And I bet if we went over to our old house, we'd find those exact loran TDs scribbled on the wall."

He shook his head. "I had the housekeeper wipe them clean about a year after you put them there."

"Why?" I smacked the table in frustration. "Because it didn't fit the government's little theories? Do you remember them? I'll bet you do, Mr. Great Brain. Were they east of two-six-six-eight-zero, north of four-two-two-eight-zero?"

I really thought I had him. His eyes widened and wandered up to Mr. Church in some sort of amazement. "That's not bad, Edwin. I have to hand it to you. It's nothing that hasn't happened to millions of other people under the power of hypnosis, but—"

"I wasn't hypnotized, Emmett! I was driving the boat! There wasn't time—"

"You were hypnotized by the water, Evan. You've got more Barrett in you than all the other Barretts put together, I think sometimes. I can just see you there on the water, seventeen, becoming a man. I'll bet it was like some sort of religious experience."

Mr. Church couldn't hold back a laugh. I guess he was remembering me trying to baptize myself in fifty-degree water.

"How'd you know?" I asked. The confirmation made Emmett look sad. He reached across the table, took my face in his hands, and pulled me toward him.

"I had one myself."

"You're kidding."

"No. I think it was more a Starn experience than a Barrett one, but hell, we've all got salt in our blood. I went out with Mom on Opa's forty-three-footer and refused to come back to shore until I had learned every last angle of every last computerized gadget on his dash. She sat up with me—we didn't sleep more than three hours. We came back because if we didn't, we'd have run out of fuel."

I rolled my head around a little, very impressed. "Wow. All I did was try to stick my face in the icy water."

He let go of me, but not with his eyes. I thought, *Damn it all. He is a great brother.* I got full of regret that we hadn't gotten closer when we were younger, and under normal brothers' terms. We shouldn't have been living in Philly with him taking on some huge burden to protect me from more pain. We should have been living down here, with both parents, keeping the salt in our blood. We should have gone into business together. We should own a ship together. I couldn't say that now. Too much time had passed. There was too much history. But maybe I could still save some things.

"I'm going to talk to Opa." I shot a glance at Grcy, who was starting to look stupor-tired. It had been a long day. "I think I can talk him into hiring a bubble drum to dive for the wreck. I want you to leave it alone. I want you to let me talk to him and stay out of it."

Emmett's eyes wandered to Mr. Church and they changed. They came back to me full of dread. "You asked why I erased those loran TDs. It wasn't because they didn't support a theory. It turns out they didn't support anything, didn't mean anything."

"How can you say that?"

"Evan, the *Goliath* never sank. It was found abandoned, by the Coast Guard and DEA nineteen hours after the disappearance. It's not in the canyon. It's in an old dry dock on the mainland still owned by Starn Industries. Would you like to see it?"

SEVENTEEN

I was in such a state of shock that I didn't even ask where we were going as we piled into Opa's car, which Emmett had borrowed. Emmett headed west over the three drawbridges. Once on the mainland, he immediately turned north toward Leeds Point, on the other side of Great Bay from Sassafras.

At that point, I finally found my voice. "Why didn't you tell me this before?"

I was sitting beside Emmett in the front seat, and I glanced over my shoulder. Mr. Church had asked if he could come, and he was sitting with his head back and his eyes shut. I thought he might be asleep. Grey just sat slumped with her head halfway down to her fingers, which she was picking at, and I thought how dejected she must feel. A dive that had given her a temporary lease on life would never happen now. I spun my head back to Emmett to see him rolling his eyes. I think he would have liked to show me all this and talk to me in private, but everyone had piled into the car.

"Because, Evan," he said, loud enough that I thought only I could hear it. "It just makes it all the more despicable, this...plotting it out so well that you're deserting your own boat to...*hide* on a smaller, less recognizable one. I was absolutely going to tell you, but I felt you had enough to digest for one weekend. The *Goliath* being here, being there, it doesn't make that much of a difference. They still made a break for it. That's the key issue. I just didn't want you to feel overwhelmed."

I had to laugh, though it felt hot coming up my throat. I didn't say anything else until we turned off Shore Road onto a little dirt road that twisted and twined for a couple of miles at least back toward Great Bay. At the end the headlights flashed on a sign that looked kind of familiar and said, STARN INDUSTRIES: PRIVATE PROPERTY." It was old and rusted.

"Besides, I didn't even know about this until I was twenty-one. Remember I told you Opa started hiring lawyers to protect us from further DEA questioning?"

"Yeah."

"Well, they questioned me the morning after the disappearance. The *Goliath* wasn't discovered until five o'clock, or I might have heard it from them. By their analysis, the ship had been intentionally deserted, not involved in some sort of accident. I guess Opa felt like we'd heard enough scandal."

We passed through a hurricane fence where the gate had caved in and came to the opening of a huge warehouse-looking building as high as the treetops. I then remembered Opa used to keep his first shipping vessel in there after he became a manufacturer. I guess it had been replaced with another one.

I got out of the car with so many questions, but I didn't want to ask any of them. Emmett had become like a vat of information. I hated it so badly that just being around him made me edgy about the next thing he would tell me.

We walked over to an enormous sliding door with a padlock on it. He had a key on his key ring, and he opened the lock, pushed hard on the huge door, and it rumbled backward. I stood outside until he'd hit a switch and flooded the place with light. My final hope was that I'd see some boat other than the *Goliath* and this would all be a bad dream or stupid mistake on his part.

My hope welled up, seeing this monster. For one thing, I had never remembered the *Goliath* being this massive. The hull went up and up higher than a house, and I couldn't see the top, the part I knew, because the fluorescent lights up on the ceiling were huge and blinding. I almost said, "This isn't the *Goliath*."

But I remembered the only other time I'd seen the *Goliath* out of the water. I was eight, helping Dad's guys paint red below the waterline, *and he hands me a smaller brush dripping gray paint.*

PHILLIP EVAN BARRETT WAS HERE.

It's faded and surrounded by paint chips and full of salt, but I leaned my head toward it. I couldn't believe this, and my voiced echoed loudly. "Mr. Church, did you know about *this*?"

I turned, and he was swallowing, finding a place on the concrete floor to stare at. "I'm afraid I didn't."

I thought of a great trip to the canyon, one of the most moving experiences of my life, going down the toilet. I was gripping the bottommost point on the bow of the *Goliath*, trying to find some way not to accept this.

"How do they know Mom and Dad and the crew didn't fall into the water somehow?"

Emmett smiled too sympathetically, and I realized how stupid that sounded. Captains and crew don't fall into the water, not in a storm that doesn't even have gale warnings. I remembered some fading photo in my head of a wave. And I remembered pen-and-ink drawings of the The She in a book. I didn't know what to believe, but I was done crying over this shit.

"*Well?*" I asked loudly, which only made Emmett's soft-spoken reply sound better.

"Evan, when the Coast Guard finally got our Mayday, they sent a chopper immediately. They didn't spot the *Goliath*, probably because the crew had it under blackout conditions. But they spotted a smaller, lit vessel, a pleasure yacht called the *Sanskrit*, half a mile off, heading south. They spoke to the owner and noted that in the log, but it didn't mean much to the Coast Guard, considering they weren't privy to the whole DEA investigation. It was probably three days later that the DEA called for the records on the chopper search and found a record of the *Sanskrit* heading south."

I didn't remember ever hearing the name of that boat and said so.

"I hadn't either. But the DEA had. The owners, a Mr. and Mrs. Diaz, from Miami, were first being investigated by the IRS because they had too many power toys to match their income—including the *Sanskrit*. When one suspicious power toy is a yacht that travels the Caribbean frequently, the IRS suspects there's been drug-related income and contacts the DEA. There was actually a Mayday sent from the *Sanskrit* after it hit Hurricane Marco. It foundered before the Coast Guard in South Florida could get to it. The Mayday said there were *eight* people on board. When the Coast Guard up here had made contact with the *Sanskrit,* Mr. Diaz had said there were *two* people on board, himself and his wife. The truth was reported in a moment of severe panic. Mom, Dad, and four crew would have made six additional passengers."

"It was seen passing through this part of the Atlantic, and then it foundered off the coast of Florida," I muttered hazily.

"Yes. Right where they marked the X on the hurricane map in my notebook."

I blinked at the shadows. I couldn't work out the confusion in my head. "You're thinking the six passengers were Mom and Dad and the *Goliath* crew."

I glanced at Mr. Church, who stared straight up with his eyes narrowed, like he was trying to hear or see something. I was back to thinking he might be half nuts.

Emmett said, "The DEA won't pay to dive wrecks unless there are millions of dollars of evidence at stake, and in this case, there was only suspicion. The wreck is still down there. There has only been one dive. A bubble drum in search of a sunken government vessel spotted the *Sanskrit* about five years ago."

He moved toward me slowly, took both of my arms, and both Grey and Mr. Church moved up, too, like they didn't want to miss anything. I flinched even before he opened his mouth, my intuition rolling big time.

"They spotted remains in a stateroom through a porthole. There was too much deterioration to say how many people it was, but it looked like enough bones to be five or six bodies. And one was tied to the helm, as if the driver was trying to ground himself while traversing a hurricane...or herself. All that remained was a dark blue weather suit. Fish were swimming through it."

Hungry fish. Both he and Mr. Church grabbed one of my arms like I might pass out, but I was done reacting to this stuff in usual ways. All I did was let out some noise, trying to bury what I couldn't help remembering. *"Mommy, why are you wearing that out there tonight? You said the Coast Guard couldn't see you if you went in the water wearing blue."*

I jerked my arms, shaking them both off, and pretended I wasn't swallowing sludge. I couldn't remember her answer—if she had told me her yellow weather suit had been torn or something. *But it just felt all goddamn wrong. Our parents were not on that yacht, Emmett, you pervert!*

A sturdy aluminum ladder glowed through the gloom, and I went over and put my forehead on it, letting the coolness seep through my head.

Emmett's voice had started shaking. "Later, the Coast Guard contacted family members of the crews from both the *Sanskrit* and—having heard loudly from the DEA—the *Goliath*. The families declined the cost of examining the wreck."

I shut my eyes, putting my hands up, like *stop*. Opa would have declined to pay for the dive because his health was so poor. The wrong DNA evidence might make it worse, and his daughter and grandkids still needed him.

This ladder trailed up and up, like Jack's beanstalk. Emmett started up it, then Grey, and I followed. Mr. Church spotted the rail at the bottom. Usually when you come back to childhood places as an older person, they seem smaller than you remembered them. I had never re-membered the *Goliath* as being so massive.

It was like walking on a pirate ghost ship. We came on board in the center, and I stared down toward the stern and the pilothouse. It was as tall as a three-story building but looked taller without all the containers I'd always seen loaded on deck. The white paint was chipped and scratched, the windows were covered with dingy film, and there were a couple of thick brown lines scudding across the lower pilothouse wall like it had been scraped with a huge metal object. I moved toward the stern, and the wall glimmered under the extra rays of the fluorescent hanging lantern that Emmett must have kept handy. I wondered where the shipping containers were.

Near the warehouse ceiling, the *Goliath*'s four tall antennas looked to be broken off, falling forward onto the deck at odd angles. I stared at them because they looked very strange. It was the main thing on this deck that gave the impression that something may have gone terribly wrong. Mr. Church must have seen me staring, because suddenly he was beside me and pointing.

"Were these broken off to fit the vessel in the dry dock?" he asked.

Emmett flinched while shaking his head. "Actually, they were found like that, and the DEA says they were cut."

"Cut with what? Why?"

"With wire cutters, to give the appearance of having been through some violence, like a whirlpool."

Mr. Church stayed quiet.

"I kept the report," Emmett said. "It's either in the galley or Dad's office. They weren't completely dismissive of an accident sweeping the crew off the deck. But they wrote that if a great trauma like a rogue wave had come to the *Goliath*, the windows in the pilothouse would have been broken out, and they were intact. They also found that the starboard valves had been opened in the engine room... below the waterline."

"So the crew was trying to sink it, help it along a

little," Mr. Church said, and my heart fell because I could hear him starting to buy into this.

We followed dark, narrow stairs up into the galley, a huge kitchen with a very long wood table that was bolted to the floor. Emmett illuminated the walls, cabinets, floor, and ceiling with the fluorescent hanging lanterns he'd picked up off the deck, and I took one. I thought I might be deluged with memories, but nothing came except gray doors.

Six rows of five small cabinets were still clamped shut on the back wall, where everything had been kept—from paper plates to canned goods to the coffeemaker. I yanked open a few cabinets, saw that things like fry pans were still in their spots, but that anything like salt and pepper and food had been removed, probably anything that would spoil. The room had always been kept spotless, with nothing out of place, because in rough seas Dad hadn't wanted anything to roll. It still looked basically the same, except everything, including the thick little portholes, was covered with a layer of grimy dust.

"What did they do with the cargo?" Mr. Church asked.

"The cargo in the hold was removed by the DEA," Emmett said.

"What about the cargo on the deck? Were the containers filled also?"

"The report says the containers had been loosened, the cargo pushed over by the crew."

"Why? If they were trying to sink the boat, wouldn't the added weight be instrumental?"

"Not in this case. There were decent winds, a hope for decent waves. The weight would have helped stabilize the *Goliath* rather than give it a list."

"Interesting," was all he said.

We went back into the crew's quarters, and I moved immediately to the upper bunk in the far right corner. The beds were actually still made in that squared-off, quarter-flipping style I remembered Dad having taught me, except the pillows were missing. They were all in a pile in the corner, and when I picked one up, a terrible smell hit me. Most of the pillowcases had turned black with mold. I heard a thump and saw that Mr. Church had unclamped a drawer and pulled it out.

"The crew left their belongings," he muttered.

"Yes," Emmett said. Mr. Church just looked at him until he added, "They left enough to make it look like an accident. We really don't know what they took with them, do we?"

"No, we don't."

Mr. Church's answer rang like a comeback line, though I couldn't follow anything. I had never liked being in this room. The bunk room was weird. It was ventilated with fans and had only two little portholes, so it had always been dark and stuffy. At the moment, I couldn't breathe because of the smell. I shot one last look to that back bunk. I knew I had slept there probably a hundred nights in my childhood, but again, it was a fact, not a memory of sights and sounds. I looked at it through a gray film in my head that seemed as unmovable as steel. Finally, we took another flight of stairs and went into Dad's quarters.

I thought I would get a decent breath of air, because his office had windows on three sides. But the musty smell in here was overpowering, some combination of dust and mold and old papers.

"What *is* that smell?" I finally asked, covering my nose with my hand.

"Just mold," Emmett said, rubbing the back of my hair with his free hand. "It's particularly strong in here because of the files. The *Goliath* floated around in a rainstorm for almost twenty-four hours, and somebody had broken the starboard windows, which meant everything got soaked, including the bottom drawer of that file cabinet." He pointed from the cabinet to a mountain of paper in a corner that now looked to be all molded together by dried seawater. It must have been every paper that had been loose in the room, and someone had taken the time to either sweep them or kick them into that corner. The rug on the floor seemed to be the biggest culprit of the smell. I had remembered it being different shades of red and blue. Now it was completely black.

"Somebody broke the windows?" Mr. Church asked, and I could detect an overly casual tone that Emmett also must have caught.

"Yes, *somebody*. If the sea had done it, by pouring *in* and breaking the windows, there would have been glass all over the floor. DEA says the windows were broken *outward*. It appears that somebody wasn't thinking through the details."

Mr. Church rolled his eyes, and I couldn't tell whether it was from having a different theory or frustration from *not* having another theory. I only saw that he did it as he turned away from Emmett, so Emmett wouldn't see it.

I froze, catching sight of my dad's captain's prayer. It was still bolted to the wall but had turned some horrid combination of pale green and black around the lettering. The lettering itself had been black, and it kind of branched outward into the pale green mold with little black mold fingers. The frame was rusted. It was disgusting, seeing the words of a good-luck charm hundreds of years old turned moldy and mutated, like some joke of the sea.

My neck bobbed around to Mr. Church, to see what he was thinking about all of this. He was staring at the same thing, and when he saw me taking in his look of horror, his eyes shot to the floor.

"Can we look in the engine room?" he asked softly, grabbing my arm, pulling me toward the door.

Emmett shrugged and moved past us. "Sure. Just be advised that the smell down there is overpowering. It was found half flooded. I've only been down there once—four years ago when I found out about this."

"You didn't know about this until four years ago?" I asked.

"When I turned twenty-one and was considered a legal adult, I approached the DEA myself. I just wanted to know if they'd gotten together a file on Mom and Dad like they'd gotten on Connor Riley. They had things like backgrounds on the crew but no further theories, being that the case was closed when the *Sanskrit* foundered. But that's when I found out about the *Goliath*."

I followed him down the narrow spiral staircases into the lowest level of the vessel. Grey was behind me, acting like the invisible person. I grabbed her hand, but her fingers fell limp between mine, and I didn't have a whole lot of strength to grip them with, to give her any sense of reassurance.

Emmett held his lantern high, and so did Mr. Church. He walked down one set of plankings and back up the other, looking at the valves, I guess.

"So they only opened two valves. Why not all of them?"

"I don't know."

Church looked at Emmett, and this stare-off as he got closer made me think for some reason that Church was going to yell. But he got right up in Emmett's face and spoke kind of softly.

"Emmett, we both know there are ways for valves to open other than by human hands. For one thing, they break under certain types of pressure—"

"That's not the opinion of the experts."

"We both know that when a ship undergoes a trauma, the pilothouse windows needn't break. If the DEA conversed a little better with the Coast Guard, they would also know that windows blow *out* if a ship is traumatized at its stern."

Emmett smiled at his shoes, too smugly, too patiently, I thought.

"We both know that crew members cutting down antennas is about as ridiculous as them hanging their underwear from the flagpole."

"There is no other explanation!" Emmett hollered, finally. Somehow it made me feel good. Like maybe he was feeling threatened.

This time Mr. Church smiled smugly, patiently.

"Look!" Emmett pointed over his head. "The report is upstairs. Read it. There were no gale warnings that night! There was hardly any weather! There was nothing big enough to wipe the crew off the deck…or blow *out* the windows in the captain's quarters!"

"You're right," Church agreed. "There was only a little weather. To assume that some dark force seized the *Goliath* is ridiculous. To assume that a crew chose to cut antennas in a sleet storm, when they could have better spent their time opening valves below the waterline, is also ridiculous. Eeeny, meeny, miney, moe."

"Church, there is no way you are ever, ever going to find a reliable report, in this part of the world or any other, of giant tentacles coming out of the water! The only tidal wave ever recorded on the Atlantic was in the Netherlands! You can check with the Coast Guard if you think I'm too close-minded! They don't have any such reports either!"

"There are other facts that don't fit into our ideas these days, and so they've been conveniently altered to fit those ideas. And if you didn't know any better, you'd have to admit they've been discarded because they would support the theory of a dark force existing over the water."

"Church"—Emmett moved over to me, stuck a hand on my arm, as if to protect me from him—"you are one sick individual. I want you to stay away from my brother."

The man must have developed some thick skin against being humiliated, I decided. He looked no more upset by Emmett than he had by me earlier that day.

"Your opinion of my mental faculties is irrelevant," he said quietly, his finger spinning circles in the air as if he were thinking of something concerning the whole boat. "There is every possible indication, every bit of evidence, pointing to an alternative notion—broken antennas, blown-out portholes, broken valves, the smell of mold you'd hardly pick up from rain seepage—that this boat has been rolled."

Rolled. I felt the hair stand straight up on my arms as it sunk in what the smell and the rust and the mold inside here actually meant. *Rolled* was a term that meant a boat did a complete three-sixty in the water, coming to stand upright again.

"You don't have to interject the story with a crew abandoning a boat and cutting down antennas with a butcher knife if you could allow yourself to believe in unsolved mysteries of the deep—"

"I like evidence, Edwin. Can you forgive me for that?" Emmett snapped. "I've never seen a Coast Guard report of...of a she-devil rising out of the water and trying to suck boats down, rolling huge ships. I'm sorry!"

"Would you believe one even if you saw it?"

Emmett just stood there staring.

"Because I think you're engaged in a circular argument. You no longer believe in such things; therefore, they can't be true."

"I *know* there are no sightings of anything the least bit weird off the coast of South Jersey—anything that could even be mistaken for a monster or a She. I checked with the Coast Guard. Their records go back to nineteen-eighteen."

Church laughed. "No records? Why, there have been dozens of such reports."

Emmett pushed me backward and stood between me and Church with his back to me, laughing. "You're talking about those childish sea-monster stories that Dad used to read Evan? Out of those cheesy, locally printed paperbacks?"

"Yes! And I beg to differ about the cheesy paperbacks. They're not published by the University Press, but someone was taking the time to chronicle honest sightings by hardworking people—"

"'Honest sightings'! You're talking about a bunch of rum-head old fishermen, with half their teeth gone out of their heads, talking about witches and dragons!"

"Which is what it looked like to them! And who are you to call those people feeble! What in hell gives you the wherewithal to be so arrogant, you presumptuous brat!

Did you have to sink your father's wisdom with his body?"

"Whoa!" I jumped in the middle of them, a hand on each chest, and put on the same cool voice I used to get out of trouble in school, only with a lot more force. Nobody was getting slugged on my mom and dad's boat. "Stop it, now! Mr. Church, if you hit my brother, I will have to defend him, which wouldn't make me too happy right now. Nobody is hitting anybody, nobody is calling names, not on this ship. We're going to figure this out."

Mr. Church backed up. He spoke very softly again, almost from the doorway. "Emmett, in my early years I really wanted my PhD, to really know things, to be a doctor of something. Do you know why I kept quitting at the master's level?"

"I would assume your methodology was the problem."

"*My* methodology. I have never called anything a fact that was not. You people, you build your facts on theories, and whatever doesn't meet *those particular* theories is dismissed as nonfactual. Where do you get off? The DEA has a theory. You stack up the facts a certain way and some of them seem to fit—if you dismiss the ones that don't. I'm not saying your brother is completely correct about the *Goliath* being hit by a wave. *I don't know.* But I do know this. He never said to me that he saw the *Goliath* sink to the bottom when he had his second sight. He said he saw it tossed. He never mentioned tonight anything about sensing the *Goliath*. I don't think any mention of the vessel ever came out of his mouth. I had the whole drive over here to remember correctly what he did say tonight. He *said* he sensed the presence of your parents."

"So? You think some fang-bearing superwitch came along, swept my parents off the deck, and ate them? Spit out their bones as an afterthought? Is that it, Edwin?"

"Don't be vulgar. It won't diminish the truth."

"The *truth*?"

"Yes. The truth is that this boat could have been *rolled* by either a giant wave or a force of nature that, for whatever reason, didn't quite suck it under and keep it there."

"You have absolutely no way of proving anything so...fantastic," Emmett said.

"Prove I'm wrong," Mr. Church replied. "I mean, really, really *prove* I'm wrong. You know damn well you haven't done it yet. You can fool those little freshman undergraduates you teach, but you can't fool me."

"How *dare* you."

"How dare *I*?"

I just rubbed my eyes with my fingers, muttering something like, "Jesus Christ. I'm going home to sleep. Come on, Grey."

I pulled her along by the hand, back up four flights of stairs, all the while looking for the right images as to what kind of a force could roll a vessel this steely and this massive all the way around under the water. While I was walking from the bowels to the deck, images of waves and whirlpools got dim, then faded altogether. I could no longer conceive of anything on the Atlantic that massive. My imagination refused to budge. I tried once again to force my brain to my brother's way of perceiving what had happened, because, like he kept saying, the alternatives were clearly impossible.

EIGHTEEN

I showed Grey into one of the bigger guest rooms at Opa's, pulled the door closed behind her, then stood for the longest time with my hand on the doorknob. She needed to sleep after this long day, and it was closing in on one-fifteen in the morning. But she had been so quiet on the way home, so empty of any emotion. I think that bothered me more than if I had seen her spiraling into depression.

I thought of her blinking at the floor almost all morning when I had talked to Mr. Church and realized she was very good at shutting down, not letting her personal feelings seep out if she didn't want them to. And considering her life was so up in the air, I really had no idea whether she was suicidal or fine or somewhere in between. I tried to force images from my head of her in a limo with some old dirtbag, but it was hard. I didn't know if she'd go back to Saint Elizabeth's and find some answers on her next move, or go out in the middle of the night and throw herself off the drawbridge into the freezing—

I knocked. I could hear her moving around in there, so I opened the door two inches and said, "Um…," since I really wasn't sure what I wanted. She walked past the crack in the door, and I could see she was in a tank top and flannel Abercrombies, so I pushed the door open all the way. She started brushing her hair upside down, looked at me sideways, and asked, "You come back to help pop my zits?"

Humor. Good sign. "I don't think you have any. At least none of the mirror-splattering magnitude."

"What would you know about hitting the mirror, Barrett? God, you're lucky. You've got skin that came straight from the angels."

I rubbed my cheeks, thinking of how I didn't like them, how they could stay flushed from cold or heat longer than anyone else's I knew.

"I hit the mirror occasionally," I lied.

"Liar. Check this out." She ran her finger over two little places, one on her cheek and one on her chin, that looked like she'd been stuck by a small pin. "I'm, like, besieged by these devils. I don't really think they're zits because they never hurt."

I kind of flinched and swallowed. "Yeah, well, stuff like that always looks worse on yourself." I had noticed at times that Grey's skin was not always perfect, but somehow it didn't take away from the overall great effect.

"Are you going to help me brush my teeth?"

She wandered into the bathroom, turned on the light, and I sat on the edge of the bed, saying nothing. I heard water running, and she reappeared a few minutes later with toothpaste all over her face.

She said around the toothbrush, "I got these bleeding gums, too. Really bad teeth. It hurts to brush them."

Now that was a bold-faced lie. I sat there laughing quietly as she went back in the bathroom, and figured maybe she was okay if she was up for weird tricks to make me laugh, and I should turn in. She came out smelling of alcohol and mint and some sweet, fresh smell I still think of only as the Great Grey Shailey Smell. Her face was shiny. She stuck a finger up to her gums as she plopped down beside me, facing me.

"Honest. I have the gums from hell."

"Grey, your mouth is perfect," I argued. "Aside from what comes out of it every now and again."

"Yeah, but these aren't my real teeth. They're all capped."

She actually had me looking for a second as she flashed this Colgate perfection in my face.

"Why are you trying to gross me out?"

She flinched a little, like she was amazed at my insight. Then she wiggled down under the covers, flopped her head back on the pillow, and put her arms behind her head. She glanced sideways and said, "Sorry, I forgot to shave."

"I'm not coming on to you, so you can cut it out."

She bit on her lip to bury a smile. When she got it

under control, she asked, "So, what do you want, Evan Barrett?"

I want to make sure you're not going to sneak past me in the middle of the night and throw yourself off the drawbridge. I want to make sure you're okay. My eyes wandered around the room and landed back on her. I just shook my head.

"You take your meds finally?"

She looked at me for a long time. "No, doctor. Why? You worried about me?"

"Yeah."

"How come?"

I didn't want to ask a lot of questions about where she was going in two weeks, stuff that would keep her awake. I think I would have sold my soul for one more chance to run my fingers through her hair, lay a big kiss on her forehead, and promise that her life would get good again, and I would make sure of it if it was the last thing I did. But I could read her defensive mood, and a glint in her eyes had me burying mine in my fingers before she even started up again.

"You know, up at Saint E's, if you don't take your medicine, they'll make you drop your drawers, and they'll give it the heave-ho up the exit door. You want to give it a try or something?"

I fell onto the floor, rubbing my eyes hard. "Grey, you are like a tarantula...or whatever type of spider it is that spits poison."

She rolled over on her side, looking down on me.

"Don't be too offended. I only get poisonous to people I really, really like."

"Now, why would you want to do that?" I could actually see some affection in her gaze that I really had no clue what to do with.

"Actually, I'm more of a barracuda than a spider. I chew my victims up and spit out their bones. I get too much pleasure out of ruining guys. It's horrible. I'm working on a remedy. But it's going to take a while. Seriously. I like you, Evan Barrett. Maybe I even...like you a whole lot. Therefore, in deference to you, I suggest you stay as far away from me as is humanly possible right now."

I sat up, thinking this was all bullshit, or even if it wasn't, it also wasn't the real issue. I would just say it, and deal with the results later.

"If you're up for destroying your love interests, maybe it's because some of your experiences have been completely putrid."

She stared at the ceiling again. "You have no idea."

"I probably know more than you think."

"God Almighty, tell me I'm dreaming this." She muttered it with closed eyes, and after a moment of silence, she opened them again. "I was wondering how long I'd have before Chandra got real drunk and real chatty. Damn. I've got to find all new friends. Or better...I've got to start from scratch. Do you believe in reincarnation?"

"Absolutely not." I was so looking for a suicide remark from her that her question brought me to my knees. I knelt over her with my hands in the air because I didn't know where to put them. She looked from one hand to the other warily, reminding me that she was in a bed, in her pajamas, which was probably too vulnerable a position for her liking. So I left them in the air, thinking of Miguel, and of Mrs. Ashaad telling me he had been abused by an uncle: "He won't know a good touch from a bad touch, so just don't touch him." I hadn't, at all, until he finally started hugging me when I left him, about the third month I was seeing him on a weekly basis.

But Miguel was a little kid. This was a girl who had passed through me and come back out again at my parents' memorial at sea. This girl had wiped spit or snot or whatever off my face a couple of times, had seen me seasick and life sick. She was stronger than Miguel. I hoped.

"Grey, I'm taking your hand, okay? This left one. Just for a minute." It was actually my left and her right. I realized it as she cracked a stupid grin, but let me slowly lace my fingers through hers. My other hand stayed in the air. "I don't want you doing anything stupid. You are not alone. I can handle your problems. I've basically raised myself. All right?"

She looked at me for a long time, and I thought maybe she was going through a little meltdown. Her fingers gripped down on my hand until we had a white knuckle sandwich going on between us. Her eyes turned shiny, filling up, and her head seemed to push back further into the pillow. Then she leaned up on one elbow, got her huge gray eyes within six inches of mine.

"It's not my problems that are the problem, Barrett. It's

me that's the problem. Do you know what I did to those guys? I charged each of them a thousand dollars. I got them halfway there and said, 'If you don't want me to destroy your favorite body part, it'll be another five hundred.' Three times I walked off with fifteen hundred bucks. I'll be going to a masseuse twice a week until I'm twenty-one. So why do I give a shit?"

She reached an arm around my neck, pulled with all those athletic muscles, and just dropped me into her face. The most horrifying part of this kiss was how my thoughts went from *She's trying to bite the hell out of my mouth* to *She's not trying to.* It was kind of like the way we all kissed in our stairwell adventures way back in fifth grade, feeling little else but stupid, and looking even stupider. A stray thought flipped through my head about how she'd always toed the line, flirted her brains out, drove guys crazy, but I really hadn't seen her go out with anybody—except for maybe a night. It's easy to get out of kissing someone if you only go out with them once, and I wondered if any of those old dirtbags had even bothered with that part.

I wiggled out of her strong arm, shook out my throbbing fingers, and she flipped around and faced the wall. I think my friends have it wrong when they say I have nerves of steel, because in certain really deadly situations my adrenaline is lighting me up like an electric chair. Her words truly had completely horrified me, and she left me gulping for air, just like she'd intended. I do think most guys would have made a mad dash for fresh air, and I wonder if they would have realized her lack of romantic experience.

Something told me if I came back with the type of remark she was used to making, it would take some of the steam out of her.

"If you find somebody interested in teaching you how to kiss, you'd probably make a lot more money than that."

She laughed. She didn't turn around, but held up a hand, which I realized she wanted me to skin. I skinned it and thumped back on the floor, staring and staring at the ceiling until my heart calmed. I watched her back every now and again, wondering how in hell much therapy it would take to make her heart, mind, and body work like a normal person's. And I didn't know what I could do for her, and it was a very helpless feeling.

I hadn't heard her breathing change, so I sat up, trying to keep my voice from quaking.

"I'm going to sleep. I'm closing your door, but I'm a light sleeper. If I hear this door open, you'd better show up at *my* door. You get any ideas of taking a little walk over the side of the drawbridge or anything, you will never get past me. So forget it, right now."

She finally sniffed, and it was full of tears. I rolled my eyes guiltily, thinking we could have filled up the Atlantic Ocean, between me today and her tonight.

"That's nice, Evan. Really nice. You almost make me want to play vulnerable, just so somebody else could be tough for a while. But I just can't afford it right now. So listen to me...Listen up." She turned over without jerking around too hard, and I could see a resolve in her eyes, despite the flood. "I spent a lot of time talking about suicide up at Saint E's. I've had doctors and nurses in my face every hour reminding me that if I did something stupid like that, I would be letting grown perverts win over innocent kids. At Saint E's, they're making me feel like I *stand* for something, something that's bigger than me. I feel important. For once. Though the truth probably is..."—she forced out a laugh as she hiccupped—"I simply have enough killer bitch in my system to be stubborn on those evil bastards, and maybe other girls wouldn't have it in them. That's all. I don't want to be a hero for others. I don't want to turn in my dad. I don't want my name in the newspaper for setting an example, or any of the other stuff they're trying to talk me into at Saint E's. I just, um...I don't want to let those perverts win. I promise you, I will not take myself out over this mess. I don't know what I'm going to do yet, but I won't do that. Do you believe me?"

"Grey, you are not a killer bitch. Stop saying that."

Her face grew blurry, because my own eyes were filling. I wanted to tell her she was amazing and a hero no matter what, but it was just the kind of remark that she didn't like to hear, that would have brought out her raunchy side, and I didn't want to be the cause of it.

"Do you believe me?" she repeated. "Because if I ever forgot myself and thought I wanted to do it, I would remember not to do that to *you*. Call it a romantic gesture. At my speed."

A laugh spilled out of me from somewhere. "Okay."

"Good. Because, yeah, I lied. I finally had to take my meds. And I really need to sleep now. And you really need some sleep." I felt her fingers on the side of my face. They were still shaking, but they were there. "Get out of here, Barrett. You look...kind of ugly, for once. Go sleep it off, 'cause I can't stand looking at ugly people first thing in the morning."

I got up hazily and walked out.

NINETEEN

I trudged down the hall after homeroom, half trying to remember what my first class was on Monday, half realizing Grey Shailey's name had just come out of somebody's mouth in front of me. My eyes were too heavy to look up, but I saw two slender, shiny bars of metal disappearing into a sock and snow boot.

"Anyway, she says to me, 'I was really mean to you a couple of days last year. And at any rate, I'm sorry.' I didn't want to laugh or anything, but I almost did...just because I was stunned. It was like waking up in some alternate universe, where everyone you run into is their coeternal opposite."

"I hope you did laugh. Either she was on something or she had an ulterior motive." The girl to the left of Soundra shuddered. "Does she want to go skiing with your family over Christmas or something?"

I flinched, remembering Grey's outburst about amputees going skiing: "Does it cost less to buy your skis if you only have to buy one?" She might feel ready to turn over a new leaf, but Grey had a long way to go before she'd be able to bite her poison tongue through a ski trip. I looked up. Soundra was walking between Amy Fontaine and Georgia Kraus.

Amy had asked the question, and now Georgia kicked in. "I think she must have heard my mom's theory somewhere along the line called the 'popularity principle.' You ever hear this?"

"No." Soundra snickered. "I don't think I've ever had the need."

"My mom says that kids' popularity never lasts. And whoever was most popular last year turns into a burned-out old windbag next year. And she says you're always most popular right before your burnout ignites. So if you ever feel really popular, look out. Your windbag stage is right around the corner."

"So... Grey Shailey was really popular as a junior, and now she's making a last-ditch effort to stay out of her windbag zone by finally being nice to people?" Amy cackled.

"Wait a minute," Soundra cut in. "This was a minor miracle here. Don't let's mock. It sort of reminded me of that girl with the blood disease six years ago who went to the pool at Lourdes. Remember her? Supposedly she came back well again? Maybe Grey Shailey went to the pool at Lourdes or something and came back human."

Soundra kept grinning while thinking of other weird

cures. "Maybe she's been touched by an angel! Maybe she went to California and walked across hot coals with those middle-of-the-night TV people. Shut up! I believe in weird stuff like that."

"You do not," Georgia said.

"Try lying in the snow for forty-eight hours, watching frostbite crawl slowly up your broken leg and wondering if someone will hear you holler before your leg isn't the only thing you'll lose. You would believe in weird things, too."

They shut up. I had a brief thought of Edwin Church in a POW camp.

"Actually? I stayed on the phone with her for half an hour. We shot the bull about this or that, and actually had some laughs. Truly, I can see why she's so popular. She's very funny and so...not afraid of people. She only said one mean thing the whole time. And I'm not really sure it was even mean. It didn't make sense to me."

"What was it?" Georgia asked.

"Well, the girl can really ski, you know? We're talking Olympic potential here, if she would take something seriously besides train-wrecking her GPA. So I told her, 'Feel free to come up to our chalet and spend a weekend with us.' She was still laughing about the last thing we said, and then out comes, 'Don't make me puke.' Why would my asking her to come skiing make her want to puke?"

I felt my eyes rolling into my head and made a quick U-turn, and I bumped into people and walls and stuff until I was knocking on Mrs. Ashaad's door. She was on the phone, as usual, but beckoned me in. I flopped in the same chair I had sat in six days ago—back when I was some naive person. The whole time she was talking about how to get the press to cover our cheerleader competition, she stared dead at me. So I couldn't change my mind and leave again. I didn't really know why I'd come.

Finally she hung up. "So did you go see Grey?"

I don't think I said anything.

"Because you look sleepless."

I rested my neck on the top of the chair back and decided on, "She got a weekend pass. I just spent Friday and Saturday with her."

She groaned. "Evan, if you would put as much into your grades as you put into your KHK projects, we might actually have a shot at getting you into a decent school. Did she talk to you about her family?"

I felt my eyebrows shooting up as I drummed two fingers on my leg.

"I take it she did. Listen, if you feel uncomfortable about anything she may have told you, I want you to know…" She sucked in breath with an O-shaped mouth, and let it out again, more relaxed. "I want you to know, this is new territory for me, too. I think we have a case of child abuse here, the likes of which I could not have fathomed before last week. At least, not in my school."

I stopped drumming. For a second. I drummed two fingers, then four.

"The problem is, I didn't hear it from Grey. I heard it from somebody else, but I believe that source is reliable."

I let my mind spin different webs, any of which would fit. Did Chandra tell somebody else when she was partying? Or did she tell Mrs. Ashaad, fully sober, her brain cells finally having boiled over? Did Grey confirm just enough to make Mrs. Ashaad start dialing phone numbers? Picking at students' heads like she was so good at?

"What are you going to do?" I asked her.

"I can't do anything. Not until Grey confesses either to me or to a person who is willing to sign a family services report. I asked her about it flat out, up at Saint Elizabeth's this morning, and all she did was laugh at me. So I can't do anything."

I took the hint loud and clear and let my eyes roll back up to the ceiling. "Mrs. Ashaad, the problems are a little worse than you're imagining. According to Grey, her father is a dangerous guy. I would so love to take him off the street. Problem is, I've got a brother whom you know and like. A brother who already lost two parents. I'm not sure I want one of Mr. Shailey's hit men chasing me around Philadelphia," I blathered.

"Evan, do you really think it's that bad? He's *that* dangerous?" She sounded shocked, and I didn't answer. I didn't know how much I should say.

"Is he in the mob or something?"

I shook my head. "In fact, Grey said actual mobsters are probably smarter, more discreet than he's been." I forced a breathy laugh. "She asked if there was a support group for men who just love to break the rules. You probably have some idea of his net worth. So put it all together."

She just sat there, shaking her head. "I don't even want to begin to think about him. I want to think about *her*. She's little more than a child, for God's sake."

You don't exactly mind your friends being called children in a context like that. And I threw my head back on the chair again, thinking of her kissing me like some dumb fifth grader, despite the greasy old men—

"I'll do it. I'll sign anything you want. I'll go to court, look him dead in the eye." I found I was blessing myself as I sat forward, but I meant what I said.

She was shaking her head. "I think I'd like to go to some of the more learned authorities first. If there is a serious risk, it *would* be so unfair to your brother...and would probably kill your grandfather."

I thumped my fist on the front of her desk a little, then put my head down on it, staring at the floor. She was all too perceptive. She said, "Evan, do not get any idea you want to be emotionally involved with her. She's going to need a great deal of help before she can lead a happy life. As for romantic interests? Forget it. She wouldn't know—"

"—a good touch from a bad touch," we chimed in together, and my breath came out hard in a blast of frustration and anger at having been detected. She sighed into the silence, and I could hear sympathy in it.

"Didn't you tell me last week you have this way of getting involved with thorny girls? This one's thorns could slice your head off. I'm not deaf and blind. You have to let her get more help."

I thought of the last remark that Soundra quoted and shuddered. "I know. I just don't know what I'm supposed to do for her."

"Maybe you're not supposed to do anything. This is in the outer stratosphere of a KHK project. We have to mix desire to help with wisdom. I have another source. You're not the only one. I can probably open this can of worms. The problem is, it might take a couple of weeks."

"Did you know she has nowhere to go in a couple of weeks?"

"We'll find her a place."

"Where? In foster care?" My voice went off more loudly than I wanted it to. "Grey Shailey does not belong in foster care, Mrs. Ashaad. Besides, who in foster care would take the risk of having her? To listen to her talk, you might think some leg breaker would show up in the middle of the night with a silencer, put her out of her misery."

"Do you think she's exaggerating?"

"I doubt it."

She groaned in disbelief, and I just stuck my arms out in some spasmodic shrug. After a minute she said, "I can have the FBI in here this afternoon or tomorrow. Maybe you could speak to them off the record."

I shook my head. "She was not very specific. She named some overall types of crimes she thinks he committed, but she didn't say how, or when, or with whom."

"Tell me the crimes."

I watched her for a minute and felt myself full of Orphaned Kid Syndrome. I loved this principal. I was wondering if she weren't too naive, might put herself in harm's way if I said too much.

"Come on, Evan."

My problem? I loved too many people, I decided. She picked up her phone and said, "I have a friend at the FBI. I'm calling him."

I said, "Fine. You know where I am," and I left. I figured I could keep her out of the middle. And as I was walking back down the corridor, I felt ripped in shreds. I was so pissed at Grey's father. I was angry at Mrs. Ashaad for not having all the pat answers. I was mad at Emmett and my grandfather for needing me so much I couldn't put my neck on the line. Then I was mad at Grey for being such a ... *barracuda* when all I wanted to do was help her. And I loved her for kissing like a bonehead child. And I hated her for leaving me scared that she could run out of strength and jump off a bridge.

I pulled my cell phone out of my pocket, dialed information, and got the number for Saint Elizabeth's. Information put me through, and I leaned on a couple of lockers, waiting for the ringing to stop.

"I need to speak to Grey Shailey. She's a patient there."

"I'm afraid that's not possible," the snippy woman's voice said.

"Lady, this is an emergency. If you won't let me speak to her, let me speak to her doctor." I was going to tell him I was afraid of a suicide attempt, not because she hadn't convinced me on Friday night that she wouldn't. I just realized how seriously *I* would have considered it, if her life were mine, instead.

"I'm afraid that's impossible, too. Grey signed herself out of the program this morning."

"*What?*" I leaned off the lockers and almost fell forward. "How could she do that? She has two more weeks!"

"Well, actually, if a patient is not signed in by the courts, she can sign herself out at any time," she told me.

"She's a minor!" I blathered.

"That rule applies to minors as well. If you'd like me to leave a message for Dr. Tartaglia, then—"

"No. Not yet." I clicked the OFF button and started back down to Mrs. Ashaad's office. I had no idea where Grey would go or why she had signed herself out. I had to pass the school entrance, and call it intuition or just a way with details some of the time—my eye was caught by a person in the parking lot wearing street clothes, when everyone else around here had on uniforms. She was hugging a blond who had her arms wrapped around her neck. *Chandra.*

I made a quick exit out of the building and gave a glance up to the windows, wondering which class I was supposed to be in and if it really mattered if that teacher saw me out the window.

I got up to Grey and Chandra, who were hugging forehead to forehead and talking.

"What the hell are you doing?" I asked, pulling Chandra off her.

Chandra shook loose of my grip as Grey stared at me

with some humor in her eyes that I didn't know how to take. It looked a little dangerous.

"So she signed herself out early!" Chandra shrugged. "She looks great to me. She's coming back to school tomorrow, after spending an afternoon at Liberty Mall, of course, and everything will be fine... *This whole thing is our little secret.*"

Chandra nudged me, and after such a long weekend I could see through to Grey's inner depths.

I said, "Great!" in some tone I hoped would be lost on Chandra but would let Grey know I didn't buy into her bullshit.

"Go to class! You've got enough Saturdays on account of me," Grey joked with her. "I've just got to tell Evan one thing, and I'll see you!" She didn't say, "I'll see you *tomorrow,*" I noticed, and studied my shoes.

"Hey, you let him come see you and you wouldn't let me. We're going to have a long talk about that!" She stuck a finger in Grey's chest, then backed up toward the entrance.

"Long talk," Grey agreed with her, nodding hard, waving. She was still waving at Chandra's back when she took hold of my blazer and pulled me up to her. "I had to do it," she said more softly. "If I hadn't checked myself out of Saint Elizabeth's, I couldn't get another two-day pass until next weekend. I needed one now."

"Grey, whatever the hell it is, couldn't it have waited? Where are you going after this?"

"Stop worrying about me, Evan! I can take care of myself."

"I don't think so," was the nicest way I could put the fact that she had just come from a psych ward and couldn't exactly go home.

"Look. Last summer a Girl Scout died in my face. The sorest problem I have right now is that I did nothing to save her. Well, call it my second biggest problem...outside of the fact that I never learned how to kiss."

She cracked up and clunked her head into my chest, laughing at the ground. My hands automatically went to the back of her neck, and she kept laughing too long, like she was enjoying having her hair rubbed. Her red face came up, which meant my hands were rubbing her cheeks. She put her own hands in between and thrust them outward, pushing me away.

"And, unfortunately, I don't have time to learn. I called Lydia Barnes this morning. She was on 'The List.' She was with me when the Girl Scout drowned, and afterward I called her a douche bag for not pushing me into action. Can you imagine her guilt?"

She didn't give me time to answer. "She was down in the Hooks for the holiday and didn't leave until six-thirty this morning. She was still on the road to New York when I caught her on her cell phone. Her dad had stopped in the Island Diner before heading north so they could get coffee and doughnuts for the road. Lydia told me Bloody Mary was in there. Bloody Mary was blabbing on to anyone who would listen that she'd heard The She once already today."

I felt my jaw dropping, and I didn't like the look on

her face. It was reckless, the same look she'd been wearing on Church's boat—when she said a new risk has little meaning when your life is already at risk.

"I thought we were doing pretty good out in the canyon, trying to figure out what that noise was—before you lost your nerve." She pinched me in the side. "At any rate, my dad hasn't taken his boat out of the water yet. He's been too busy visiting me and playing superdad. I'm going back—"

"Oh, no, you're not."

"Oh, yes, I am. I want to hear it again. I've got to face my demons. I want to see them, if I have to. If that noise is nothing but an air pocket and the girl died in a riptide, then I'll have to deal with it. If it's something worse... something I could never have conceived of before recently, well, then, I just want to know it. I have a right to."

"Grey..." I knew car keys were gripped in her right hand, because it just had been in my face. I looked somewhere else, thinking I could grab them if I didn't attract her attention to the fact that I was aware of them.

"At any rate, if there is a She who kills me, I'm dead. If she doesn't, I'm still leaving, Evan. I've got to head out of here. I came to say good-bye."

I gripped her by the shoulders, though she tried to pull away. "Where in hell are you going?"

"I can't tell you. But you have to believe me. I'll be fine. Very safe."

I didn't believe her for a second. I would have shaken her if I thought I could shake the information out of her without giving her a hemorrhage. But she was so stubborn.

She was stubborn, but she wasn't so fast. I grabbed her right hand and snatched the car keys. I almost took her finger off and had to listen to her curse.

"Just stop at my house. I need clothes."

"You can't go where I'm going, Evan."

Watch me. "I can go as far as West Hook, can't I? Since when did this become just your problem?" I would take care of what followed West Hook after West Hook.

"You've got a brother to think of! Do you know how lucky you are? Don't do anything stupid, Barrett."

"I've got demons, too. If Bloody Mary is really hearing something, then it's as much my problem as yours. If that something kills you, then I don't get any answers. Unless I want to go see Bloody Mary and call you back from the dead. Is that what you want?"

It was like something she would say. I think she was a little stumped to have met her own face in the mirror. "No...Okay, just bring your damn Dramamine. You puke really loud and it's gross."

That was a total lie. "Bargain."

We got into her car.

TWENTY

Our problems started before we'd even crossed the Ben Franklin Bridge into Jersey. Emmett's number showed up on my cell phone and I took the call, figuring if he heard I'd left school and didn't know where I was, he would drop his whole day to hunt for me. I could think of a way to soothe him over, maybe.

"Evan, Mrs. Ashaad called. She said you disappeared from school, that you were very upset this morning, and that she'd set up a nine o'clock meeting tomorrow with you and some important people. She wouldn't tell me with whom."

I glanced sideways at Grey, as innocently as I could. "Oh, I'll be there. Tell her not to worry."

"Where are you now? Why did you leave school?"

If Emmett ever acted like a father figure, it was always in a very diplomatic way, and I didn't have the type of re- lationship with him where I lied about too many things. I settled on, "Emmett, I can't tell you right now. I'll be home late tonight. We'll talk then."

"*Late* tonight."

"Yeah." I had to be careful, or he would figure the whole thing out. I remembered how easily he'd found me on the islands when I came cruising home on Mr. Church's boat. He was in his car, I could tell by the hum, on the way to school. "Look, go teach your classes, go to your meetings, and whatever else you have today. I'll be fine, I promise, bro."

"Evan, I don't like the sound of this. If you're not up to something that's either dangerous or involves poor judgment, why can't you tell me?"

It might be both. I had no answer, so I just hit END, clicked the power off, and handed it to Grey.

"He's very smart. We'll have to steer clear of Opa's, Mr. Church, the diner, The Docks, anywhere he would think to call. He'll figure this out. Where does your dad park his boat?"

"At the Basin, which would not be hard to figure out either. My dad's name is as well known there as the president's is in Washington."

My head bobbed around to stare. "The Basin? What the hell does he have? Something the size of the *Goliath*?"

"It's a thirty-eight footer." She whipped out her wallet, laughing in a way that sounded half victorious, half evil. She flashed a photo ID of herself in my face. Seaman's license.

"You can drive that monster?"

"As long as I'm not in a typhoon."

"Listen." I thumped my fist on her knee, spouting some of the worries that had been running through my head. "We're going to get a Basin weather fax first thing when we pull in. If there's any sign of weather east of Kansas, we're staying on land, okay? God knows you can hear what you want to hear from land, too. And let's go pay a visit to Little Miss Mary first. I'm a pretty good judge of people, and if Bloody Mary is lying, I'll be able to tell."

Grey pulled off her coat, stuck it in my lap, and fell asleep on it. I thought it was a very strange time to be falling asleep, but for some reason, she looked more peaceful than I'd ever seen her.

I went to the Basin weather station first and figured I had some good luck. A weather fax showed a new warm-water eddy starting over the canyon, with clear skies all the way to Oregon. The air was forty-five degrees. I waved it victoriously under Grey's face as she was passing off what looked like a good load of cash to a very young dockworker. He was giving her a list of things he would check besides the fuel, including fuses and oil. She laid another twenty on top, and said something to the guy about her father going into West Hook to get his favorite bait. I guessed she wanted this prep guy to think we weren't alone.

She grinned, looking over the fax, and I watched the guy walk off counting this wad. "What'd you do, stop home this morning? Raid some money-laundering nook?"

"I took just as much as I need and no more," she said. "Dad took his little button skiing in Denver. I think she feels neglected from all the time he's spent trying to nuzzle up to me. Mom was making a good appearance at one of her few remaining charities."

Her dad being in Denver gave me an even better feeling, like I wouldn't have to worry about him showing up here for some stray reason. It would take at least an hour for the boat to be gassed and prepped, so we went over into West Hook and pulled up in front of Bloody Mary's tattoo parlor. This time of year, there were lots of vacant parking spaces.

"What are you going to say to her?" Grey asked, and I sighed.

"Why beat around the bush?"

Bloody Mary was in there, filing her nails. She had on this green, blanketlike cape that matched her pale green eyes. She had long, ropy blond hair and, this time of year, pale Nordic skin, so she looked like she could pass for a corpse if she wanted to. She was probably only around thirty, but her eyes and way of talking made her seem weirdly ageless. And it didn't help at all when she said, "You don't want a tattoo. You want...something else."

I tried to ignore how creeped out I felt. I didn't look like the tattoo type, so it was a logical guess.

"Right, no tattoos." I cleared my throat.

Grey was standing behind me, like maybe she didn't want to deal with this part. But she laid an arm on my shoulder and a twenty-dollar bill dangled in my face. I swiped it, handed it off to Bloody Mary.

"You were down in the diner this morning, talking about something you'd just heard."

"I hear zee She!" She nodded heartily. I looked from one of her eyes to the other, and back again. I couldn't see anything in them except enthusiasm. If this was a hoax, I couldn't tell. "She comes again. Last August, I hear her. First time in two years. This time, she gives warnings. Short shriek...Friday night after dark. Again this morning. *She comes. Tonight.*"

I turned my back on her and looked at Grey as a sickening feeling rolled through me. I could have done without the accuracy about Friday night. But Grey gazed stubbornly around my shoulder, and I turned again, this time ready to face something I might have to believe. I held up the Basin weather fax to her.

"How can you say she's coming tonight? Look at this."

She waved a hand, dismissing it, and pointed one of her long, filed fingernails up in the air. "That means nothing! You are confused. You confuse zee She with zee weather. She is *alive*. A *being*. She does not need zee weather. She needs no reason. Except that she is hungry."

I put my fist in front of my mouth, thinking I was going to burp if I didn't actually heave again. I wondered if I'd lost ten pounds over the weekend, just from people inspiring me to lose my lunch. Grey stepped in front of me, passing another twenty to her.

"We're driving out to the canyon. Tell us when you think she'll come."

"Oh, no! You mustn't! You will not return! Not zee two of you! You are *in love*! You will arouse her jealous wrath, bring a bad thing down on many."

Grey backed into me, laughing in her face in a way only Grey could do to people. And I put an arm across the front of her, wanting to ward off this lady or something.

"She comes at the fall of night." Bloody Mary leaned up to us, drumming ten fingers on the counter. "You will need protection. I can offer it to you." She disappeared behind a curtain where she tattooed people, and Grey turned to look at me. I really hated the look on her face. I didn't see anything romantic there. It was laughing—reckless, daring, stubborn, and, somehow, still skeptical.

Bloody Mary returned with a couple of necklaces full of broken shell pieces all strung together on a leather chain. "I have holy water, comes all the way from Haiti. I will bless these. You wear them. Maybe she will not eat you."

Grey started stepping backward away from her, forcing me backward, too. Bloody Mary looked at both of us like we were a mystery to her.

"What? Zee protection of your very lives is not worth fifty dollars?"

Grey kept backing us up, and she was good enough not to laugh again, though I could feel it bouncing around her insides. Bloody Mary's eyes went to me.

"And you! You have lost to her before, your own flesh and blood!"

I froze. Her pale green eyes bored holes through me, and I tried telling myself she remembered me from childhood, that was all. I turned and walked out as calmly as I could, but Grey took the car keys from me.

"Let me drive," she said. "That was horrible. Are you all right?"

I got in the passenger side, trying to figure out what I actually felt. It had been sickening in there, though I couldn't quite decide why. I couldn't say Bloody Mary was absolutely a liar. She'd been pretty accurate about having heard The She the same time we'd heard it. There just would have been something even more sickening about thinking you could be protected by broken shells. I couldn't say why. I guess maybe I sensed they would be blessed with tap water.

"Evan, you don't have to go if you don't want to," Grey said. "In fact, I wish you wouldn't. You've got everything to live for, no reason to take risks."

I snatched her hand up in mine absently and laced my fingers through hers tightly, like I didn't want her going anywhere without me. Certainly not out there.

"If there's something out there, something that could eat my folks right off their boat, I don't want to live in this world." I bumped my head on the headrest a couple of times with my eyes shut. "And if there's nothing more than a scandal, I don't think my gut will ever let me believe it until I've found out more. This is not the time to just drop everything and try to live a normal life. How in hell could I do that?"

I think any other girl might have tried to encourage me, anyway. Grey seemed to understand the value of a supreme risk. She said nothing but squeezed my fingers, letting me know she was watching me. I kept letting scenes from my last trip out there roll through my head—my face in the water, spitting over the stern.

"That water is my friend," I said. Whatever that meant.

"Your friend has killed a lot of people," Grey pointed out, but it was more like she was feeding me thoughts to conquer rather than arguing.

I had to nod, though. "It's killed a lot of *good* people. But everybody has a time. God takes everybody, and sometimes he doesn't leave a very reassuring explanation. And yet, somehow, we end up coming back to the thought that he's a good guy."

"Unless we're Emmett."

"Yeah." And yet Emmett is such a good guy. "Maybe Emmett's just...good enough within himself. Me? I'm not so good." I sat there for a while trying to figure this out. I decided I couldn't.

"Let's go," I whispered, realizing I was releasing her hand to make the sign of the cross on myself.

She didn't do likewise, but she kind of laughed, closed her eyes, and shocked the hell out of me by saying what was a very common captain's prayer, or my mother wouldn't have had it on the *Goliath* when it had been hers.

"Lord, give me a stiff upper lip."

III

"The only real valuable thing is intuition."
—ALBERT EINSTEIN

I thought we would have a smooth ride, at least out to the canyon, but when we got back to the Basin, my Sherlock Holmes brother was standing on the dock, to my amazement. He did not look thrilled. His cell phone was in his hand again, and he left the dockworker standing beside the Shailey boat and marched toward the car.

"Shit— Shit," we echoed.

"I'll handle him," I said to her, though I had no clue how.

He got within six feet of me, stopped, and shook his cell phone at me. "If you set one foot on that boat, I'm calling the Coast Guard. You are not leaving port, Evan. You ought to be using better judgment. And you, *you* ought to be taking better care of yourself."

"I'm taking care of some business that's highly therapeutic," she said, and as they exchanged a couple of argumentative lines, it gave me time to think a little.

"You can call the Coast Guard," I said. "Grey has a seaman's license. On what grounds are they going to tell us to not take this boat out?"

"How about that it's the last day of November, the most dangerous month on the water?"

I pulled out the weather fax, showed him the clear skies and the warm-water eddy over the canyon. I really loved showing him paper proof of stuff. It made him angry because he had no real replies.

"You're not going, Evan," he said. "The Coast Guard could stop you on...the issue of truancy...and I'm not sure if it's even legal for two seventeen-year-olds to take a boat this size out alone. I will call them and find out."

I wasn't so sure the Coast Guard would get involved in an issue like truancy, and I decided to meet him on his own turf.

"What are you afraid of, Emmett? Outside of me getting suspended? That's an issue I will handle, I assure you. What's out there? Nothing?" I shoved the weather fax at him again. "According to everything you believe, there is nothing out there. No waves, no whirlpools, certainly no life force that could bring any harm to us. Right?"

His jaw bobbed for a moment. Struggle was written all over his face. "Okay. I'm not worried about the weather on this trip. I'm worried about your lack of good judgment. You're supposed to be in school. She's not well. This is ludicrous."

Grey said, "Someday soon, I'll be better than I am now. But you've got to know, I'm better *now* than I ever was. I'm much more equipped to do this than last summer when I looked to be on top of the world." She looked so sincere, I think it stumped him for a minute. He changed direction.

"Would it be a terrible imposition if I asked the nature of this trip? Or is this just another 'I feel things' expenditure of what could feed a dozen children of Zimbabwe for a year?"

I just grabbed his arm, figuring the only way to win this argument was through the back door. "Bloody Mary heard The She this morning."

"Evan, there is no She."

"Are you sure?"

"Of course I'm sure!"

"Then why don't you come with us?" I really didn't want my brother on this boat giving us heartburn the whole way out and back. But I didn't feel we'd get out of the harbor any other way. "There's no She, no gigantic waves, no nothing but a warm-water eddy, clear skies, and maybe a couple of drug runners looking to cook up an excuse for a disappearance. Right? And for whatever reason, you've been renewing your seaman's license every year. You know the dash of a big fishing boat, Emmett. The way you were talking in the diner Friday night, about learning how to use Mom's instruments, you couldn't forget all that stuff, not the way you baked it into your brain. Why not come? Help us out? What are you afraid of?"

He sighed. "I'm not afraid of anything."

"Are you afraid you might be proved wrong?"

It took him a minute to finally say, "No."

"Maybe you're afraid you'd have to throw out your whole dissertation and start from scratch."

"That was a cheap shot!" He pushed me in the chest with his finger. "Don't you ever imply my integrity isn't intact!"

"Well, maybe it's really not!" I got back in his face, fighting my conscience for a moment. "You've got a perfect opportunity to prove something. In fact, the burden of proof is on us! All you have to do is come along, see nothing, then you can laugh at us all the way back to shore. Why won't you do that?"

He threw his arms up and down and said, "Am I allowed to simply say that I have a bad feeling about this? Would that be a crime?"

I let my head bob downward so he wouldn't see me smile. A *bad feeling*, huh? Lord knows I'd given him enough unsound arguments over the years. I rubbed his arm. "Of course you can say it. But you have to come. Say you'll come, Emmett. This is about our parents. I have to do this. If you're right, then nothing will happen. If you're wrong...you need to know, too."

He'd been rubbing my right arm as I'd been rubbing his left. He pulled me by the back of the neck up to him so we were forehead to forehead. "I know this is a hard time for you, Evan, and I want to do anything I can for you. I'll go. But I want you to promise me, when we get back and nothing has happened—*if* nothing has happened—you will start to accept the things I've been trying to tell you."

The *if* part was a real stretch for him. I knew that. I promised.

And he was an extremely good sport, I'd have to say. He got at the helm of this huge boat and went happily nuts over the dash, like I hadn't scared the hell out of him for the past two hours. Grey had to take ten minutes, explain every monitor, radar, both handsets.

"You must let me drive some." His eyes lit up like torches as he clutched the throttle. It sent these fireworks through my insides, which went off a second time when Grey handed him a yellow weather suit that looked exactly like his old one. He'd gotten heavier and softer in the body since he was seventeen, but the weather gear covered that. A person's eyes are always their own. Except for the beard, he looked like the guy who used to flip me the bird across the table, sit on my head and fart, and tease me until I was laughing and crying at the same time.

He brought us out of the harbor with little problem, remembering like I did about the following sea. We hit the surf coming in off the Atlantic City beaches, and the size of this boat being what it was, he barely had to zag. I got goose bumps watching him stick a finger in his lips, then set out against this monitor, some ultramodern, ultracomplicated loran receiver. After a couple of tries he plugged in the loran TDs for the Baltimore Canyon and looked not the least bit impressed with himself.

Grey had picked up hoagies again, and I looked at mine a little warily as we sat in chairs on the stern. It was right around noon, and I turned mine over and over in my lap, watching her grin. She unwrapped hers, handed me the papers, and took a huge bite, laughing at me. I laughed right back, until she started this ungodly game of "see food." I swear, she chewed one mouthful for over a minute.

I decided her games of gross-out, whichever ones they were, had a purpose. They were more of her endearing defense mechanisms to keep men and boys at bay. I just didn't respond to it with anything more than a grin and a thumbs up.

I watched the Atlantic City horizon disappear, then did little else for two hours, save go into the cabin a couple of times to get warm. But we didn't leave Emmett alone on deck for too long. He confessed to being "squeaky," though I couldn't feel more than a couple of jolts when he caught a six-foot swell head-on. There were a lot of four-footers. I noticed, on my watch, that it took me a half hour longer to start feeling seasick. I didn't say anything to Grey, who had eventually devoured half my hoagie, too. Emmett gave her the helm finally, sat down in the other fishing throne, and stared off the stern.

He was smiling. "That was great. Very refreshing."

He watched Grey for about ten minutes, then, convinced she could do the same job as him, he turned to me. His grin looked a little lopsided.

"How you feeling?"

"Green," I confessed.

"Me, too."

We stood up as discreetly as possible, leaned over opposite corners of the stern, and heaved our guts into the water. I could hear him laughing along with me.

Finally we both turned. I wiped my mouth on my sleeve, and watched him take a more gentlemanly approach. He put his fist up to his mouth, then put a hand on his chest.

"You lost it *first*," I told him, in case there was any question.

He took his hand off his chest very slowly, formed the bird, and flipped it straight up at me. I hooted as he shook his hand out and took his seat again. I flopped down, too, and he leaned close so I could hear. "Dad said it takes six trips out to get a seaman's stomach if you're not born with one."

"Guess we weren't born with it. We'll get it back, bro." I punched his arm.

He was staring down at his thumbs, picking one with the other. "*You'll* get it back."

I watched him and finally nudged him. "All this really sucks. We should have bought a boat together, Emmett."

He shook his head. "I'm where I'm supposed to be. I'm very happy. You, on the other hand, will probably come back. It was written all over you last weekend. It's cold. Let's go inside."

We walked past Grey to get into the galley. She just shook her head, handing me a pack of spearmint gum.

We fell into either side of the booth, and Emmett said, "The house is in both our names. I could just sign it over to you, Evan. I don't have any problem doing that."

He was talking about our old house in West Hook, which was a beauty in my eyes. It was old but not falling down, and Opa had mentioned it was worth close to a million dollars, just because of the location. One thing I could definitely say about my socialist brother—he was no hypocrite.

"You're not parting with half a million dollars with no more than a shrug. Over my dead body." I punched a fist lightly on his hand. "Besides, we're moving a little fast here."

"Maybe," he said. "But I just have a feeling."

"Oh! You have a *feeling*, do you?"

"I suppose it's all right. I mean, you have an actual *thought* every once in a while." He pulled the gum pack out of my hand with a glint in his eye I hadn't seen in a while. "You rancid little wet fart."

I was driving when we got to the canyon. I cruised over a few white waves, watching the lorans for where the shelf would drop. Emmett pointed to a monitor on the computerized dash that actually read depth numerically and on a graph. I saw a black line tumbling downward on the neon green screen.

"You just hit thirteen hundred yards depth. See that?" He pointed to the numbers. He was chewing a fresh piece of Grey's Wrigley's spearmint, which means he'd just gotten sick again—in the cabin bathroom, I figured, because Grey was sitting with her feet up on the stern railing.

I gave him the helm and went to stare over the stern, deciding I liked to look at the water this way rather than on that little green monitor with its lines tumbling downward.

It was almost a mile down, here. *A mile down.* I tried to think of it. It was less than a mile from our town house in Rittenhouse Square to the art museum. I thought of turning half of center-city Philadelphia onto its side and shoving it downward off this stern. It was a fucking city deep. And yet, the top was smooth in the late afternoon sun, giving no hint of what lay beneath. Little ripples turned to dancing diamonds in patches, and there weren't any swells big enough to rock this boat enough to feel it, all of a sudden.

I knew Emmett was now heading toward the loran TDs of where we were the other day, and it gave me time to think this thing through again. I had said I felt my parents down there. I had actually been thinking of souls and loved ones and not the *Goliath* at that time. Mr. Church had been right when he said that to Emmett. Maybe, just maybe, my intuition worked okay, if I didn't try to get too specific about it. Maybe they *were* down there. The hair on my arms stood up as we passed one remaining yellow flower, floating and waterlogged, that hadn't managed to drift away in the Atlantic. A short time later, the engine was cut down to neutral, and Emmett came back to the stern.

I pointed downward. "This is about where we were when I thought we were over Mom and Dad. You feel anything?"

He put his hand on my back with a shaky laugh. "I'm afraid I don't."

But he rubbed my back sympathetically, looking all around. "I've rarely seen the water this calm. Beautiful, isn't it? Diamonds dancing. It's probably calm enough to cut the engines. If you want."

I shrugged, looking into the gray water. "Let's drift around."

I gave Grey the thumbs down, and she cut the twin engines again, so we were left in silence. It's considered a somewhat daring thing to cut all your engines in the canyon, because a stray swell could get out of hand, and then you had no way to maneuver yourself against it. But there was nothing but little flat ripples to the horizon in every direction today. The surface looked almost like it was covered in bobbing Saran Wrap.

"Could you just live out here?" I asked.

Grey had taken a folding deck chair, plopped it between us, and slouched there, just staring off the stern into the late afternoon sun. "Absolutely."

Emmett didn't reply. I turned my eyes to Grey, got a sneaky feeling in my gut, and said, "You're not thinking of…"

"I would never." She put a hand up, like, *Stop with that thought*. "The boat would be the first place my dad would look for me."

I got the feeling Emmett absorbed more of that comment than most people would have. In fact, he put a hand on her knee, patted it, and said, "No matter how big your problems get, you must promise not to run away. There are too many organizations available to help minors in trouble. It's not necessary, if you know where to go."

She turned her head slowly to look at him. When she saw he was looking, she turned frontward again and laughed. "I'll be all right."

It didn't sound convincing—at all. I figured no matter what she tried, I was bigger and stronger, and if I had to tie her up to keep her from running, I probably could. The problem would be what to do with her, where to take her, after I had to tie her up.

Emmett went on. "I'm friends with Myra Ashaad. In fact, I talked to her this morning after she discovered Evan had left school. She doesn't know you left Saint Elizabeth's. But she did say she was working on something for you."

Grey just got this little sad grin and said, "She's a nice lady. I owe her my sanity at this point. What there is of it." A stray laugh rose up. "But I wish she wouldn't get in the middle. It's probably dangerous."

"Your dad?"

"Yeah, he's a real sweetheart."

"All she implied was that you were abused." He slumped a little further, and I could see that in his good-hearted way, he was trying to dig information out of her. "But people who abuse have boundary problems all across the board."

"You a shrink? I thought you were a philosopher," she joked.

"Most of the truly dedicated academics try to be a bit interdisciplinary these days. If you're feeling that you can't report your family, that's a very normal feeling, especially if it's dangerous."

I figured he would throw out a solution, but he didn't, and I wondered if that wasn't smart. See if she wouldn't talk first.

"I'm...pretty certain it's dangerous." She sighed. "I got to thinking last week that he'd talked so much business in front of me because he was stupid. Now I'm wondering if he wasn't very, very smart. It kind of puts me in check...though I'm not ready to scream checkmate."

Emmett kept nodding, and she shifted around. "He's got a money-laundering operation that's gotten pretty substantial. Loose mob ties, though I wouldn't call him a mobster. Let's call him a friend. Ha-ha."

"Which mob?" Emmett asked, and I just gazed over the stern like this was of no interest to me at all, but I was figuring what I could tell the FBI if I had the chance.

"Irish. He takes a lot of trips up to Boston. I really think his heart was in the right place when he came out of law school. That was a long time ago. He had something to do with the IRA. Then...I don't know what happened, except he did some coke, and then did too much coke. Got greedy, full of himself, full of his own sense of power. He thinks he can do *anything*," she said.

I took her hand in my lap and held it, sensing her feeling of aloneness. She just let it lay limp there, but she didn't snatch it away. She finally said to Emmett, "Your brother suspects I'm suicidal. I might be, except that I feel like I have a divine purpose in my life that I haven't completed yet. My divine purpose is to show a lot of people that guys like him can't do just *anything*."

I flinched, thinking of the men in the limos for the hundredth time.

"Well, do you have a plan?" Emmett said.

"Yeah, I've got a plan."

He waited, but she stayed quiet. Too quiet. The lowering sun had turned the sky, and the water, all sorts of orange and red and white and yellow. It was like being inside a crystal ball. I think, no matter what we were discussing, we would have had to stop and pause and consider. For me, part of pausing and considering was thanking heaven and everyone who lived up there for an amazing sight like this. It made me feel closer to heaven, and I wondered if Emmett didn't feel some void, not feeling like he could thank God for things.

Maybe he managed by keeping his mind on the needs of others. He was far better at it than I was. He spoke first.

"Grey, I cannot encourage you strongly enough to find some adults who can help you. Up at Drexel, there's a list of charities as long as your arm and people who would know about things like this."

She reached over, took his hand, pulled both our hands into her lap. It was beyond a cool gesture—it was a miraculous gesture. She was out on a boat, isolated from the world, with two full-blooded guys. If she trusted no one else in the world, she trusted both of us.

"I don't know which of you has the biggest heart." She shook my hand a little. "I'd be tempted to say this one, because he puts up with my endless abuse. But I don't know. You both have hearts of gold, I'll say that much."

And we sat like that, holding hands in her lap, watching the sunset change from yellow to orange to red to purple—over the shine of Saran Wrap—and, finally, to black.

Emmett stayed quiet after night fell—diplomatically quiet, I should say. He read the dash on the helm a few times, went into the cabin a couple of times, and I started to get antsy about him.

"I don't know what I want more," I mumbled to Grey. "To see The She or not to see The She."

"What's your gut telling you? Some gusts blew up after sunset. Feel that?"

"My gut is telling me I'm seasick." I put a hand on my stomach and didn't mind confessing. It seemed like we'd heard enough about each other over the past few days to say just about anything. "I guess my ultimate wish list would be to see The She and then find some way to escape her. I suppose people have escaped her wrath, or there wouldn't be any of those accounts in the cheesy little books I've seen."

"I'd just like to ask her if she's got a taste for Girl Scouts, and then kill her with my own bare hands. Is there any way to kill a sea hag? Like...a silver bullet or any-thing? Maybe we should have thought of that before we came out here."

I stared into the black abyss, and the gusts made me edgy. Wind dies down at sunset more often than it rises up. I could see little whitecaps dotting off the stern. In the black, they looked like neon dots lighting and disappear-ing. I listened past them, but there was no sound beyond the slight wind kicking in. I shook Grey's fingers around, thinking of my mother's description: "black-bean soup, coming to a boil." I swallowed, realizing that was a way creative statement for my mother, who didn't have a drop of imagination in her, and remembering how Emmett had later said the line was rehearsed.

It *was* a far reach for Mom. But the more I looked at these neon dots lighting and disappearing, the more it seemed like a perfectly natural thing to say. I was looking at them so closely that when they changed, I flew out of the deck chair, grabbed the rail on the stern, and stared harder.

"What is it?" Grey asked.

"Something..." I didn't know how to describe it. I felt like I was on LSD again. "You didn't see that?"

"See what?"

She had a hand on my back, and at this point, I knew she wouldn't think I was losing it. "All those dots out there. They just dropped about thirty feet and came right back up again."

She looked and looked, up, down, up. "Well, maybe you're seeing a reflection of the sky or something."

She looked up again and I forced my eyes off the water. The stars were bright like flashlights, all the way to the horizon, leaving a pretty clean line where the sea met the sky on all sides. The half moon overhead was full yellow, giving these whitecaps their neon.

"Maybe." I sat down again slowly.

"I feel very selfish having you guys out here," she said. "Though I guess if I really and truly believed I was going to die by coming out here, I would not have come. I'm not ready for serving myself up as a hot lunch."

I tore my eyes from the deep and laid them on her sad, determined face, glowing in the stern lights.

"I want you to tell me where you're going," I told her flatly.

Her eyebrows rose and fell. "I'll be safe. Believe me. Maybe someday I *will* tell you. Someday when I'm not so busy trying to become a different person."

"I like you the way you are."

With some stunned awe, she leaned sideways in her seat and completely cracked up. "You are nuts, Barrett. If The She is out there, you'd do better to go out with her than me."

"I don't think you've ever really been out with anybody," I finally said.

Her eyebrows did the up-and-down routine again, and she didn't deny it. "I've had my nights. I chew them up, spit them out, and have enough good sense not to put them through it again. Someday I'll be a different person, Evan. Then I'll come back."

I cramped her fingers totally, pulling them into my lap like I wouldn't let her go. She didn't respond to the loss of circulation. She just said, "By that point, you'll be married to some lucky girl and will have three kids as perfect as yourself, Prince William."

I hated when people called me that. I leaned away from her, then spun in annoyance as a hand came down on my shoulder. Emmett leaned over, and I could see he had a hand on Grey's shoulder, too.

"Evan, I don't need to remind you that you need to go to school tomorrow. You have an important meeting in the morning, and you can't be late."

In other words, outside of a slight breeze kicking in and my misguided eyes, nothing at all was stirring out here.

"I'm not ready to go back yet." I stood up, not knowing whether I wasn't ready because I hadn't seen any She, or whether I knew when we got back to Philly, Grey Shailey might walk out of my life and be stubborn enough to not show up again until years had passed.

Grey stood up, too, looking at me with eyes that didn't lie. She didn't want to go back to shore either, back away from this place of make-believe and magic and answers and mysteries. Emmett moved back to the helm without saying anything else, but I knew we couldn't stall him out here for more than twenty minutes or so.

I went into the galley, and Grey followed me.

"I don't want to go back," she whispered, and it was the first fear I'd heard break in her voice.

Her eyes looked afraid, but then they changed some-how, filled up with some sort of resolve again. She bit her lip and stepped up to me slowly and wrapped her arms around my neck. It was hard looking down into her eyes with her that close, leaning into my chest. Usually, when a girl gets that close, you shut your eyes. You just kiss her. Our noses bumped. But her eyes were wide open, looking purely curious for once, as if the hardness that usually possessed them was sound asleep. I realized I had wrapped my arms around her when the ski tags on her zipper flut-tered sideways and my hands felt the back of her soft sweater. It was good she was still biting her lip. I couldn't do anything but speak up.

"Grey Shailey, I don't want to become part of your problems."

"I don't know that person," she whispered. "I'm not her. Maybe I left her back on the shore. Maybe I'm some-body else now. Maybe I don't...have those problems anymore."

I knew the feeling of being in a different world when you were out here, past the horizon. And I knew her eyes looked more empty of pain and distrust than I had ever seen them. It was almost startling, seeing that big a change, her eyes with nothing in them but some innocent curiosity, some desire that was devoid of self-consciousness. It was still awkward, in a kind of endearing way. Her elbows were up on my shoulders, and she was tapping the back of my head with her fingertips. I realized she was pushing, not tapping, some sort of shyness breaking through.

"Okay." I wrapped her all the way into my arms and whispered, "Let's see if we can make The She jealous. Let's say...we're tempting the devil."

She liked my reasoning, I think. Her little whispered laugh blew on my mouth. She liked being close to the edge, and so long as she wasn't killing her friendships, I had a feeling that love of danger would always live on in her. She kissed me, those short kisses where you're not trying to take somebody's face off. I didn't want to take her nerve away.

Her sweater got rumpled up, and I let my hands rub across the smooth skin on her back. This little moan fell out of her, and I just had the thought, *Yeah. That's what you've been missing. That's what it's supposed to feel like.* And then I was really kissing her, and she was wrapped around my neck like she wanted to pass through me again. I don't know how long we stayed that way. An eternity and about three minutes beyond it. The boat even kicked in with a nice little rock back and forth that felt so peaceful, so comfortable.

"We'll get us our own boat, and we'll go to Marrakech," I whispered, kissing her more. "Then Madagascar. Then Australia. And New Zealand. And the...whatever islands, where Amelia Earhart disappeared."

"Oh, lord," she whispered. I could feel her struggling inside. I kissed her down her neck and around to the other side. She sighed, and I could feel her starting to tighten up.

"Okay, just Madagascar." I looked at her hard. Her eyes were shiny, glazed, bright. I felt like I almost had her.

"The boat's rocking," she whispered.

"I know."

"Something's happening, Evan." I didn't really even care, considering what was going on inside my own skin. It was hard to apply her words to anything but the fireworks going off in my gut.

However, Emmett stuck his head down, and I loosened my grip a little. Sometimes reality sucks, even out here. He shook his head, like he was a little annoyed but not angry.

"Grey, I suddenly seem to be having trouble with your dash. It's a great dash. But the depth finder is acting crazy."

She had put her elbows between us when he appeared. She drummed on my shoulders lightly in frustration, and I let go of her, followed her out to the stern, thinking, *More later. She won't leave me now.*

To my surprise, a wind really had kicked in.

"There's no weather," I reminded Emmett.

"It's not weather I'm worried about. The sky is great. It's that water seems to be disappearing out of the canyon. Look at this." He pointed to the little green monitor that drew the graphs of the depth. Everything looked okay to me. The line was definitely pointing downward.

"Look at the loran TDs," he said. "We're in the deepest part of the canyon. I can match them up with your map. But look at the depth. We've misplaced about nine hundred feet."

TWENTY-TWO

Grey glanced at the graph on the dash, but then, like I would have done, she looked over the stern, curiously.

"Well, we all know the canyon doesn't have a leak in it, right?" she said, but would not stop staring. "Unless The She has something to do with it."

I think Emmett was annoyed that he had found us kissing, and that comment made him very, very annoyed. He flopped his arm down on the wheel and scratched his beard impatiently. The map he'd been talking about was folded in fours, and he grabbed it off the dash.

"We've been drifting around for a few hours. It could be that we moved further, and the receiver didn't pick it up. There's not much current. Look." He pointed a finger at a far northwest corner of the canyon. "The depth we're registering would put us about here, which would mean we've drifted twenty miles."

He looked at the loran receiver. "These numbers say we haven't moved more than a mile."

"Which I would say is accurate, given that there's hardly any current. Or hardly waves." Grey cast another glance over the stern, which sent me back there to stare into the night. I heard her say to him, "We couldn't drift twenty miles."

"Unless we got pushed in a rush from the Gulf Stream," he countered. "It's been awfully warm out here."

"No Gulf Stream. Put your hand over."

She meant we would feel water that was about seventy degrees instead of forty-five if we were in a rush from the Gulf Stream. But those rushes never came out past the shelf, if I remembered things right. While they were busy arguing, I let my internal rhythm fall into in the heave and sway of the boat, realizing there was something weird about the rhythm. It would bob up, then bob way down, bob up, then bob way down. The down bobs were always stronger than the up ones, and that was a sensation I could not pull out of my childhood memory.

"What direction are we facing?" Emmett asked.

"West." I backed up to the helm, staring off the stern, trying to see anything but black and little whitecaps.

"How do you know?" Emmett asked. "Are you watching the stars?"

I shook my head. I just knew. My heart revved up a little as I tried to bring my hands up to stare at them. It took a bit of effort. They felt clumsy, like I was holding two-pound weights in each hand. I wiggled my fingers, trying to decide if this was my imagination. I looked at Grey.

"Do you feel that?" I asked.

She rolled her shoulders around a couple of times, staring over the stern. "Like a...like something's standing on your shoulders. Not bad, but...definitely weird."

I nodded. From the corner of my eye I could see Emmett looking back and forth from her to me.

"Don't let's get carried away with ourselves," he said patiently. "But I think I'll start the engines."

I didn't think that was such a bad idea, so I let him do it, then touched him in the chest. I made a thumbs-down sign while my eyes were glued to the stern. He kept the throttle in neutral, leaving a hum, so that we could still hear each other pretty well.

"We're moving," I insisted.

He jerked his head back to the dash and shook his head. "Not enough to notice, here. What direction are you, er, sensing?"

"Downward."

He looked at me, and I heard his gloved fingers beat on the dash. "Don't do this to me, Evan," he said. "It's unfair."

"I'm just telling you what my body is telling me."

"Listen to me." He pulled me up to him by the shoulders. "If you think I don't remember every last moment of what happened the night Mom and Dad disappeared, you are sadly mistaken. It is a torturous memory. Horrible. Don't pull me back there, no matter how badly your psyche wants to create a drama. It is totally cruel—"

"Do you remember running back up to the widow's walk? The second time?"

"Of course I do."

I stared at him, stared into his tortured eyes. I saw everything there. Embarrassment, pain, horror, shame, regret, even terror.

"Please," he said. "Let's not engage in any sort of psychodrama that could take either of us back. It was harder for me to get where I am than you would ever imagine."

I shut my eyes and tried to get rid of the rhythm of the boat in my mind. *Down, rock. Down, rock. Down, rock.* For the love of your family, you can come a lot further away from the truth than you normally could.

"Okay. Maybe we're not moving downward, Emmett. If we're not then...Can you just relax a minute more?"

"I'm not exactly relaxed!"

"Just a minute more."

I moved back to Grey, who was staring over the stern. "Black-bean soup?" She repeated my earlier description.

I could see the whitecaps appearing and disappearing without seeming to move. I nodded, wanting so badly to draw Emmett back here and ask him to look more closely. But I was so sure we were losing water underneath us, which made no sense, and I set my mind instead to figure out what that meant. Water has to be somewhere. If it's not under you, then it has to be somewhere else—beside you, behind you....I spun around in a little paranoid frenzy, searching over the bow and then the stern again.

The stars were brighter over the stern. No immense, water-logged creature was rising anywhere.

Grey climbed up onto the bridge, looking all around. She hadn't heard my whole conversation with Emmett, I don't think, because she was indiscreet enough to say, "Definitely. It feels like we're falling."

"Well, that's goddamn impossible," Emmett snapped.

"Then why are you so nervous?" I snapped back. My own nerves were snapping.

"I don't know," he said. "I think it's the two of you giving me the creeps."

"Can you hear that?" Grey jumped down from the bridge, and her feet hit the deck with a bang. "*Shh...* listen."

Against the downward sway that was dominant in our rocking, I started to hear a little gurgling on the side of the boat. *Rock, down, gurgle...Rock, down, gurgle, gurgle.*

"We're being sucked," she told us.

"Let's go," Emmett said, and reached for the throttle. But Grey jumped in front of him.

"No! Don't you want to see?"

"Not particularly!"

"How are you going to feel tomorrow if you say you ran tonight? From something you don't even believe in?"

Their stare-off was lost on me. I moved back to the stern, listening to Emmett finally agree, persuaded by her combination of logic and dashboard readings, that we had somehow lost about three hundred yards of water.

Any great intellectual would want to figure that out, she told him. Three hundred yards of depth. Where in the hell does it go? *The Hole?*

And I felt every hair on my body standing straight up as I gazed off the stern, though I wasn't quite sure what I was seeing yet. I only got the idea the water *could* rise. And just keep rising.

The sucking and gurgling was unmistakable now, and water smacked as if the stern were unhappy and fighting it. Grey punched me in the arm and I looked at her. She was pointing off the port stern—not straight out and not straight up.

If she were a clock, her body and her arm would have made about 10:30. I know, because I've seen it in my head five hundred times since, her halfway point between the horizon and straight up in the sky. When she found her voice, it was too loud.

"Guys, why are the stars disappearing?"

She was absolutely telling the truth. Emmett came back and gripped both of our shoulders, saying, "It's in the sky. It's a cloud!"

I thought the line was too thick, crawling slowly upward, without showing any stars behind it. "It's water," I breathed.

"It's a cloud!"

"It's her," Grey said. "Oh, my God, what have I done?"

I had about two seconds to realize I had no idea how far away this black thing was rising, because there was nothing to help me gauge distance. It could have been twenty yards off the stern or ten miles away.

I screamed. "It's a wave! I just know it!"

Emmett's eyes grew immense, and I had a flash of a second to enjoy the fact that he finally believed me. He all but threw himself at the throttle, but before the engines filled my ears, I heard one short line screaming out of him.

It was the first line of my dad's captain's prayer.

The engines cut in at the same time as the shrieking, which dropped me to the deck in a moment of sheer pain and utter heaviness. We were flying west, away from the impending black at top speed, but it was too late.

Almost right over our heads, but way up, I saw a telltale white line rip across the black, a line any petrified sailor might have taken as a couple of long eyebrows. They got thicker, and I shut my eyes, knowing I would be seeing a wall of white behind me any second.

"Emmett, drive! It's a fucking wave!"

He was still shaking his head in denial, though his mouth was moving. I didn't need to hear. I couldn't hear anything except that shrieking, and then Grey shrieking just as loud. It was as if the water quit shrieking long enough to inhale. Then a rumbling, crashing boom split my head, like the sound barrier was breaking.

"Drive, Emmett, drive! It's a fucking tower, man—"

I lurched to my feet, jerked my back to the thing. The throttle was all the way forward, but this boat wasn't moving fast enough. We were heavy, paralyzed mice trying to crawl away from an angry lion. I couldn't look anywhere but straight ahead, but I felt a huge breath blowing my hair forward, and the picture drilled through my head of a huge avalanche devouring a small cabin in the dark. Spray followed the hurricane breath, pouring onto us, forcing my eyes shut.

A blast of water shot me in the back, and I smashed into the cabin door. I grabbed the helm from Emmett, slamming the wheel all the way to the right.

"You'll kill us all, goddamn it! We're gonna die, we're gonna die!" He kept screeching. But I'd just had time to cast one glance over my shoulder, which showed me nothing but white as high up as I could see. Call it intuition, or just an eye for detail, but my sight caught one black streak off to the far right, and I drove sideways into it, falling, falling. It was a spot where the wave hadn't broken yet, and I was flying into some spot between a giant thumb and a giant finger that could squash us like a fly.

Grey threw herself down and grabbed the bridge ladder, waiting for the boat to roll in this little piece I caught near the far end of the wave. We were falling sideways, bouncing, managing on the last little thread of my driving power to keep from spinning over and rolling. The flood in the stern forced the boat to list into the wave, into starboard, and I knew we needed to straighten before it washed back the other way. Mercifully, we were straightening. The boat trembled in seizures, in violent attempts to obey me, finally pulling up, up, sideways into the black.

I could not conceive of the height we were reaching in

this endless climb, up over a hunched, black shoulder and the white, shapeless face screaming in outrage.

Emmett had fallen and just laid at my feet, so I screamed, "Grab something!"

Finally hitting the crest was no consolation prize, because this mountain had a backside that made the headlights of the boat seem like we were looking straight down to the canyon floor, to the hole. I tried to slide us down it sideways, but that screeching started in again, and I could barely hear Emmett screeching back as we spun downward. There were twenty times we could have rolled; we were like a little peanut rolling down the front of an unconcerned, heaving chest. I could finally feel the force with which the *Goliath* would have struck the surface as it fell. It would not have made it this far, could never have hit the backside of this wave, or it would have crashed into the deep and split into four or five pieces. The water was a solid wall to port, and I hugged it, half driving and half bumping, down, down, until I couldn't resist the urge. The only way to keep sanity enough to stay at the helm was to screech back.

"Get away from us! What in hell did we ever do to you?" I stopped short of name-calling, some idea in my gut cutting off my air, as if to remind me to show some respect.

The wave moved out faster as I yelled, with the shrieking turning to a deep *OoooOOOOooooooooooooo* that got less and less overpowering until it finally bottomed into little more than an echo. We were rocking finally, moving, but not dropping anymore. Somehow I had lowered the speed to nothing to look at the white line disappearing toward the shore. Almost at the horizon, it evaporated to nothingness. I knew what had been out in front of that white line could easily have toppled Opa's house.

Emmett was sitting in water up to his waist while Grey clamored to her feet beside him. My own screeching having stopped and the wave having been silenced, I realized he was still yelling.

I dropped to my knees and shook him, as he screamed in my face without seeing me, *"You fucking whore! I'm gonna kill you!"*

"Emmett! It was a wave, buddy. Calm down...It was a wave." I looked through the black and added, "I think..."

TWENTY-THREE

I couldn't stop Emmett from freaking out, even after I got him to his feet. We were up to our knees in water, but he just swayed there, pointing where the thing had disappeared close to the horizon

"It's going to hit Opa's house! It'll level Opa's house!"

"Emmett, they never make it to shore."

"You don't know that!"

"Yeah, I do."

"Evan!" He hugged on me. "It was just a wave, right? It didn't...come after us. Right?"

Grey was behind me sending a Mayday, saying we'd flooded one of the engines and had been hit by a rogue wave, and she was spitting out lorans. I could feel Emmett trembling violently and couldn't decide how much was from being half soaked in the cold wind, and how much was from being out of his tree. Grey was turning up the ballast pumps, and I decided the best thing to do was get

Emmett moving. A bait bucket floated past, and I grabbed it, stuck it in his hands.

"Bail, my man! I'll get us moving on one engine, but you've got to get some weight off the top or we're going in the water! Do you understand?"

He started bailing, but like a zombie. I turned to Grey.

"The Coast Guard has a cutter about twenty minutes from here," she said. "They're ripping this way. They'll give us a tow. We ought to be okay. Unless you think she's coming back."

She...she...she. All the theories were mixed and mashed together, making my brain split into quarters.

"I don't think she's coming back that fast." My voice came out like metal on metal. "It was a wave, Grey! Right?"

"Uh, *yeah*." She looked at me like I was nuts. "It was a wave. What a killer bitch! It put me in my place...I'm going to have to be nice now, just from knowing I'll never match the competition—"

"Um..." I took her by the shoulders and moved her in front of the helm. "Just drive toward that cutter. And don't talk about that thing in front of Emmett as if it were alive. Okay?"

I found a hand pump in the galley, and under the anemic sound of one engine, I figured I'd better try to calm him as we bailed. He was muttering under his breath, like a crazy person. It was part reality about we could have been killed, part captain's prayer, part seizure breathing because he was cold and wet.

"Okay, bro. Let's figure this out while we bail, okay?"

He threw a bucket of water over the side, and I started in. "There's a fault in the canyon floor, right?"

"I don't know..."

"And the fault trembles every so often and throws up a reaction, right?"

"I don't know..."

"And it never hits shore because it just keeps refilling the canyon. Maybe?"

"I don't know, except that it is fucking cold out here now."

"Keep bailing, keep your blood moving. They're coming. Okay? Talk to me." I watched him toss another bucket of water over the side. "And since there aren't enough witnesses who live to tell about it, nobody takes it seriously enough to investigate."

I thought it would have to help him to think of the thing in his own terms, so I blathered on about funny eardrums and heaviness in your limbs. He kept bailing, and I couldn't tell for sure whether he was really hearing me, just because his head kept nodding up and down. He hadn't heard the screeching, but he seemed to want to agree with me about everything. "It's got to be suction, something about the force of gravity pulling on sensitive bodies, right?" I said.

"I would guess."

"Well, you're going to have lots of fun up at school after this, my man! I want you to promise me you'll call all your cronies over in the science department, and we'll work on something together for once, all right?"

"We're not sinking, right?"

I figured he ought to know that much and fought to keep from yelling at him. "No. The ballast pumps are working good, and so am I. Just keeping bailing and get a hold of yourself."

He bailed until the cutter lights came over the horizon and finally drew near.

A Coast Guard officer offered us a bigger, motorized pump, and another jumped on board with a clipboard. The guy was writing down basic info—our names, name of the boat, size of the boat.

"We got hit by a rogue wave," I told him.

"What, you tried to ride it straight up?" he asked.

"No, I zagged it. The water load is from where it hit us in the stern. Believe me, if we hadn't been on the edge of it, we would be dead and gone. I zagged up a piece of the swell that hadn't broken, came down behind it."

He didn't look too impressed. "How big?"

I realized he thought I was talking about a twelve-foot rogue wave. My mental alarm bell went off. He would never believe me. Should I lie? Make the thing sound smaller? Just so I wouldn't have the Coast Guard thinking I was nuts? I wondered how many people might have caved in with that thought, especially if their last name happened to be Barrett.

Grey put a hand on my back and put herself up close to the officer. "It was halfway up to the sky, mister."

I cleared my throat as a flood of Mom memories struck. "...*another pitfall of me being a captain...the*

Coast Guard doesn't hear women very well. Unless they always remember to keep it in really, really manly terms, it's downright dangerous—"

"It was sixty-five foot," I put in quickly.

The guy looked away from me quick, back down at the clipboard, and his pen made a few random circles above the page. I sensed he felt we were trying to blame the weather rather than my bad driving.

Emmett waded over, and I nudged him. "How big was it, Emmett?"

"It ate my parents," he muttered, and I rolled my eyes heavenward, realizing I had won something, but wondering how quickly Aunt Mel and I could get him some therapy.

"You lost passengers?" The officer grabbed for his handset.

"Not tonight," Emmett said. "Our parents were out here eight years ago, and it took them off a three-hundred-foot freighter. It is big enough to roll a freighter—"

"Which one of you is the captain of this voyage?" He sounded confused.

"I am." Grey raised her hand.

I felt my mother's bones roll as his eyes looked right through her, like maybe he ought to talk to a guy, and they swam back to me. "It's just that there's no weather tonight, Mr...."

"Barrett. I'm Evan Barrett. This is my brother, Emmett. This is the *owner*, Grey—"

"Barrett." The guy looked me up and down. "You guys are related to those people who sent a Mayday and disappeared a few years back?"

"They were our parents," Emmett croaked.

"Oh."

I watched in amazement as he circled his pen over the place where he was about to put the size of the wave, and skipped it again. His complete thought came to me in a flash: We either fucked up our driving or created a hoax to prove something about our parents. Mr. Church's words clattered through my head: *The Coast Guard rewrites these reports to fit a belief system they can tolerate.* He didn't leave the height blank on purpose. I just think his fingers couldn't write what his brain refused to acknowledge.

The Coast Guard was good enough to give us a tow to shore. I forced Emmett to go on the cutter, but Grey and I stayed on board, watched the ballast pumps, manned the Coast Guard pump, and kept ourselves busy. We were almost back into port when I went into the galley and found Grey loosening a couple of floorboards with the help of a wrench.

"The engines are pretty well drained by now," I said, thinking she shouldn't waste her time.

"They are. Just…there's something down here I need." She pulled up the floorboards, then reached her hand almost under the pumps. It came up dripping with a very large, sealed bubble envelope in it. She handed it to me.

"Hiding place number one," she said. I opened the envelope. It was full of cash, six fat bricks of hundred dollar bills. I stared at her and she laughed, tired. She shoved it down her coveralls and hooked her jacket again.

I helped her screw down the floorboards, trying to convince her that she would not run away so long as I was living. She kept insisting she was not running off, but I couldn't imagine what she needed this wad of cash for if that wasn't the case. It looked to be about twenty-five thousand dollars, maybe more.

My tongue was thick, and my arms were still weighted down, like they sometimes had felt when I'd heard The She. I could only sit there on the floor, soaking wet and cold, trying to decide what The She really was.

I had driven her. I was supposed to be convinced it was a wave more than anybody in the world. But there were those elements that squeaked through my head that made the wave seem alive...those things I could never explain and maybe wouldn't want to. Like the fact that she started to rise up in some jealous seizure while I was kissing the love of my life. Like the fact that, afterward, I remembered feeling that I was fighting something alive, and that we'd all talked about her as if she were alive.

That wave had a pulse, a heart throb, an anger, a sense of humor. She was a thing that laughed at me...something that maybe didn't want to hurt us as much as show off her fury and then spare us...maybe so that someone else might go back to shore and brag on her. And like maybe there was some small maternal instinct in her. She had rolled the *Goliath*, taken my parents, yet wanted me to know that maybe she was no ugly hag, that she was offended by some of the horror stories that echoed back on shore. She takes whom she will, but she doesn't eat. Her passions are more sensual, having more to do with her heart and spirit than her mouth and belly. She's a graveyard, not a kitchen. She's a woman, not a witch. When the church bells ring in memoriam in East Hook, she takes a graceful bow. She's never wiped her mouth.

I knew I could never prove to another human being that my description of The She was valid in any way. But I also kept hearing Church reminding me that no one could take her from me again. Because even if the next terrified soul had the presence of mind to get pictures and send them to publications all over the world, it's easy to photograph nature but difficult to photograph soul and character. And if somebody found the fault in the canyon floor and validated that great mystery, nobody could ever photograph a massive idea, a will, or a decision to place a fault where it lies.

You can't photograph the hugest mysteries of the universe that really have nothing to do with what shows up before your eyes, under a microscope, through a telescope, in the pages of books. I can't prove much, but I decided, as we pulled into the Basin, that when the next person tries to pull that argument on me—that great spirits aren't real because they never show up in our faces— I'll see that vengeful, hateful, graceful, merciful killer wave—which I knew in my heart was sent for our eyes only, for a once-in-a-lifetime answer to some deep needs of three orphaned souls—and I'll say, "Well, maybe divinity just isn't that artless."

IV

"But who's to say what's true and what's not,
what's real and what's imagined, what's the way it is,
and what's what you want it to be?"
—ED OKONOWICZ, author of
Terrifying Tales of the Beaches and Bays

EPILOGUE

I threw my mortarboard in the air with a hundred other fools out in Fairmount Park on a clear spring day. The sun was warm, and I should have been extremely happy, except I was still numb from having heard Grey's name announced among the graduates. I'd last seen her six and a half months ago. I made my way over to Mrs. Ashaad and saw my brother doing the same.

He caught me just before I reached her and gave me a bear hug, laughing a little. "I have to say, Evan, you gave me a few scares during the past four years. Congratulations, my man."

He stuck out his hand, and I skinned it, turning to Mrs. Ashaad.

"You gave *me* a few scares, too." She hugged me, and I caught her by the shoulders.

"You graduated Grey."

"Yes, I did. She completed the work."

"From *where*? If she did that, then you have to know where she is."

"No, I don't. Her last work came in late. What else is new? We were able to process it in time. Come to my car with me. There was something in the last bit of work addressed to you."

I followed along half thrilled, half angry, knowing that this was not possible if Mrs. Ashaad didn't have an address. While we were walking, my mind roared back to how she had slipped through my fingers—by throwing me a curveball I never would have expected.

I'd docked her dad's mangled boat when we reached the Basin, and I had actually cut a stern line and had it in my hand. I was playing cowboy or something I hadn't really thought through, except if she didn't tell me where she was going, I had some game plan to tie her up.

I looked up on the dock, and there were two men standing there in trench coats, with what looked like business suits on underneath. It was after midnight. One reached a hand down and pulled Grey up onto the dock. Neither said "hello," but the second one said, "We were listening to the Coast Guard radio and thought we might have had a fatality. Are you all right?"

"I'm fine." She turned, reached into her weather-suit pocket, and tossed me her car keys. I caught them. "Will you drive my car back to Philly?"

I looked back and forth between her and these two men I had never seen before, figuring she would introduce them. She asked them, "What should I do about the boat?"

"Leave it. We'll have it taken care of," the first one said.

"Evan, just leave it. Leave everything, okay?" She took two steps backward up the dock, and the two men fell in with her. She walked backward like that, staring and staring at me, until she finally blew me a kiss and turned. I didn't know if they were uncles or people from Saint E's. And I never saw her again.

I figured I would smooth talk Mrs. Ashaad out of her address somehow, some way, though she had denied having any knowledge of Grey's whereabouts up until a month ago, when I had finally stopped asking.

Mrs. Ashaad was parked in a VIP spot, so we didn't have to walk very far. She opened her back door, and sure enough this package she pulled out was merely a FedEx envelope. It was misshapen, as if it had once been full of papers, but now there was only a small envelope left in it. She handed the envelope to me, and I saw my name in pretty handwriting that sent chills down me.

"She said to give it to you on your graduation day," she muttered. "It's a present of some sort."

I tore it open, expecting a lengthy letter of explanation—where she was, why she'd never contacted me, and why she came to our town house and picked up the car without saying squat to me, without even ringing my doorbell. I still had the keys.

But it wasn't a letter. At least, not one from her. It was a report. A lot was blacked out with thick black marker, like the name of the company, the names in the to and from lines, and any part of the address except the state, Florida.

The report said, "This is in response to the dive of the wreck of the *Sanskrit,* owner operator James Diaz, having foundered off the coast of southern Florida. Remains from eight victims were removed via photo arms of Bubble Drum II, and analysis of those remains took place on May 3 at the LabTech facility in east Miami.

"Be advised that based on the dental records and DNA samples provided, none of those remains belongs to Wade E. Barrett of West Hook, nor his wife, Mary Ellen Starn, also of West Hook.

"A transcript from LabTech is provided. We hope you found our bubble drum and diving facility as accommodating as you expected.

"Yours truly." And a blacked-out name.

I slid down the side of Mrs. Ashaad's car, staring at this piece of paper, until Emmett finally grabbed it from my hand. He dropped to his knees and let out a loud yell, half from shock, half a victory whoop. He's a much faster reader than I am. I didn't know where to land a thought. I wanted to think about taking that letter to the authorities, though I didn't really know which ones would change the status of my parents from "missing at sea" to "died at sea," or even if that letter would be enough evidence that they died up here in the canyons.

And I couldn't get rid of the image of Grey stuffing that money envelope down her coveralls. I had guessed it to be somewhere around twenty-five thousand dollars, and she'd most likely used every dime getting herself down in a bubble drum, finally. She should have used it to live on. She used it on us, and I had no way to thank her.

I reached around and grabbed the FedEx packet off Mrs. Ashaad's seat as Emmett passed the paper to her, while giving more shocked victory yells.

The words WITNESS PROTECTION PROGRAM stared back at me. I dropped the envelope, dropped my chin to my chest as my heart fell. The two men in suits had been FBI, I realized, and Mrs. Ashaad's broken-record lecture made sense all of a sudden. "Evan, she's not coming back, or if she is, it will be in a long, long time. You have to remember her in the wonderful way that you do, and move on with your life." I could just never accept it. Now, I guess I had to.

There was a little note attached to the report, in her pretty handwriting, but all it said was, "Thought this might come in handy. Have a great life. I will think of you every day. Stay good, Grey."

During the summer, I looked at the pages over and over, and I would hold that report up to the light, trying to see something through the black lines. It would be her new name, new address. I could see only a couple of little indents, and I could have sworn, when I held the paper in just a certain way, that the last name she had chosen was Starn.

I knew this report didn't mean that she was actually living in Florida. She could be living in goddamn Wyoming and just went down there with a new ID, with whatever the government gives you. Her name did come up in the Philadelphia newspaper, starting in June. I was staying with Opa that summer and might have missed the whole thing if Emmett hadn't been good enough to check every Philly paper's Web site daily. She had not been exaggerating about her father.

The FBI had arrested fifteen men in a sting that involved extortion, bribery, drugs, and money laundering. Her testimony implicated her father and two of the other men, and the stories read like the thing had snowballed. After she told what she knew, they all started to turn on one another. Some of the more gabby newspapers liked the idea that a daughter would turn on her father; they put out a bunch of articles, and one even ran her picture. I was made so sick by the whole thing, the only one I would read all the way through was the *Inquirer*. Even that was sickening. After the story blathered on through the counts of everything in the world that had been thrown at "Philadelphia Attorney Kevin Shailey," it listed child abuse, including incest and prostitution of a minor.

Another story told even more. If the people at Saint E's had convinced her she'd get some sort of heroic reception, they had miscalculated. Youth and family services had gotten her some kind of specialized lawyer, because one set of defense lawyers actually planned to "use the sex charges to discredit her testimony," to try to show that she made up the extortion charges against the other two men because she was mad at her father. It just looked like an enormous mess and the ultimate test of a girl's sanity.

This trial started in August, and I knew she would be in Philly for three days. I was staying with Opa, working the docks and trying to start a fishing boat rental business, at least on paper, with Opa's help. It took everything in my heart and soul not to get in my car and drive up there. I got as far as the mainland twice, and forced myself to turn around. I was just remembering her pride and how difficult the newspaper said the questions would be. I didn't want her looking into my face while she was telling it.

They kept her on the witness stand for three days, from eight-thirty in the morning until five-thirty at night. When I knew she had left Philly again, I went over to my house in West Hook and sat there and wept a few times. I could feel her great will to do good for people, which made the horrors of her mouth seem so minuscule in comparison. Then I felt my mother's presence come around and tell me nicely to get a stiff upper lip.

On August 16, a year to the day after the Girl Scout's drowning, Grey's father was sentenced to fifty years in a federal prison with the possibility of parole after twenty years. That final newspaper article said that he and one of the two other guys went down based mostly on what Grey had to tell. One of those newspapers had joined forces with Saint Elizabeth's, apparently, and they started some sort of fund in her honor to help kids who had to turn in their parents for criminal activity. Grey wasn't around to receive anything from it, and the newspaper even said she might never know about it.

In August, I got the idea to call the LabTech place to

find out what DNA evidence she had presented on my parents. They said two toothbrushes and two hairbrushes, which could mean only one thing. At some point, she had come to West Hook and had gotten into my parents' house. It wasn't hard. That window Emmett left open the night of the disappearance never shut well or locked.

When I figured that out, my intuition drew me back there, and I went around inhaling. In certain places I could smell that combination of fabric softener, shampoo, soap, and that just Great Grey Shailey Smell that had stamped itself on my brain. One of the places I could smell it the best was on the pillow in my old bedroom. It was unmistakable. She had laid on my bed.

I moved into the house in September, and I started sleeping in my own bed again, and I slept with that pillow beside me, afraid that if I lay on it too hard, the smell would disappear.

And I guess all that sounds a little crazy, especially since I don't remember feeling that horrible about my own parents' loss. I guess maybe I felt it horribly, but not in this way of having had my skin ripped from my body. It was a hard autumn, which had been preceded by a hard summer.

Though it was a good time in many ways, too.

When I came to stay with Opa for the summer, I took a room that had a view of the harbor from three sides. I woke up every morning and looked out for about half an hour before I got up.

My first day at work on the docks, I showed up expecting just to pitch in, scrub floors, and fill bait buckets, which is about what happened. But when I first got out of the car with Opa, about a hundred people flew out of the marina building holding balloons, throwing confetti, and holding up photos of my parents. It was nuts. I had no clue while I was sitting up in Philly how much my parents had meant to the islanders, or how many of the islanders' opinions of them were like Mr. Church's.

One lady had painted seamen's portraits of Dad and Mom and reminded me that Dad had portraits of all the ancestors in the attic. I figured I'd get them all down someday soon and try to hang them.

Emmett was up in Philly that day, and I wished he had been in East Hook. I thought our experiences at sea might have changed his mind about his life's direction. But not even surviving a sixty-five-foot wave had managed to do that. The changes I saw in him were slow, painful, yet sometimes funny. He came down for the annual Maritime Memorial Service, and he blessed himself after the prayer. Afterward, we walked home on the beach and he threw something into the surf—a black book, though I'm not sure whether it was the DEA report or his dissertation.

I do know his dissertation had been rejected a few days earlier. He had tried to stick with his basic premise, but he laid in some added things: "Quotes by weird guys like C. S. Lewis and Michael Polanyi," he told me, as if these names were new and intriguing to him. I'd never heard him mention either before. He said the department was right to reject it, because the quotes toppled other arguments, and he could see that now. He needed to start from scratch.

He spent the month of July with us in East Hook, thinking the change of scene would help his writer's block. And when it didn't, he turned into more of the Emmett I used to know. He would lose his temper, then become extremely apologetic, as if I cared. I would try to bait him, like I did when I was a little kid and I knew I was within arm's reach of Mom. We were grown now, and I didn't need Mom or Dad holding him off, but we frequently ended up in a wrestling match on the floor of the family room, which sent Opa into peals of laughter. It added some kind moments to a difficult period for us.

One day when he couldn't write, Emmett got to clicking around on the Internet, something I'd noticed him doing a lot of, and he started to laugh hysterically.

"Read this," he said. I wasn't surprised by the title, "Danger on the Seas As Walls of Water Sink Tankers," because he was always surfing for something to "prove" my parents got taken by a wave. It was published in a newspaper called *The Observer* out of the United Kingdom, dated Sunday, November 10, 2002.

"They are the stuff of legend and maritime myth: giant waves, taller than tower blocks, that rise out of calm seas and destroy everything in their paths," it read. "For years scientists and marine experts have dismissed such stories as superstition. Walls of water do not rise out of the blue, they said. But now research has revealed that 'killer waves' do exist and regularly devastate ships around the world. They defy all scientific understanding and no craft is capable of withstanding their impact."

"They don't know about you, my man." Emmett held out his hand for me to skin, and I kept reading, though only one other line was understandable to me. "These mammoth events are not tidal waves or tsunamis, however. Nor are they caused by earthquakes or landslides. They are single, massive walls of water that rise up—for no known reason—and destroy dozens of ships and oil rigs every year."

"Looks like they don't know about The She, either," I said. "Are you going to send this to the DEA?"

Emmett sighed for a long time before shaking his head. "Maybe when I have about twenty-five things like this. Maybe when we can finally explain that shrieking, too. It's insidious, their mindset. I'm telling you. I would know."

He's found nothing yet to explain a shrieking that one person can hear and another can't, and nothing to really explain the heaviness that would come and go in my limbs, Grey's limbs. He's patient, but I think the most unsettling thing for him, beyond his struggle with his dissertation, is having to believe in something that he knows but can't prove. He says it's deeply humbling.

It's still difficult for us both sometimes. A year has passed since that Thanksgiving trip to East Hook, and everything has changed. But being that it's November again and the smell of that pillow is starting to leave, I spend time with a face that's wet and a gut that is bone-dry of any intuition as to where Grey Shailey is...or if I will ever see her again. It's almost as if she were strong enough to will away my intuition, or as much of it as concerns her.

It's also difficult to live without having any evidence as to exactly where my parents' resting place is, but that is a common problem for seafaring people, and I have enough friends around here to take the same comforts in them as Opa did when the ship rolled and sent the crew and his daughter to the bottom of the deep. I visit Edwin Church a lot. I call him Edwin at his request, and he treats me like a man. We sit outside his cabin on milk crates on nice days and drink brandy, and I swat the shit out of my neck and hands to keep the green flies off me. He's immune or something. Maybe he laid hands on himself, who knows. We don't talk about his hands. We don't need to, and there's nothing really to say about it.

He says things that give me peace somehow, in some way I don't understand. I'll say to him, "Edwin, it's been a year. When are other girls going to start to look worthy to me? I'm supposed to be a young, horny guy."

He'll clamp down on my shoulders and say, "I don't know," and shake me a little, like he's trying to shake something positive into me, something from his glinting eyes, his ornery grin...and it works. I get filled up with a peace. It doesn't always last long. But it does the trick for the moment.

1. Do you think Emmett mixed up the sequence of events on the night of his parents' death subconsciously or intentionally? Why would he do so on purpose?

2. Do you think Emmett was right to keep the information about the DEA investigation a secret from Evan for so long? How might Evan's feelings about his parents and their disappearance have been different if he had known the information when he was younger?

3. Describe Evan's original feelings for Grey. When do his feelings for her change?

4. Why are Emmett and Aunt Mel opposed to religion?

5. Edwin Church and Bloody Mary are both said to possess supernatural powers, and because of this they are perceived to be just two crazy people by the townsfolk and tourists of West Hook. How do Mr. Church and

Bloody Mary differ in the practice of and their attitudes toward their powers?

6. How did Grey justify stealing her father's money? Do you think Evan was right for not accepting the money that she offered for the dive?

7. If someone close to you were to disappear mysteriously, do you think you'd react more like Emmett—obsessively searching for scientific explanations; or Evan—remaining open to explanations that seem illogical to most people?

ABOUT THE AUTHOR

Carol Plum-Ucci's first novel, *The Body of Christopher Creed* (2000), was a Michael L. Printz Award Honor Book, an ALA Best Book for Young Adults, an IRA Children's Choice, and a finalist for the Edgar Allan Poe Award for Best Young Adult Mystery. Her second book, *What Happened to Lani Garver* (2002), earned much critical acclaim and was named an ALA Best Book for Young Adults and a New York Public Library Book for the Teen Age. She has received numerous citations for her entertainment and business writing, including the Kneale Award in Journalism Excellence in Feature Writing from Purdue University, and has worked with groups that funded the smuggling of classic literature behind the Iron Curtain. Carol Plum-Ucci lives in New Jersey.